DEFENDING CAIN

Shimon Walner

Published by: Shimon Walner, Oakland CA

Please direct all queries to: DefendingCain416@gmail.com

Version 2020.09

ISBN
978-1-7355381-0-5 (trade)
978-1-7355381-0-5 (electronic)

Library of Congress Control Number (LCCN)
2020914649

This book is dedicated to:

The Master of the Universe,
for everything

My mother,
Leyah bas Avraham (z"l),
for many gifts,
including the love of language

My late wife,
Hadassah Esther Simcha bas Avraham (z"l),
for her love, support and courage,
and her wonderful children

My dear friend,
Dr. Jerry Beker (z"l),
for his warmth and wisdom

My racquetball partner,
William Shrears (z"l),
who taught me grace and balance
on and off the court

Cain spoke with Abel his brother;
and it was that they were in the field,
and Cain rose up towards Abel his brother
and killed him.

Genesis (4:8)

Prologue

The blue ball floated down from above, forcing me to choose. I could charge ahead for a rushed shot on the ball's first bounce, or back up to the rear wall for an awkward swing as the ball arced downward a second time. What I couldn't do was stay where I was.

I backed up. When the ball arrived, my coiled right arm burst into motion, the racquet executing an angry backhand shot, driving the ball quickly to the ceiling. It hit too far from the front wall, dropping to the floor to give Josh the point. I shook my head. I could do better.

I *had* to do better; the game was now on the line.

I assumed my ready stance in the back court. Josh set the ball in motion. As it bounced, I raced forward, aiming to pass Josh on the right. Instead the ball angled straight back to the middle, where Josh had an easy kill shot.

I had lost the third straight game. I rapped my racket on the wall next to the back door as I escaped the court.

It's a stupid game.

No, really; racquetball is a stupid game. Two men close themselves up together in a high-ceilinged room and smash a rubber ball against the six sides according to arbitrary rules about which wall to hit first and how many times the ball can bounce on the floor. This was not worth getting excited about. It just wasn't.

Josh ducked through the transparent door and joined me outside.

"It's a stupid game, Larry."

"Yeah, I know."

"A man should never let a few humiliating losses ruin his whole day."

I followed Josh down the stairs to the fourth-floor

locker room. He was a gangly fellow with a sharp mind and pleasant repartée. Not one to get bent out of shape when he lost a game. The man was infuriatingly satisfied with his life. Happy with his computer programming job, his marriage of six years to his high-school sweetheart, and his fathering of two young boys; he'd show off family pictures at the slightest provocation. Josh could be the poster-child for satisfied.

I opened the locker room door with a flourish and bowed low. "After you, sir."

Over the top of my locker door, I asked, "What's your secret source of equanimity, Buddha-man?"

"Hmm. When I was twelve I tipped over the chessboard after I lost a game. My dad forbade me to play for a month and he made me write a story-- what it would be like if I weren't smart enough to play chess at all."

"Yeah?"

"The next time I lost, I realized that I could either be angry I had lost, or grateful that I was able to play. It was actually a choice."

Josh smiled and disappeared toward the showers.

In the Beginning

1

"Au revoir, mon Sonny."

Andy dropped me off with his father's favorite pun lingering in a heavy faux-French accent.

Inside my apartment, I set down my bag, closed the door, and sank into my living room recliner.

The Chicago bridge tournament had been a great adventure, and on the drive back Andy and I had relived the memorable moments, laughing at the characters and reviewing the play. I ribbed Andy about running into an old flame, Gayle, and he razzed me for not asking out her bridge partner, Ruth. Last night the four of us had eaten Chinese together for dinner. Sitting in the restaurant, I had beheld a stunning, refined brunette, with a delicate jawline and glittering emerald eyes over a perfect nose. Her lips were full, and her dark hair was pulled back with a small braid circling like a crown. Ruth was exquisite, a princess, and I had sat staring stupidly.

Andy and Gayle had spent the evening together, but I had failed to muster up the courage to invite Ruth out. She seemed somehow too classy to approach, and in the end I had found myself alone in my room, surfing the Internet on my cell phone. But that was okay. The breakup with Mary was recent; my phone had made a good companion. And now it was Sunday afternoon and I was back in Saint Paul, alone in my empty apartment.

The light on my land line was blinking; I dialed voicemail and sat back to listen.

"Thursday, 7:13 pm... Bring your life into balance by eliminating your old—" I hit delete.

"Friday, 9:40am... This is Dr. Silverberger's office calling to confirm your appointment for Monday at 9:30..." It took me a moment to remember that Dr. Silverberger was the psychologist Mary had suggested I go see to "explore my issues". After much prodding, I had finally agreed to see him exactly once, and had made the appointment for two months in the future so I could focus on the *Hernandez* case. Probably rude to cancel at the last minute, but I sure as heck wasn't going now. Placating was a thing of the past.

I replayed the message and canceled the appointment using my cell.

"Saturday 9:32pm...Hello, Larry? This is Cindy, Josh's wife. Um, he won't be able to play racquetball Monday. He's-- well, he's sick. I'm not sure-- why don't you call me when you have a chance? Thanks, Larry. Bye."

Strange that Josh wouldn't just call me himself, or give Cindy my cell number. I dialed.

"Hi, Larry. Thanks for calling."

"Sure. What's up?"

There was a pause that lasted too long.

"Um, I've got some bad news, Larry. It's actually very bad news. Josh--" Her voice caught. There was a long silence. I strummed my fingers on the leather armrest. Whatever it was, it was bad. She took a deep breath and let it out, "Josh has cancer, Larry." I heard a muffled sob.

Cancer? The healthiest, organicky vegetarian who biked to work in all kinds of weather, played racquetball three times a week and wrestled with his two boys over the weekend when he was not meditating himself into nirvana? Who had never smoked a day in his life? Cancer? Josh? It was impossible.

"Larry?"

"I'm here. Sorry."

"It's okay. It's a shock, I know."

"How did it happen? I mean, how did you find out? What kind of cancer is it?"

"Well, you know he had a cold last Tuesday, but by Thursday he was fine. He seemed so-- normal, you know? And then Friday night we all went to my folks for dinner in Saint Paul, and he, and he--" She broke off. I heard an indistinct sound. "He went to the bathroom and he just never came back. My brother knocked on the door and there was no answer... Mort actually broke it down and we saw him just lying there in a heap."

She was crying now, but she controlled her voice. "He and Phillip tried waking him up, and they-- they had to carry him to the car. He actually tried to fight them off, although he doesn't remember it. Together they probably outweigh him by 300 pounds, you know, but he's so strong." There was a touch of pride in her voice. "Anyway, they finally subdued him and we took him to the ER, and, when they couldn't find anything at all the matter with him, they did a, a CT scan, and... and that's when they found it."

The silence stretched out. I studied the weave of the tan carpet. Each strand poking up just enough to be counted. As if taller strands had been shortened with a quick strike of a scythe. I was about to say something to bridge the widening chasm of silence, but she picked up again.

"They found a tumor in his brain, Larry. They showed me the picture. It's like a big— spot or something." She was quiet again. I slowly let out the breath I hadn't realized I had been holding in. "They're hoping to operate on it, but they might do a biopsy or radiation first. They're not sure. They're— consulting a specialist in Baltimore."

"I'm sorry, Cindy." They were the only words I could think of to say. I pictured Josh's graceful motion as he set the racquetball in play, not even a week ago. "Where is he?"

"United Hospital, room 2515. I'm sure he'd love to see you if you can make it over there. If he's awake and all. He's been sleeping a lot. They have him on some sort of anti-seizure meds and they're, you know, monitoring him."

"Thanks for letting me know, Cindy. I'll go see him. I'm-- really sorry."

After a few more inadequate mumblings, I hung up.

I sat. Cancer. Impossible.

2

The pleasantly unruffled woman who answered United Hospital's information line confirmed that a Joshua Levin was in the oncology ward and accepting visitors. I headed out in my beamer, a refurbished M3 I had gotten a good deal on two years before. It might be old, but it was still a BMW, and I kept it in good shape.

As I made my way to room 2515, none of the people I passed were smiling. On the other hand, I probably wasn't smiling either.

Did anyone ever really recover from brain cancer. *Brain* cancer? Breast cancer, if you're lucky. Lung cancer, probably sometimes. But brain cancer?

I arrived at the oncology ward. A nurse looked up from her station.

"Can I help you?"

"I'm looking for Joshua Levin, Room 2515?"

"Around the corner to your right, first door on your left." She gestured past me from the desk, "I think he's still sleeping, but you can look in on him."

I nodded and moved along. What was a person supposed to do when visiting a brain cancer patient? Chit-chat? Talk about how long the doctors had given you to live? The whole idea suddenly seemed really stupid. Awkward silences, depressing reality, and nothing that could be done about it. I was going to be a big help. *Hi Josh, how's the dying coming along?*

I steeled myself and turned through the doorway. I stopped in my tracks. An old man in a rumpled black suit and an old black hat swayed as though exorcising a demon from the patient in a bed I could not yet see. He held a small bound book in his spotted left hand, and mouthed words I could not hear as his gnarled right hand punctuated his incantations. He turned slightly toward me, without pausing, and his right hand formed a single forefinger, as though to say he'd be just a moment.

In a minute he came to a close. He slipped the book into an inside jacket pocket in a well-worn gesture and extended his hand in greeting.

"Moishe Friedler," he announced with the joy of a first-grader meeting his new classmates, "at your service."

"Larry Cohen."

"Are you a friend..?"

Who *was* this man? He seemed right at home intruding in Josh's private room. His youthful energy and smiling eyes contrasted with his dusty jacket and the graying beard that straggled from his chin down to his ill-fitting tie.

He was probably a rabbi, making the rounds.

"Um, yes. Friends. We play racquetball together three times a week. Or I mean, we did. We usually do."

"Ah."

"Did-- do you know Josh, Rabbi Friedler?"

"No, I have not yet had the pleasure. But I was visiting on the floor and when I heard the name 'Joshua Levin', I said to myself, 'Now that sure sounds like a yid if ever a yid there was', so I stopped in to say some Tehillim and a misheberach prayer for healing."

It took me a minute; it had been a long time. As a kid, I had attended a Jewish day school, but I had left that world many years ago.

"Tehill... Psalms?"

He nodded agreement as he made room for me to come past him and around to the bedside. We had been talking softly, so I had assumed Josh was asleep, and he was. For some reason I had expected him to have a tube up his nose and an oxygen tent over his bed, but there he was, just sleeping comfortably. Just another day napping in the oncology ward. With wizened rabbis pronouncing psalms, and friends stopping in to sit helplessly by as rain started falling outside the window.

"Does it help?"

"Reciting Psalms? Well, it never hurts." He smiled. "That's what we do, you know. We cry out and beg the Master of the Universe to have mercy and heal our brother. Sometimes He answers our prayers, and sometimes... sometimes He doesn't. Or doesn't seem to. But we do know that He wants us to ask."

The fluorescent lights seemed harsh on Josh's face, giving him an unearthly chalky texture. I glanced at the monitor to see his pulse tracking across the screen. I sat down in a chair by the bed and looked at his still body. If I looked closely, I could see the covers barely rise and fall with his breathing. There was a thin metal post next to the bed with a plastic bag hanging from a hook; the tubing disappeared under the covers.

I said, "Must be nice knowing what to do."

Rabbi Friedler looked at me thoughtfully and put his right hand alongside his face. He reminded me of the rumpled police detective, Columbo. Or maybe what Columbo's grandfather would have looked like, if he'd been a rabbi.

"Sometimes," he said slowly, "Sometimes people do something in the merit of the patient, you know. Lay tefillin--" he gestured with his right hand circling his left arm, "or study Torah, or take on another mitzvah, even something small, something seemingly very small. We do that and we ask that the merit of our actions be given to the sick person, so that he might be healed."

My gaze fell to the floor. The tiles had been worn smooth from thousands of sad shoes walking over them. Each was about a foot wide and a foot long, light cream with some blue highlights in no discernible pattern. Laid out in an intricate code that only the knowing could penetrate. In time, the blue markings would be worn away by the passing footfalls, and the secret of the pattern would be lost forever.

Rabbi Friedler said, "Did you meet through work?"

"Oh, no. We're in totally different worlds. He's a computer programmer over at Wells Fargo in Minneapolis. I'm an attorney in Hennepin County Attorney's office. We met at the Y, both looking for a racquetball partner..."

The rabbi's face lit up; he had uncovered a vital clue.

"You're a lawyer?"

"Yes..?"

"Then you can put your lawyerly skills to work; you can plead your friend's case before the Heavenly Court."

"If only I could..." I shook my head. "Prayer is not my thing, Rabbi."

"But you can! Anyone can pray. Just ask The Almighty to grant your petition."

"I'm good in the courtroom, Rabbi; give me a legal proceeding, and I'm there." I looked down at Josh, motionless in the bed. "But I work in the County Court, not the Heavenly Court...."

Rabbi Friedler cradled his chin in front of the windows. Outside, a late afternoon storm was darkening the sky, adding to the gloom inside. It reminded me that my days working in court might be numbered.

"I have a thought," Rabbi Friedler announced. "What if you asked for a hearing? To ask the Judge of all creatures to be merciful and kind, in the merit of all your friend's good deeds --the deeds he has already done, and the deeds he can yet do, if given the chance. You could use the same lawyerly skills you have perfected in your courtroom. Here, come stand over here and I'll help you."

Rabbi Friedler beckoned me. "Of course," he said with mock slyness, "such a request is much more powerful if made while wearing tefillin--!"

I smiled in spite of myself. "Why's that?"

"Two reasons. First," he raised the gnarled forefinger of his right hand, a hand that had probably strapped on the little black boxes every day since he had turned thirteen, "the spiritual power of the tefillin themselves amplifies the power of your request. By doing the Will of the Master of the Universe, you are binding yourself to His Desire, and so of course your prayers come more quickly and clearly before His Throne."

He smiled at me. "And secondly, well... you're asking the Master of the Universe to do something that *you* want *Him* to do, yes? So perhaps it makes some sense to do a little something that *He* wants *you* to do..?"

He tilted his head and raised his eyebrows encouragingly.

I held out my arms. Like an expert tailor, he gracefully rolled up my left shirt sleeve. "You're right-handed?" I nodded. From a pouch on the chair he removed the two black boxes. One he put on my upper arm and had me intone the blessing, repeating after him word for word, winding the long leather strap down my arm to my hand; the other went high on my forehead with a separate blessing.

And then, the Shema. That one I knew. Six words. The world of my childhood embodied in six words. The ancient prayer, the first prayer a Jew learns as a child, and the last prayer a Jew says before he dies. I had forgotten that I still knew it, but there it was, on my lips, as if it had never departed from them in the intervening years. *Shema Yisroel, Adonoi Eloheinu, Adonoi Echad.* Hear O Israel, the Lord Our God, the Lord is One. It felt clean. It felt good. And it felt strange, too.

But Rabbi Friedler was not done with me yet.

"So now, take a moment to focus on your friend. Think about the times you've had together; think about what a good friend he has been to you. Think of how much he means to you. Think about how you'd do anything you could to help bring him back to his full health. Take a few moments." He spoke quietly, almost hypnotically.

I thought about Josh's ready smile, his encouraging words. His sense of humor and his unflappable equanimity, on and off the court. And his wife and his boys, to whom he was so dedicated.

"So when you are ready, in your own words, ask the Master of the Universe to allow your plea to be heard on the Most High. It's important that you actually say the words out loud, not just think them. Whenever you're ready."

Strangely, the words came fully formed into my mind. I said slowly, "Master of the Universe, please grant me a hearing that I might bring my legal skills to bear in entreating You to -- restore -- him." On the word "restore" a small flash (lightning?) drew my attention to the window and I faltered, recovering enough to say "him" as I beheld the strange reflection of myself wearing the traditional black boxes on my head and arm. For a moment I feared my stumbling speech had ruined the prayer, but Rabbi Friedler's resounding "Amen" put my doubts to rest, and I felt a burden lifted as he patted me on the back and then began to help me out of the tefillin.

I felt like I had actually done something. I had come wondering what to do, and somehow this had been exactly the thing that needed doing. Rabbi Friedler shook my hand warmly and congratulated me with Yiddish words I didn't understand but whose meaning was plain in his smiling face.

And then, a moment later, as I saw this kindly old man putting the black leather boxes into their little cases, I wondered what exactly I thought I had accomplished. Maybe I had made an old man happier, and maybe I had tripped a little down memory lane. But did I really think the doctor would examine Josh in the morning and find he was miraculously cured from the cancer growing in his brain? Or even the slightest bit improved? A little perspective might be helpful, Mr. Cohen; a little reality check might be in order. Get a grip on yourself.

After he left, I stood watching Josh breathe.

I found myself wondering if, in the end, making an old man happy might not have its own merit worthy of consideration.

3——

I let myself into my apartment and fell into my chair. My hand went reflexively to my cell to dial Mary's number, but I caught myself. I had burned that bridge. Or, rather, it had come crashing down unexpectedly like the 35W bridge many years before.

And Josh was certainly not available. I could just imagine calling him at his hospital bed:

Josh, this is Larry. I'm having a hard time with your having cancer, man.

Me, too.

Why'd you have to go and get cancer?

Been asking myself that same question.

You can't die, Josh. You can't.

I hear you have to sooner or later, Larry. Although I don't have much personal experience with the whole death and dying thing.

Well, I do, and I don't need any more.

The sad truth was that I had no one to talk to.

I punched up my cell phone and left a second message with Dr. Silverberger. I would take the appointment after all. Let them think I was crazy for canceling the cancellation. That was their stock in trade, right? Dealing with crazy people. He should be able to handle me just fine.

I am—

4—

What--? Where--?
Bed.
Bedroom.

Darkness around the window shade.
Big red numbers. 4:16. Air.

Breathe.
Air.
It's all right.

Shapes, colors, surfaces. No substance, no reality. Would I fall through into nothingness?
Get a grip, Cohen. It's a floor.
My heart beat wildly. *Get out of here.*
I jumped into sweats, grabbed socks and running shoes. Out the door with wallet and keys.

Fresh air.
Cold cement sidewalk.
The lampposts looked real. The trees stood as they always did.
I breathed in. I let it out. Same old air.
My feet hit the path. I headed north along the river trail. Nobody here this early in the morning. The ground smacked my feet with a solid rhythm, and the river ran reassuringly along its course. I kept an easy pace.
Everything was okay.

5—

There was no line at the Highland Grill, and in short order I had a veggie omelet, hashbrowns, and a side of bacon in front of me. I looked around the diner. Mary and I used to come here often. Tuesday nights were our unofficial date night. If she were here I would tell her about this dream.

She would have listened attentively with those blue eyes. Would have said I was special to have had such a dream. She would have scoured the Internet for clues as to what it could symbolize. But it was pointless to think about what she would have done, because she wasn't here to do any of it.

At 8:45 I paid my bill, leaving myself extra time to get through rush hour traffic. It would not do to be late for a first appointment with a psychologist. He would probably infer all kinds of neuroses and rebelliousness from it.

I expected the traffic to be terrible.

It was.

6

Dr. Silverberger's office was in a nondescript brown building of 1970s vintage. Inside, the cramped reception room held fading yellow carpet, six black plastic chairs, two end tables with old magazines on them, and a water cooler. A hallway led off to the right with rooms off either side. I had expected a receptionist, at least. Dr. Silverberger did not seem to have hit the big time.

A sign said to have a seat and if no one helped me within 15 minutes I should let them know. I looked around at the five other empty black chairs. Let whom know? Maybe one of the other patients would walk in and could help me if the good doctor forgot he had a 9:30.

I got a cup of water and sat back down. Maybe they had a hidden camera and evaluated new patients based on their behavior in the empty waiting room. How long would they last before they cracked? Reminded me of the old Twilight Zone episode. Fellow comes to consciousness in an abandoned village and wanders around looking for other people. He thinks he hears sounds, but he sees no one anywhere. He eventually loses it and starts ranting and raving. Turns out he's in an isolation booth as part of a psychological experiment. He had created the abandoned village completely in his mind. I looked at the blank wall opposite me. Maybe Herr Doktor would ask me what I saw in the faded wallpaper.

At 9:32 a pear-shaped Dr. Silverberger strode confidently into the waiting area, and correctly identified me as Larry Cohen. He shook my hand, and asked me to come right this way. I followed his portly figure through a little maze of fluorescent-lit corridors. Finally he opened a door and asked me to enter.

Inside was a warmly lit office with windows on the opposite and left walls. The vertical blinds were bent at a careful angle to allow light to enter but prevent outsiders from looking in. On my left, two cherry-stained bookshelves filled the wall with texts, topped with dangling plants. To the right, a desk with papers sat under framed diplomas, and the chair in front of it was turned to face the room.

Dr. Silverberger urged me to have a seat as he closed the door. Under the windows to the left was a leather couch, old and comfortable, and closer at hand was the matching chair, forming a right angle with the couch. I took the chair. Dr. Silverberger sat down facing me.

He was an older man than I had thought at first, easily in his early 50s. His round face was brightened by intelligent brown eyes and a smile that seemed more friendly than polite. He wore a simple dark suit with a hint of color in the piping, a white shirt, and an unimpressive tie. Altogether probably $300 at a discount store.

"All right, Larry, how can I help?"

It was a reasonable question. What did I really expect Dr. Silverberger to be able to do? Poor little Larry is flipping out a little, doctor.

"I'm not sure, really." I shrugged. "I had originally made the appointment because my girlfriend-- well, my *ex*-girlfriend now-- had talked me into seeing a therapist at least one time. She thought I needed some help."

Dr. Silverberger nodded to show he was paying attention. "I see." He sat quietly, looking at me expectantly. I stared back at him.

"Well, now that you're here, why don't you tell me a little about what's going on with you?"

Where to begin? Every event felt connected to what came before it. The dream, the hospital, the diagnosis...

I decided to start with racquetball. Racquetball is always a good place to start.

.7___

I took a long breath and looked up at Dr. Silverberger.

"So that's pretty much it." I summarized by ticking off the events on my left hand. "I broke up with my girlfriend. I had an outburst in court that may have cost me my job. I have a major birthday coming up. And my best friend has cancer."

Dr. Silverberger eyed me thoughtfully. "That's a lot."

"And I had a weird dream last night. Really weird." Psychologists are supposed to love hearing dreams.

"Yes?"

"I was in a courtroom. It was-- well, it was like Courtroom 14B at the Federal Building, which I'm in all the time for work, but in the dream it was-- it was--" I shook my head helplessly. "I don't know. It was totally different. Intense and unnerving. And I woke up all sweaty and shaking. Everything was... unreal."

"How was the courtroom unreal?"

"No, no. When I woke up, everything in my bedroom was unreal. It was like-- like painted scenery or something. A holographic projection that could collapse into nothing at any moment. Poof." I noticed I was clutching the sides of the chair and casually unclenched my hands. "No, the courtroom in the dream was actually vividly real. Too real. Like no dream I've ever had before. The setting was familiar on the surface, but it was alien and strange somehow."

"Say more about that."

I licked my lips. My mouth was a little parched.

"Everyone was watching me, and I felt really small.

Yeah, like a, a grasshopper or something. And everyone else sort of belonged there, and they knew what was going on, what the rules were, you know? But somehow --even though this is the court I know inside-out and it's my job and everything-- somehow I felt like a second-grader thrust up on a Broadway stage in the middle of Hamlet, with the spotlight on me, and a packed house of critics and important people. All watching me. All waiting for me to-- do something. And not having a clue what that something was. Not just not knowing the words to say, but not even knowing the rules of what's expected of me. It was-- it was humiliating. And scary. Like my life depended on it and I was clueless."

I sat back, laying my arms down on the chair's arms.

"And another thing," I suddenly remembered, "I was on the wrong side of the courtroom."

He raised his eyebrows in a question.

"I'm a prosecutor. But in the dream, I was standing at the defense table."

Dr. Silverberger appeared to reflect on what I had told him. He steepled his hands below his chin.

"So, what do you make of it?"

"What do I make of it?"

He nodded.

I could not believe it. "Dr. Silverberger," I groped for the right words, "I come in here and I pour out my life to you and I'm paying you --or my health insurance is paying you-- something like $150 an hour and you're asking me what *I* think of this dream? *You*'re the expert! *You*'ve got the PhD. *You* tell *me*!"

He looked at me calmly, as if waiting to be sure I had

finished before he responded. He nodded slowly. Then he launched into a speech which he clearly had given many times before.

"Larry, therapy is kind of a funny thing. It's usually categorized in the medical field, but that can be quite misleading. In the medical model the doctor is a kind of glorified plumber, a Mr. Fixit." He leaned back in his chair. "When you have a leaky faucet at home, Larry, what do you do?" He gestured widely with his hands. "You might first look at it to see if you can fix it yourself, but if you can't, well, then, you call a plumber. So the plumber comes in and you show him the problem. He looks at it, makes his diagnosis and gives you an estimate."

I nodded to show I was paying attention.

"If the estimate seems reasonable and you think he's reliable, then you hire him to fix it. And he does. He gets parts if he needs them, rolls up his sleeves and sets to work while you go about your business. When he's finished, he calls you over, tells you what he's done, maybe shows you the old parts, demonstrates that the faucet now works the way it's supposed to, and you pay him, and off he goes. Very straightforward."

Dr. Silverberger leaned his bulk purposefully towards me. "But Larry, therapy is not plumbing."

He paused. Since it was clearly a dramatic pause, I restrained myself from responding caustically.

"Therapy is more like coaching, Larry. My job is to help you work your way through whatever difficulties you face, so that you not only solve the problems right in front of you, but you become a better problem-solver in general. I'm supposed to work myself out of a job. There are some things I know, from life experience and from professional training, and I bring those to the table. I'll share my opinion when you're grappling with an issue. But ultimately, you're the one who has to do the work. I can only assist."

He looked at me. I noticed his brown loafers. Tassels. I have never understood why people think brown shoes can match a black suit. At least his belt matched his shoes. Not everybody gets that right.

"So what do you think, Larry?"

I shrugged. What was I supposed to say? "Makes sense."

"All right, well let's see if we can work together on this dream. As you were telling it to me, what kind of feelings came up, what kind of thoughts entered your mind?"

I shook my head. "It was just so weird. That's the thing that keeps coming up. Weird. Intense. Spooky. It was like no other dream I've ever had. It was so... real."

"Hmm. You mentioned several major things you have going on: recent breakup, friend with cancer, your work... does this feel related to any of those?"

"Well, the setting was work-related, but--" I suddenly remembered Rabbi Friedler and the whole prayer thing. I sighed inwardly. This was going to sound nutty.

I related what had transpired with Rabbi Friedler, from the psalms, to the tefillin, to the prayer request, watching him while I did so. He listened closely, and, when I had finished, said, "So you think this rabbi bringing up pleading for your friend in the 'Heavenly Court' is what triggered the courtroom setting in your dream?"

"Well it-- seems plausible. Doesn't it?"

"Could be. Could be." He nodded and pursed his lips. "Larry, one thing that stands out to me is the anxiety in your dream, the feeling of inadequacy and smallness. It sounded like a major element; did I hear that right?"

"Yeah. It was definitely overwhelming."

"Have you had dreams with that kind of feeling before? Maybe not so intense, and maybe not in the courtroom setting, but-- same kind of feeling?"

I thought about it. "Not especially. I mean, not since I was a kid anyway."

"I see."

He nodded as though to himself. I couldn't tell if he expected me to speak, or if he was pursuing his thoughts. The silence stretched.

"So, Larry, you clearly have a lot of things going on. How do you manage the stress? Do you have people you can talk to? Really unburden yourself with?"

"Well..." An eyelash stung my eye and I tried to wipe it free with my right hand. Dr. Silverberger offered me a tissue box. He probably thought I was crying. I waved him off. "Just an eyelash."

He sat back, setting the tissue box on the couch.

"I don't know. I just do my normal things. I play racquetball. Well, I had been before Josh got sick. I play bridge with my friend Andy, but he's not exactly someone I can talk to-- not to relieve stress." I shrugged. "Obviously I can't very well talk to my girlfriend any more. My 'ex-girlfriend', I should say. I'm not too close to my mother. Or my sister..."

Inexplicably, my mind fastened on an image from my recent trip; I pictured Ruth's penetrating green eyes, a face listening intently across the Chinese restaurant table.

Dr. Silverberger glanced at his watch. He was probably itching to get on to his next appointment. "Well, we're coming up towards the end of the session, Larry. I'll tell you what I see and how I would suggest proceeding together, and you can decide if you think I can be helpful to you."

"Okay."

"You're under a lot of stress, and sometimes dreams like this come from stress in a person's current life, or sometimes, when we're under stress, unresolved issues from the past arise. And often, it's both at the same time. Some stressful issue of today taps into something from the past, and suddenly, wham!, things can seem to fall apart.

"So my suggestion would be twofold. First, focus on your stress management skills to help you deal with all that you have going on, and second, increase your understanding of the dynamics of how current events may be triggering old patterns of thought and emotion. The homework I would give you --yes, that's right, I give my clients homework-- would be to buy a small journal and carry it with you throughout the day. At least twice a day, write in it non-stop for five minutes. Whatever comes to your mind."

He raised a thick forefinger. "Now, I can almost

guarantee you'll find yourself thinking it's a stupid thing to do, and avoid it for a while. That's okay, but try to write anyway. How you're feeling, what you're thinking, and so on. You can write, 'This is so dumb; I just can't believe Dr. Silverberger thinks this is going to help!' Whatever comes up. If you wanted to, you could keep it by your bed and record your dreams as soon as you wake up. The idea is to increase your awareness of what's going on in your mind. What triggers what, what follows what."

He shifted in his chair. "Now the thing is Larry, this journal would be just for you. You wouldn't 'turn it in'; I wouldn't even see it. It's for you. Before you come in each time, you might want to review it, but only if you found that helpful." He held up a second finger. "The other piece of homework would be to write a list of things that you enjoy doing. Could be alone, could be with other people. Whatever you find pleasant and relaxing. Or things you get so engrossed in that you forget yourself, or lose track of time." He smiled. He tilted his head slightly to the right.

"So that's what I'm thinking, Larry. How does that strike you? Does it sound like something worth trying out?"

I considered. Dr. Silverberger seemed like he knew what he was doing. And it wasn't like I had a lot of other things going. "Sure. Couldn't hurt. Your homework sounds kinda like a blog."

"Yes, like a blog." I noticed the corner of his eyes crinkled when he smiled. "Well, the next step would be to find a time that will work for you to come back in..."

"Oh, I'm on leave from work for the next three weeks while they figure out if I'm coming back. Any time is fine."

My schedule was wide open. My boss, Mr. Hansen, hadn't lectured me. He hadn't felt the need to say, "You can't talk to a judge like that." Instead he had suggested I use the time off to regain my equilibrium. He had gone to bat for me, preventing an immediate dismissal. I owed him a lot. He was a good guy. When I first started, I noticed everyone else called him "Harry", but to me, his grey hair and stolid demeanor required a more respectful address. He had said calling him "Mr. Hansen" was fine. "Just don't start calling me 'Pops'!" he had quipped.

Dr. Silverberger's eyes were on my face. "Well, we can either meet weekly, or, if you want, we can meet more intensively while you're off work."

"What do you mean?"

"Oh, something like Monday-Wednesday-Friday."

"That would be great, as long as my insurance covers it."

Dr. Silverberger assured me he had made similar arrangements in the past with my insurance company, which apparently covered twenty sessions, regardless of how they were spaced over the year.

Which worked out well, because I had to start sleeping again and regain control of myself before I got back to work.

In order to be allowed back to work.

8

Josh was lying with the bed cranked up to a semi-sitting position. A smile broke through his tired face as he saw me.

"Hey, lawyer-man. Good to see you."

"Good to see you, too. I would have come sooner, but-- wait, actually I *did* come sooner. Yesterday, in fact, but you were sleeping."

"Been doing a lot of that lately."

I nodded. He looked haggard and his voice sounded weak.

"So how are you holding up, Josh?"

He looked up at me, "The waiting is the hardest. And seeing Cindy suffer under the strain of it. It all feels a little unreal to me until I see her face, trying to be calm or reassuring. Especially to the boys."

"Yeah. That's got to be rough." Like I knew anything about it. "They treating you all right here?"

"Oh, the staff is great. Anything I want at the press of a button. What about you? You look like you could use some sleep yourself."

"Well, I woke up way too early. I had the strangest dream. Sort of spooked me."

"Hmm?"

"Yeah. I was in this intense courtroom scene. I mean it was so *real*, that was the thing. Vivid and intense, you know?"

Josh might have nodded; it was hard to tell.

"When I woke up, everything around me seemed so flat and detached. It was like I was in a bad cartoon or something. I didn't know who I was, where I was."

"Chuang Tzu."

"Huh?"

"Chuang Tzu!"

"Gesundheit."

Josh throated a sound that would have been a chuckle if he hadn't been so dry. He sucked on a straw in a cup by his bed. He set it back down carefully, like an old man who knows his hand betrays him occasionally.

"Master Chuang Tzu was a Chinese philosopher. He dreamed he was a butterfly fluttering around, completely happy with himself. He didn't know he was Chuang Tzu." He looked up at me. "Then he woke up. But he said he didn't know if he was Chuang Tzu who had dreamt he was a butterfly, or a butterfly dreaming he was Chuang Tzu."

"Yeah. Something like that."

"So what was this dream about?"

I told him what I remembered of the courtroom scene.

"A grasshopper, eh?"

"Yup. I mean, it wasn't like your Chinese guy and his butterfly. I wasn't actually a grasshopper in the dream, it's just how I described the feeling afterwards. The first thing that came into my mind in Dr. Silverberger's office."

"Still," he mused, "most people would have said 'ant' or 'insect' or 'fly'. But 'grasshopper', now that's interesting."

"Why's that?"

"Well, I can't help but think of Kung Fu, you know.

An old TV series from, oh, the seventies I think. A Kung Fu priest wanders the Wild West spreading the ideas of tolerance and peacemaking." He smiled. "While occasionally beating the snot out of bigots and bad guys, of course."

"Sounds like a fun show. What's the connection?"

Josh explained that interspersed with the Wild West scenes were flashbacks to the Chinese monastery where the hero had trained all the years of his youth. One of his primary teachers was blind, and early on, the young child pitied the old blind master, commenting that the blind man must be missing out on so much. The master responded that his other senses were sharpened because of his blindness; he pointed out a grasshopper at the young hero's feet that the boy had been oblivious to. The astonished kid learned his lesson, but from then on, the blind master called him 'Grasshopper' as an affectionate nickname.

"He called him 'Grasshopper' particularly when our young disciple got stuck in his limited view of the world which, for all his sightedness, he couldn't see as well as the old blind master." He smiled up at me. "A cool show. Found it when I was first getting into Zen and meditation."

"But I don't see how my thinking of a grasshopper to describe my dream could have any connection to that show, when this is the first time I've heard of it. I mean, it sounds cool, but my subconscious wouldn't have had a chance to make the association."

"That's what happens when you have a tumor up here." He tapped the side of his head. "Strange illogical connections abound, Grasshopper."

"Speaking of strange illogical connections, when I was here yesterday and you were asleep, I met an old rabbi in your room! He said he had heard your name and had come in to say a prayer for you." I told him the story of our encounter.

"So, do you think your dream is related to meeting this rabbi?"

"Well, I thought it could be. It occurred to me at the shrink's office this morning. Although now that I think about it, I don't know if I even mentioned the possible connection to Rabbi Friedler. He must not have been too impressed with it if I did."

"Oh? When did you talk with him about it?"

"This morning." *Like I just said.*

"Busy morning for you. So what did the good rabbi have to say?"

"Good rabbi?"

Josh gave me a puzzled look. "Didn't you just say you talked with Rabbi Friedler about it and he wasn't too impressed with the connection?"

"No, no. I talked with Dr. Silverberger about my dream; he's a psychologist, after all. Why would I go tell Rabbi Friedler about my dream?"

"Why *wouldn't* you talk to Rabbi Friedler about your dream?"

"Because I barely even met the old guy, and it would be presumptuous and intrusive to ask him to listen to a crazy dream."

"Well, maybe. But don't you think he might be interested in the, um, conveniently coincidental fact that you had this intense courtroom dream the very night he instructed you to make this prayer about 'pleading my case'?"

"Hmph."

"A dream in which you're defending someone, instead of prosecuting?"

"All right, all right. But it doesn't make me want to embarrass myself to a complete stranger who probably wouldn't remember me from Adam."

Josh nodded. "Just a thought, Grasshopper-man. Just a thought."

9

The hospital gift shop sold spiral notebooks so I thought I would try the journal homework thing. I had some time to kill before meeting Andy for dinner and bridge.

I sat down at a table in the cafeteria and tried to look inconspicuous. A lone man losing himself in the crowd. Except everybody else was with somebody. Orderlies and nurses clustered together on break. Families visiting their loved ones. The kids looking bored and more than ready to go home.

I opened the notebook. The spaces between the blue lines stared blankly up at me. I wrote the date. Dr. Silverberger had said just to start writing and keep writing, no breaks. Starting now.

I'm sitting here in the hospital cafeteria writing in this notebook. Well, obviously I'm writing in this notebook. How else would these words be appearing?

A stupid start. But no stopping.

This definitely feels like a waste of time. Just as Dr. Silverberger predicted. Of course, if he knew it would be a waste of time, why did he tell me to do it? So obviously he thinks it won't be a waste of time. So even though it feels like a waste of time to me, and a waste of ink and paper, it's not. Or it shouldn't be. Or it wouldn't be if I did it right.

Just what am I supposed to write about, anyway?

Whatever comes into your mind, he said. 42 seconds and I'm supposed to go on for five minutes of this? What garbage. My friend's dying over in the oncology ward and I'm sitting here writing idiotic thoughts about writing in a notebook and glancing at my watch every eleven seconds.

Not that there's anything productive I can do anyway. If writing words in a notebook could kill cancer tumors, the world would be free of them in a hurry, that's for sure. And if that weird dream last night was connected to the ~~prayer~~ request to plead Josh's case, then I certainly blew that opportunity. Stood there in court stunned out of my mind. How can you be stunned out of your mind in a dream, anyway? Stood there like a perfect idiot. Felt like a fool in front of billions of --I don't know-- people, or beings or something. Naked in a dress suit, and completely unprepared. Trembling. Overwhelmed. Totally out of my league.

One minute fifty-one seconds. This is impossible. How hard can it be to write for five minutes? And me a lawyer, no less.

It was a start, anyway. He said it wouldn't be graded. "There's no right or wrong about it."

I went back to watching people. A young boy holding his mother's hand in the checkout line looked at me and our eyes met. I smiled at him. He shrank back uncertainly to his mother's side. Don't scare the nice boy, Larry.

I wasted another hour there, writing a little in the journal, watching people come and go, scaring other young children. Then I headed out to Barnes and Noble. When nobody was looking, I browsed their self-help and dream interpretation sections, but nothing caught my eye.

I drove to meet Andy for dinner. Crosstown traffic would be annoying at this hour, and Andy was occasionally close to punctual when we had a game at the club. But I bet I would order before he got there anyway. We had come to an agreement on pre-game dinners: after waiting fifteen minutes I ordered for us, and after twenty minutes he paid for both meals. Kept us from missing the bridge game. Kept me from getting too irritated with him. New Yorker.

10

If Andy had been another two minutes late, I would have ordered our dinners. As it was, I had just requested a large orange juice chaser to the glass of ice water I had almost finished. As he came to the table the pert little waitress hurried up. He ordered a cherry Coke.

"So how's the vaykay?" he asked.

"The what?"

"The vaykay. Your time off."

"Oh, as in vay-kay-shun?"

"Exactly. I knew you could get it in two syllables."

"It's syllable-conservers like you who are ruining the English language." I sipped my water. "It's not exactly a vacation and it's not exactly going so great."

"I told you to take a trip, get out of town. What are you doing, just sitting around moping?"

To change the subject, I gave him the news about Josh. And, since his New York roots had familiarized him with various Jewish sects, I told him about Rabbi Friedler.

"Full beard, wide-brimmed black Borsalino hat, dark suit and a ready pair of tefillin?"

"Wouldn't swear to the hat style. Looked more like a cowboy hat to me. But otherwise, that's him. You know him?"

Andy shook his head. "Gotta be a 'Neener'."

"A what?"

"A Slovodjaniner. It's a Jewish Hasidic sect headquartered in Brooklyn. They run around brainwashing unsuspecting Jews into doing the traditional rituals: putting on tefillin, lighting candles for Shabbos, keeping kosher, praying three times a day. The works. Starts off innocently enough 'just this one time, you'll like it', that kind of thing. Ends in... cult-like disaster. You've never heard of them?"

I shook my head.

"They're all over the world. Sent on 'holy missions' by their beloved, saintly Rebbe, whom they revere as the Messiah Himself."

"I thought all Hasidic sects thought their rebbes were the Messiah."

"Theirs has been dead for over twenty years!"

"Ah. That would put a damper on things."

"Not for them!" Andy gathered in some air. "You have to understand, Larry, these people--"

We were interrupted by the waitress, returning with our drinks.

After she left, Andy looked at me. "Anyway... Sorry about your friend, Josh. That's terrible. Is that why you look so sleep-deprived?"

"I had a dream."

"Little black boys and girls joining hands with little white boys and girls as sisters and brothers?"

"Very funny."

I described the dream, but he had little response.

I said, "Didn't you go to a yeshiva high school or something?"

"Guilty as charged, counselor. Went to cheder as a young child, yeshiva for high school. Even survived a year of Yeshiva University before I escaped to the Midwest. University of Chicago for undergrad. Then back east to Columbia Law School. They cured me."

"But you still remember a lot of the religious stuff you learned before."

Andy's narrowed eyes probed my face. "What are you getting at?"

"Just wondering, Counselor... Do you think I blew it in the Heavenly Court?"

"Huh?"

"Was that the Heavenly Court?!"

"How should I know?" He took a pull at his coke. "It sounds like a nightmare set in the Hennepin County Court. Didn't you say that's what it looked like?"

I nodded.

"Okay, so you were on the defense side. Big deal. It was a dream."

"Yeah. But the thing is, Andy--" I looked at him, trying to figure out how to convey it. "It just wasn't like any other dream I've ever had. It was totally, like, other-worldly. And if it was-- I think I blew it."

"You're serious." Amusement, incredulity and irritation flashed across his face in quick succession. Then he was shaking his head vigorously. "Not at all. Okay, look. Say it *was* some kind of Heavenly Court case. It wasn't, but never mind. Okay. So it's coming to you in the metaphor of the County Court. That means it has to follow County Court procedures the whole way through, not just here and there, randomly." He held up his left hand and began ticking off fingers with his right forefinger. "Which means you need to have an arraignment, discovery, an Omnibus hearing and a--" he broke off. "What is your friend charged with in this dream, anyway?"

"I don't even know! People may have been talking, but I stood there the whole time stunned out of my mind!"

"Look, if it was said in your dream, then you know it. Your subconscious has stored the memory of the entire dream." He leaned back in the booth. "I bet if you were hypnotized you could remember it." He swung his spoon playfully in a pendulum from side to side. "You are feeling sleepy. Very sleeeepy."

Something caught. Like a fragment of a passing conversation overheard as noise and then, a few moments later, the noise resolves into words and the meaning suddenly hits you.

I smacked my hand on the table. "Someone did read the charge. He was accused of 'the crime of crying b...'" I slumped.

Andy raised an eyebrow. "The crime of crying..?"

"I can't make it out. It's gibberish. The crime of crying 'bendawma'?"

Andy shrugged. "So google it. You'll figure it out. Somewhere in there" --he reached over and tapped the side of my head-- "you already have the answer. Once you unravel it, you'll understand your dream and it won't have this power over you. My father always says, 'It's what you don't understand that scares you.'"

"But what if I can't figure it out? What if I lose the case?"

"You win some, you lose some. It is just a dream."

"But, Andy," I blurted out, "what if Josh's life hangs in the balance?"

Andy shook his head slowly. He looked down at his plate and lifted his last forkful. "Okay, so if it's that important to you, win the case, Counselor. Find out what this 'bendawma' thing is and win the case."

11

The bridge session had started off poorly and had gotten worse from there. I was thankful it was over. Andy and I were watching the last four players in the corner finish a late play, after which the final scores could be calculated. We would finish last, or close to last, I knew, but no matter how pathetically I had played, I stayed at the end; only a coward would leave before seeing the final scores.

I had made a bidding error on the first hand, and, on the next hand, I played my first card without thinking. Later I realized that I could have recovered if I had kept my wits about me. But no. Dumb and dumber. Like dominoes falling over in a line, an interminable evening of increasing frustration and failure.

Andy had taken it in good stead. It was one of the things that made him a good bridge partner. He took no joy in crowing over his partner's mistakes, the way we constantly heard other partnerships sniping at each other. He kept holding out the possibility of a turnaround.

The late group was done now. A couple of hardy souls lingered around the director, probably in contention for coming in first. Otherwise, the place was deserted. Funny how depressing the room seemed when it emptied out.

"You know, Larry, about those Slovodjaniners." Andy's voice broke in on my thoughts, but lacked its characteristic lightness. He raised a palm. "I don't want to tell you what you should do--"

"Sure you do."

"No, no. It's just that-- well, I've seen it up close, you know. I know what can happen-- and, well, it can be pretty devastating the way things turn out..."

"I hear you."

He paused, considering how much he should say. "Just-- well, just be cautious, okay?"

"Yes, mama." And seeing he was still looking intent, I added, "Don't worry, Counselor; I'll be careful."

Andy nodded to himself and seemed to relax; having completed his duty, he let go of his burden. We went over and confirmed a rock bottom showing in the standings. Andy peeked at the results for two of the deals, but apparently came to no profound conclusions. He nodded his readiness to leave.

"Thanks for your advice on this dream thing." I glanced at his profile. "I know you think it's stupid."

"Of course I think it's stupid," Andy said. "A dream is a dream, Larry. By any other name is still just a dream. You're a trial lawyer, so you have a courtroom dream. Very simple. End of story."

The hint of a smile lurked behind his suddenly formal demeanor. "But tell me, Counselor, how are you going to plead?"

I looked at him in mock amazement. "How can you ask, Counselor? The defense *always* pleads 'Not Guilty'."

12

The empty apartment felt funny when I let myself in. Like ghosts haunted the corners or something. I tried to shake off the feeling, but failed. I startled at the sound of the floorboards creaking.

I realized that I had been away the entire day, avoiding the place. But that hardly explained my jitters. The truth was that I was nervous about going to sleep. Which was silly.

I stayed up in my chair watching late-night television and eating corn chips. *Defending Your Life* came on; Albert Brooks was funny, but I started falling asleep, so I finally turned it off, willing myself out of my chair and across the living room. Just a dream.

I brushed my teeth and prepared for bed. Tonight I would probably have nightmares about competing in the Bridge World Championships. After my performance at the club, that would be terrifying enough.

I turned out the light and laid down. The bed was comfortable. And no need to set the alarm. The luxury of leisure time.

I am standing behind the table.
Right thumb pointing to left thumb on formica.
Two white moons.
Perfect curves of flesh. Perfect curves of thumbnail.
Mirror images.
On the one hand. On the other hand.
Two necessary parts of a whole.
Let's just be together, you and me, you and me.

A sharp clap of thunder reverberates throughout the chamber, the sound rippling outwards from the Judge's gavel. A butterfly flapping its wings in the remote jungle causes a hurricane halfway around the world. One thing leads to another, to another, to another.
The wheels on the bus go round and round, round and round, round and round.
The people on the bus go up and down, up and down, up and down.

Down. Knees bend, chair creaks.
Two white moons blush pink as blood returns, traveling through arteries, expanding capillaries, bringing nourishment to each and every cell. Skin cells, tissue cells, bone cells, jail cells, battery cells, sex sells. Everywhere a cell, cell.
Old MacDonald had some thumbs, E-I-E-I-O.

And in those thumbs he had some cells,
    E-I-E-I-O.
Oxygenation here and mitosis there,
Hairy cell, there a cell, everywhere a cell, cell
Old MacDonald had some thumbs, E-I-E-I-O.

And on those thumbs there were also thumb
prints, formations unique in the universe, made
just for these thumbs,
special for these hands, only for you. Ridges and
bumps and whorls, lines and curves and spaces.
A world in miniature with each part in its place,
fulfilling its purpose as part of the whole.
Individual patterns on opposable thumbs.
Thumbs that oppose in harmony with the hand.
Apart and together, distinct yet inseparable.
Who could oppose that?

Thumbs up, thumbs down; thumbs , thumbs, all
around.
Thumb a ride, into town, thumb your nose 'til
it's upside-down.
Thumb through a book, thumb down the cook.
Put in his thumb and pulled out a plum.
And said,

"How do you plead?"

The compelling voice reverberates in a tomb of
silence.
How do you plead?

That is the question. Whether 'tis nobler to suffer
The slings and arrows of outrageous fortune,
Or to take thumbs against a sea of troubles,
And by opposing end them?
To sleep: perchance to dream: ay, there's the rub
For in that sleep of death, what dreams may come?

A question needs an answer, and an answer must be spoken.
Speak the speech, I pray you, as I pronounced it to you, trippingly on the tongue, but if you mouth it, as so many of our players do--
Better to remain silent and be thought a fool than to open your mouth and remove all doubt.
But the time has come, the Walrus said, to talk of many things...

Speak. This is your moment. The time is now.
Speak!

A raspy voice issues from my throat:
"Not"

Not worthy.
Not on your life.
Tongue tied in a knot.
Double-knot.
A man is a bundle of relations, a knot of roots, whose flower and fruitage is the world.

The world awaits. You must complete it.
Half done is half undone.

"Guilty."

Done!
But a thunderous, oppressive silence waits expectantly. There is more to be said, more that must be said. A collective gasp fills the sickening silence; the unthinkable unfolds with each yawning moment.
The pitiful grasshopper flailing; melting in a puddle of shame.
The universe of all beings waits.
The Judge waits.
Expectantly.
Something still unsaid.
And finally, as if of their own accord, the lips part and the throat croaks out:
"...Your Honor."

The gavel thunders.

13___

I jerked awake. Chest pounding. Sweating. Raspy breath. In and out. Raw on my throat. A stage set. The lingering presence of a million souls looking on, somewhere just out of view. The grasshopper in a glass jar.

The bed felt solid beneath me, and the clock on the bedside table shone forth 4:16 in its reassuring red lights. I jumped up to shake off the mood. I stamped on the floor. Solid. This was crazy. I was losing my mind.

The next moment I was in my running gear, stretching out on my front steps as my shins protested.

What was I doing?

Running away from my own apartment. Not okay. I forced myself to walk back inside. This dream was not running my life. I sat down in my chair and picked up the spiral notebook. I wrote. I recorded the dream and my reactions to it-- thoughts, feelings, the works. I kept writing until I had nothing left to say. I set the pen down on top of the notebook. Enough of that.

I laid back down in bed, but sleep wouldn't come. After twenty minutes I gave it up, showered and got dressed. It was too early to call anyone. I checked my email. Spam. I logged in to Facebook. Nothing. I googled 'bendawma'. Zilch.

I looked up Slovodjaniners. Wikipedia said they were a mystical chassidic sect that emphasized a personal relationship with God over formal Biblical studies. They were named after a small town in Poland where their first Rebbe had lived in the 1800s. He had been a student of the famed Baal Shem Tov, the father of all the chassidic movements, and had been known as "The Elder Rebbe". His most famous quote was, "Each and every moment in this world is about our relationship with God."

There had been a dynasty of these Slovodja rebbes, ending in the one who came to the US as a boy in 1932. He had grown up and taken over the position after his father died in 1959. The rest was history. The new Rebbe had the inspiration of sending out Neener families around the world to spread Jewish practices.

I went to their website. They had an emissary in every major city and a search engine to find the rabbi nearest you. I looked up Rabbi Friedler; his Twin Cities operation had its own local web site showcasing his picture, home phone number and an encouragement to call him with any question I had, large or small. "The only dumb question is the one left unasked." Well, I certainly had some things to ask him about.

I looked at the clock. Somehow I didn't think Rabbi Friedler meant to encourage six o'clock phone calls. I looked closely again at the web site. Morning prayers were scheduled from 6:45 to 7:30am every morning. Perfect. I had time for breakfast at the diner.

14

Back home after a hearty meal, I reclined in my chair and punched up Rabbi Friedler's number. His wife answered and happily gave out his cell phone number to a total stranger. Rabbi Friedler answered on the third ring.

"Moishe Friedler."

"Um, Rabbi Friedler, this is Larry Cohen. We met Sunday in the oncology ward at United Hospital. My friend Josh Levin was asleep in his room there and you had stopped in to say a few prayers for him..?"

"Oh, yes." I could picture him nodding in remembrance. "The lawyer!"

"Exactly. You see... ever since you had me-- well, ever since I put on those tefillin and, er, you had me ask to 'plead Josh's case', I've been having these strange dreams. Really strange."

"I see."

A pause. The silence felt awkward. At least he hadn't laughed out loud.

"I was wondering if I could meet with you and talk them over..?"

"Sure." Rabbi Friedler sounded like nothing could be more natural than a stranger he had accidentally met in a hospital calling and asking to get together to share his perplexing dreams. "Let's meet at my house; I should be home in a few minutes. 1478 Vermont Ave."

"You mean-- now?!"

Rabbi Friedler chuckled. "If not now, when?"

The Friedler house was a modest one-story affair with peaceful horizontal lines. The driveway came up on the right of a smallish front yard, surrounded by a low white picket fence. On the far side an old maple tree shaded the windows, and the walk from the driveway led through a decorative trellis and up to a low stoop in the center where an oak door beckoned from beneath a sheltering overhang. I rang the bell.

A young man of barely twenty years opened the door and motioned me inside. His wrinkled white dress shirt draped carelessly down his thin frame and hung out over his dark pants. He was wearing tefillin and seemed to be mumbling to himself. As I stepped in, I started to introduce myself, but he had already turned and headed back into the rear of the house, calling out "Nuuu!". I stayed where I was and looked around.

The foyer was maybe eight by ten with grey slate tiles covering the floor and a closet with wooden folding doors on the right. Straight ahead was an open archway, through which the young mumbler had disappeared, and just to the left of it, at eye level, was a two-by-two feet patch of unfinished sheetrock. It contrasted sharply to the rich cream-colored walls all around it, on which were hung pictures of pious-looking bearded men staring out at me, or singing in huddled groups around long tables, glasses and bottles held high.

Rabbi Friedler bustled into the room and shook my hand vigorously.

"Larry! Nice to have you." He led the way through the archway. "Shall we start with tefillin?"

I smiled to myself. Rabbi Friedler was no fool. How

could I refuse when I had come over to ask for his help? I rolled up my left sleeve in surrender. I would pay my dues. The procedure went as before, and afterwards I thought about how to tell my story as I rolled my sleeve down and buttoned the cuff. But Rabbi Friedler had something else in mind.

"Have you heard the shofar yet?"

"Um, no," I responded. "Is it Rosh Hashanah already?"

"No, that's not for another week yet, but each day during this preparatory month of Elul, we sound the shofar to remind us to return to God in repentance before the big day of judgement." Rabbi Friedler located the ram's horn amidst the papers covering the near end of a long table. The table filled what would usually be a living and dining room, but which was clearly used as one long study hall and dining room combined.

He brought the horn to his lips. Blasts filled the air. Short sounds, long sounds, different combinations. Ancient, eerie sounds, mixing the triumph of a war cry and the whimpering of a small child. The reverberations died down; my ears were ringing. I took a deep breath and closed my eyes. I cast my mind back; I was pretty sure I had only heard that sound in synagogue on Rosh Hashanah.

"You do that every day of the month before Rosh Hashana?"

"Well, *almost* every day." Rabbi Friedler smiled, "We don't sound the shofar on Shabbos, and we skip the last day before Rosh Hashana to fool the Adversary. I'm not sure how effective that is --the Adversary is a pretty clever fellow, you know-- but it's our custom to try." He gestured towards the near end of the long table. "But let's sit down and you can tell me all about these dreams."

I described the "courtroom", simultaneously familiar and strange, the overwhelming fear and the disoriented awakenings. He took it all in thoughtfully.

"So what do they mean, Rabbi?"

Rabbi Friedler spoke softly, almost to himself, "*Beelahdai, Elokim yaaneh es shlom Paaroh!*" He lifted his eyes and smiled into my confusion. "Joseph's answer when he is asked to interpret Pharaoh's dreams. He says, 'It is beyond me-- God will see to Pharoah's welfare!'"

He stood up energetically, walked a few paces holding his forehead, and then turned and started interrogating me like a trained attorney. Or maybe like the kindly grandfather of a trained attorney.

"There was only one judge in this courtroom?"

"Yes, I'm pretty sure-- yes, just the one."

"And what did he look like? What kind of throne, or chair, did he sit on?"

"Well, I couldn't see the chair, but the setting was definitely the Hennepin County Court, if that's what you're getting at. That is, it *looked* like the County courtroom, but it, it *felt* like..." I trailed off.

"Mmm?"

"It felt like it was, somehow-- I don't know how to say it. Like it was the one *true* court or something. Like every other court was just a pale imitation and *this* was the real deal."

Rabbi Friedler nodded as if this confirmed a theory. "And the judge's face? Did you see his face?"

"Well, no, I never actually saw his face. I was too, um, overwhelmed to even look up, I guess."

"And you were at the table for the defense counsel?"

"Yes."

"Was anyone with you?"

"No!" It suddenly struck me as odd.

"That's unusual in your court?"

"Yes. Very unusual. I hadn't thought of it before, but the defendant is always present at the arraignment, and I would expect him there for the Omnibus hearing, too." I frowned. "Unless he can't attend for some compelling reason." I returned Rabbi Friedler's gaze. "Like if he's lying sick in the hospital."

Rabbi Friedler paused and nodded slowly to himself. He seemed to make a mental note. Then he was pacing again.

"Was there a prosecuting attorney present?"

"I'm not totally sure. I kind of *think* so, but I never looked away from the table. But-- yes, there was. I'm sure of it."

"Was there a jury?"

"No, but there wouldn't be at an arraignment, where the charges are read. After that, you have the Omnibus or pre-trial hearing, where the defendant enters his plea, and any issues of evidence and witnesses are handled. If the case survives that without being dismissed or settling, you go to trial, which can either be in front of a judge or a jury, depending on the charge and the defendant's choice..." I trailed off, realizing I was giving a law school lecture.

"Very interesting. Very interesting." Rabbi Friedler

stroked his beard in concentration. "And you woke up at exactly four-sixteen both mornings?"

"Yes. Is that significant?"

Rabbi Friedler turned towards the head of the table where a doorway opened into what was surely the kitchen.

He called, "Sruli?!" and in a moment Mr. Mumbler reentered the room, looking attentive. "Yes, Ta?"

"Four sixteen?"

Sruli furrowed his brows and sank his chin to his chest. He raised his left hand and began touching different fingers to his thumb, as he murmured what sounded like nonsense syllables to himself. Finally he raised his head with a slow shake and a frown. "Nothing I can think of."

"Nothing?" Rabbi Friedler tried not to sound disappointed.

Sruli shrugged. "It's six fourteen backwards, which would be 613 plus the One who gave them."

Rabbi Friedler turned back to me. "Gematria is my son's specialty; he has a gift."

Seeing my puzzled look, Rabbi Friedler spelled it out for me. "Every Hebrew letter is also a number, so every Hebrew word can be associated with the numerical sum of the letters it contains. Two words with the same sum share a spiritual connection, and the study of those numbers and the spiritual connections is called 'gematria'."

Sruli nodded. "And I can't think of anything for four sixteen. Sorry."

"Well, thanks for trying," I said. "What was that

about 613 and 614?"

"613 is the number of commandments in the Bible," Sruli explained. "Adding one for God gets you to 614 and then reversing it is 416. But it's pretty thin; what could reversing the direction of the commandments signify, really? Ta, you guys want tea or anything?"

Rabbi Friedler nodded; I asked for coffee. We sat back down as Sruli headed for the kitchen.

"Now you said that when you told your friend your dream, you remembered the charge being made in this court?"

"Yes, it was something about the crime of crying 'bendawma', or something like that. Is 'bendawma' a word?"

Rabbi Friedler puzzled over the word. "'bendawma'... 'bendawma'..."

He looked up. "Could you have it slightly wrong? Could it have been, say, 'Bin Laden'?"

"No, it definitely wasn't Bin Laden. But it could have been part of a longer word, maybe. It was one of those things where you hear it while you're busy with something else, and then later you remember it, you know?"

Rabbi Friedler nodded. He got up from his chair and, pacing, started repeating to himself in sing-song, "The crime of crying 'bendawma'. The crime of crying 'bendawma'..." After a while the words lost their meaning and became mere sounds, echoed over and over again. He varied the pitch and the accent he gave the syllables, repeating them as he walked back and forth, trying to coax meaning out of the vocalizations.

Sruli returned with his father's tea and my coffee on a small tray with spoons and saucers, sugar and creamer. He looked at his father, and raised questioning eyebrows at me as he quietly set down our drinks.

I whispered, "He's trying to figure out 'the crime of crying bendawma'. It's from a dream I had."

Sruli listened to his father for another moment and then interrupted him without ceremony. "Ta, it's not the crime of 'crying bendawma', it's the crime of 'Kayin ben Odom'."

15

The base of my spine tingled and I shuddered. That was it. That was what the court reporter had announced in my nightmare. "The crime of Kayin ben Odom". Whatever that meant.

I turned to Rabbi Friedler expectantly. He said something in Yiddish to Sruli and squeezed his shoulder. As Sruli returned to the kitchen, Rabbi Friedler turned towards me.

"Kayin ben Odom," he said slowly, "is the formal name for Kayin. Or in English, Cain."

"Cain?"

"Yes, Cain, son of Adam. In Hebrew, Kayin ben Odom."

"Cain as in Cain and Abel?"

"Mm-hmm." Rabbi Friedler sat down to his tea. I slumped back in my chair.

"How could Josh be guilty of the sin of Cain? He doesn't even *have* a brother." As far as I knew.

"The interpretation of dreams can be a delicate thing." Rabbi Friedler stirred two heaping spoonfuls of sugar into his tea. He made a blessing and sipped cautiously. "You know, Pharaoh had a whole palace full of advisors and magicians. He asked them what his dreams meant. And they each gave him very plausible explanations The cows symbolized this; the ears of grain represented that. But none of the explanations satisfied him; he knew his dream held something more, some truth he would recognize when he heard it. When none of his advisors spoke that truth, he became desperate. That was when he sent for Joseph." He took another sip of tea and looked at me over the top of his cup. "The Talmud tells us that only the dreamer can be sure of the interpretation of his dream."

For this I had put on tefillin? Surely Rabbi Friedler could tell me *something* about these dreams that would help me make sense of them, or make them go away.

"Rabbi, are these dreams for real? I mean, are they from...?" I pointed to the ceiling.

"From God? Of course!" Rabbi Friedler smiled. "Everything is from God. Nothing is outside of Him; He is the Source of everything we see--" he spread his arms inclusively, "--and everything we don't see. Every single experience, every event, every happening in the entire universe, comes directly from The Master. There *is* nothing else!"

Andy's warning to be careful sprang to mind. Rabbi Friedler might look like a cuddly grandfather and his eyes might twinkle like a gleeful child's, but he definitely had the mindset of a religious fanatic. He brought his hands back to his teacup.

"But of course, we still have free will. And just knowing Hashem sent you these dreams doesn't make clear what the message is, or what you should do about them. Take the case of Yitzchak Yenkel, for example."

"Yitzchak Yen--?"

"Why, yes! The famous story of Yitzchak Yenkel." Rabbi Friedler gathered himself for a storytelling adventure. "Yitzchak Yenkel was a poor man who lived with his wife in a dirt hut in a *shtetl,* a Jewish community in rural Poland. He was constantly looking for work, while his wife sold the bagels she made on the iron stove in the center of the hut.

"One night, Yitzchak had a dream. In the dream, a voice instructed him, 'Go to Krakow. Outside the palace of the Czar is a bridge, and under the bridge is buried a large treasure!'" Rabbi Friedler's eyes widened at the prospect of treasure. "But Yitzchak Yenkel was not a believer of dreams, so he ignored the message."

Somehow I knew that ignoring this dream was not going to work for poor Yitzchak.

"The next night, he had the dream again, and the voice was louder and more insistent. But Krakow was over a hundred miles away, and the prospect of walking it in wintertime was frightful, so Yitzchak Yenkel ignored the dream again.

"On the third night however, the voice in the dream was louder still, 'Go to Krakow, find the bridge and claim the treasure!' Yitzchak Yenkel could no longer ignore this dream. He told his wife, and she packed him what little food they had, and sent him off walking to the great distant city of Krakow to dig up the treasure." Rabbi Friedler started pumping his arms as if he were walking briskly along.

"So off he goes. Many, many days later he arrives in Krakow. He finds the bridge, only to see the captain of the Czar's guards stationed atop it! The captain eyes Yitzchak suspiciously, so he maintains his distance and waits until nightfall, hoping the guard will leave. But instead, another guard takes his place!" Rabbi Friedler sagged his shoulders to signal Yitzchak's disappointment.

"But Yitzchak Yenkel has come too far to be easily

discouraged. He waits day and night for three days, hoping to find an opportunity to dig under the bridge. On the third day, however, the captain approaches Yitzchak Yenkel and demands to know why he is snooping around this bridge outside the Czar's palace!

"Terrified of arrest and imprisonment, Yitzchak Yenkel tells the man of his dreams and his trek to discover the treasure under the bridge. The captain laughs, 'You walked for days through the bitter cold and snow because of a silly dream?! You fool! Do you see how stupid you are? If I listened to every dream I had, I would not be captain of the guard outside the Czar's palace! Why just last night I dreamed of a small *shtetl* where there lives a poor man named Yitzchak Yenkel, and under the stove in his house lies a buried treasure. Do you see me tearing off into the countryside because of this crazy dream?!'"

"So Yitzchak, hearing his own name issue forth from the mouth of the Czar's captain, hurries back home and, to his wife's great surprise, tears out the stove in the middle of the house, and sets about digging with his bare hands. After a time, he discovers a chest filled with silver and gold." Rabbi Friedler looked up from where his hands had been clawing under an imaginary stove.

"There's more to the story, since the captain of the guard eventually decides to dig under the Czar's bridge, and he, too, finds a treasure, but the point here is... Yitzchak Yenkel acted in a way we might consider crazy today, right?"

I nodded. I wondered if such a man had ever really existed.

R. Friedler clearly had no doubts. "You might say Yitzchak Yenkel should never have left home, that chasing after his dream was insanity. But, of course, that was the only way he could find out that there was treasure in his own home all along. Right under his very feet!"

Rabbi Friedler had told the story well, but I couldn't see the relevance.

"So what exactly should I do with these court dreams?" I couldn't go down to the County Court and check with the clerk for 'God vs. Joshua Levin'.

"It's a good question." R. Friedler considered. "I think the important thing is to take these dreams seriously. But as to their meaning-- is it possible that your friend has committed the preliminary crime of Kayin? Jealousy?"

"I guess he could have." I thought about Josh. "But I doubt it. He's just not the type." I finished my coffee.

"We should also consider the possibility that this Kayin case has no direct bearing to your friend's life in the World of Action. It could be coming to you for a different reason altogether."

"Such as?"

Rabbi Friedler wagged his finger at me. "You ask the tough questions. And the truth is, I don't have any good answers. But whatever it turns out to be... may the merit of your time and effort be given over to your friend and may he be healed speedily and completely!" Rabbi Friedler smiled. "And putting on tefillin two days in a row is certainly a lot of merit."

I thanked him for his time, and he wished me well

and suggested I call him if I thought he could be helpful. He ushered me to the door, and I made my way to my beamer, a final Yiddish phrase echoing over the threshold.

16

I drove home. Two short miles and one long world away. I sat in my armchair and reviewed my visit with Rabbi Friedler. At least the 'bendawma' mystery was cleared up; I knew the charge was the crime of Cain, son of Adam. But it didn't make any sense. Josh and Cain?

Maybe I was totally on the wrong track. Herr Doktor had said I had a lot going on right now. This whole thing could be a stress reaction, and the dreams would go away on their own. It was possible.

But the dreams had to stop. I couldn't live like this.

And there was something else bothering me, too, but I couldn't quite put my finger on it. Something about this 'crime of Kayin ben Odom' thing that eluded me.

I leaned back in my armchair.

The courtroom is empty, abandoned. On the otherwise barren table lies a standard discovery disclosure form. My eyes are drawn to the list of the prosecution's evidence and witnesses:

Evidence: The Book of Remembrances
Witnesses: HaKadosh Baruch Hu

I shake my head slowly. I am lost. All is lost.

17

I sat up and shook off the scene of the dream. I reached for my notebook; I had to write this down before it faded.

Evidence: The Book of Remembrances -- ?
Witness: HaKadosh Baruch Hu -- God?

I called Rabbi Friedler. He would know what the "Book of Remembrances" was. I got his voicemail and left a message asking to meet with him.

I tried Andy. He answered on the third ring.

"Hey, Counselor. Only got a minute; I'm on a stretch break from a deposition. What's up?"

"Andy, does '*Hakadosh Baruch Hu*' mean God?"

"Uh, yes--"

"And 'The Book of Remembrances'-- what is it?"

"Larry, what's this--"

"In a second, Andy. Just tell me. What is it?"

"The Book of Remembrances is the book -- supposedly-- where all the deeds of man are recorded. What's this about, Larry? Did this rabbi--"

"No, no. It's not him. I had another dream. It's-- weird. Listen, are you free for dinner or something?"

He agreed to squeeze in a drink with me at the Rock Bottom Brewery before he took JoNella to dinner and the opera.

"JoNella--?"

"Surely you remember her, Larry, she's that Greek girl. The one with--"

"Yeah, Andy, I remember."
"Okay, gotta go. See you at four-thirty."

18

I stopped by the hospital to see Josh, who looked completely worn out. Still, his tired face lit up to see me.

"How's it going, Grasshopper Man?"

"Pretty well. How are they treating you?"

"Well, they won't let me ride my bike, but otherwise they're pretty helpful." He watched me sag into the chair by the bedside.

"You look a bit tired yourself; you sleeping okay?"

"These dreams are making for a short night."

"Still that courtroom thing?"

"Yeah, it's weird." I told him about the "crime of Kayin ben Odom".

Josh's eyes widened, "Really?"

"Yup."

"Well, that's fascinating. Just fascinating."

"How's that?"

"You remember that Chinese Western I was telling you about; the show with the wandering Kung Fu priest?"

"Um, yeah— lonely martial arts master looking for his long-lost brother or something."

"That's the one, the solitary seeker nicknamed 'Grasshopper'."

"So?"

"Well, his real name was Cain, too."

19

At the Rock Bottom Brewery, I prepared myself for the usual wait, but Andy was surprisingly prompt. Either he was worried about me, or he was worried about being late for JoNella the Greek. Maybe a bit of both.

We were seated and ordered Heinekens. Andy barely glanced at the waitress, and I started right in. I told him about the two latest dreams, my meeting with Rabbi Friedler and the discovery of 'the crime of Kayin ben Odom'. I even retold the story of Yitzchak Yenkel, which Andy immediately identified as the Yiddish roots of The Wizard of Oz. Of course, Andy could find Yiddish roots to just about anything.

I told him how non-committal Rabbi Friedler was in judging the dream to be my opportunity to plead for Josh in the Heavenly Court.

"Well, got to agree with him there." He took a long pull from his bottle. "Larry, you do know that this is all in your head. It's all coming from your subconscious mind. You shouldn't make a Twilight Zone episode out of a few scary dreams, okay?"

Andy had it all down pat, but he wasn't the one suffering through the nightmares. *He* was having an evening out on the town with a beautiful, shapely woman. *I* was in for a terrifying dream and a sleepless night. What did he know about it anyway?

Suddenly that little niggly thing that my foggy brain had kept just out of reach earlier in the morning came charging out of the mists.

"Okay, Andy, say it's all in my head. Okay. Fine. Then

how come I'm dreaming of things I've never heard of before? 'Kayin ben Odom'? 'The Book of Remembrances'? 'Hakadosh Baruch Hu'? They're turning out to be real things, Andy. How do you explain that? How could I *know*?"

Andy set his bottle down. "You've got to do better than that, Riddler. Come on." He started ticking off his points on the fingers of his left hand. "First, 'Kayin ben Odom'. You went to a Jewish day school. You certainly know the story of Cain and Abel; it's in the first section of the first book of the Bible. Everybody who's been to a Torah service knows that a man's formal Jewish name is his name 'ben' his father's name. So you heard the Hebrew name of 'Kayin' in school, and you know that Cain is Adam's son. Ergo 'Kayin ben Odom'."

I broke in. "But I've forgotten all that. *If* I ever learned it in the first place. And if I do know it, as you say, then how come I couldn't figure it out when I woke up?"

"Because it's trapped in your subconscious. Of course your conscious mind doesn't have access to it. That's why it comes out in a dream in the first place."

He took a swig from his bottle and ticked off another finger on his left hand. "Second, The Book of Remembrances. That's in the High Holiday prayers that you said every year for-- however many years it was that you went to synagogue. I think it's-- Yom Kippur, maybe the Musaf service?-- but whatever. It's there." His eyes dared me to challenge him. "And third, '*Hakadosh Baruch Hu*' is probably the most common expression for God after 'Adonoi', 'Hashem' and 'Abishter'; there's no way you could have gone to day school and not picked that up; it's in the *Aleinu* prayer at the end of every service. In fact, you even mentioned on the phone this morning that you thought it meant God."

He smiled triumphantly and held up the three outstretched fingers of his left hand. "And there you have it, Counselor; it's all there in your subconscious. All the mystery accounted for."

"Except for one small thing, Counselor."

"Yes?"

"Why am I having these dreams at all? Why is it all coming out like this? Even if all this stuff is coming out of my own head, why did it start now, what does it mean, and what the heck am I supposed to do about it?"

"Excellent questions, Counselor; excellent questions." He drained his bottle. "But now we're above my pay grade. What does your shrink say?"

"I don't know yet; I'm supposed to see him tomorrow."

"Okay, so tomorrow maybe you'll figure some of this stuff out."

"Yeah, but, Andy... what about tonight?"

20

Andy flagged down the waitress for another beer. I was still working on mine. She took the order with a smile and Andy resumed as if there had been no interruption. "What are you going to do tonight?! Why, you're going to defend your client, of course."

"Huh?"

"You're a lawyer, Counselor. Mount a defense."

I shook my head. Andy was full of surprises. "But, Andy, you said it wasn't real!"

"Of course it's *real*. It's a real *dream*. It's not some whack-o Heavenly tribunal. It's a manifestation of some underlying conflict in your psyche that needs to be worked through. Okay, so what better way to deal with it --until you can unravel it with your shrink, that is-- than planning out a logical and coherent legal defense." He grinned. "Who knows? It might even be therapeutic!"

It sounded bizarre on the face of it. On the other hand, it would keep my brain occupied for the evening. "Okay."

Andy straightened himself up, all business. "All right, Counselor, where should we start?"

"Well, the first thing to do would be to disqualify the witnesses, exclude the evidence..?"

"Now you're talking."

The waitress came by with Andy's second Heineken. We started talking about "the case".

The Book of Remembrances turned out to be an interesting problem. According to Andy, the holiday prayerbook described it as a book recording all the actions of man, and it could not be repudiated because its entries "bore the signature of every living being". By engaging in an act, we automatically "inscribed" it into the Book of Remembrances. It was like a signed confession. The perfect evidence for a criminal case.

We moved on to Hakadosh Baruch Hu. God. That was going to be a tough one to counter, too. God would be the most irrefutable witness possible.

Then there was the whole question of my client. "I just can't see Josh committing this 'crime of Cain'. Neither the jealousy nor the murder."

Andy shrugged. "Sounds to me like you're defending Cain himself. His name was read out with the charges, and it would explain why your client was not at the Omnibus hearing."

I thought about it. It felt impossible that Josh had committed the crime; it just wasn't in him. Andy had nailed it. I was defending Cain.

And then I had an epiphany. Two of them, actually, one right after the other.

Andy signalled for the check. Before it arrived, I outlined for Andy my approaches for excluding both the evidence and the witness. Andy considered, tilting his head first to the right, then to the left.

"Well, usually you would use that approach to disqualify the *judge* rather than to exclude the *witness*, but that might not even be possible in these dreams. Both moves are a gamble, but you need to find out what rules you're playing by right away anyway, or else you won't be able to do anything. And they just might hold up, Counselor."

The waitress returned with the check and Andy examined the bill and wrote in the tip.

"And I thought I'd see Rabbi Friedler tonight."

Andy sighed. He looked across the restaurant. "The Slovodjaniners were so renowned for drinking at their gatherings that we used to call them the 'Sloe vodka neeners'. They would raise a glass of schnapps with anyone. The yeshiva rabbis made it sound like there were Neeners on every corner, snaring unsuspecting souls into their fold with the lure of free liquor."

Andy stood up and shook his head slowly. "You gotta live your own life, Larry, but... as your friend, I have to tell you. You're playing with fire here."

21

The good rabbi himself answered the door and welcomed me in. My eye was again caught by the unfinished patch of wall in the foyer. Rabbi Friedler explained, "That's our *zaicher l'churbon*. Our remembrance of the destruction of the Temple in Jerusalem. No matter how luxurious we make our homes, we always remember that we are mourning the loss of the Temple. It's easy to forget here in America, where our lives are so comfortable. So when we build or remodel a house, we leave a little portion undone. In the midst of our happiness, we remember that our joy is not yet complete."

"Like breaking the glass at a Jewish wedding."

"Exactly!" Rabbi Friedler led the way into the large room and we stood in front of the barren section of the wall. "We are a people that remembers. We remember the destruction of the Temple, we remember our history, we remember our ancestors, and we remember our traditions and our customs. We even remember the names of all our enemies! Even the three whose memory we'd like to obliterate. The German madman --may his name be erased--, the tribe of Amalek --the first to attack us after the revelation at Mt. Sinai, -- and of course," Rabbi Friedler seemed to lower his voice as he finished, "the Sutton."

"The Sawten?"

"Rhymes with 'glutton'. Otherwise known as 'the adversary' or, in English, 'Satan'. Keeps trying to trip us up. That's his job, you know. Sent by the Abishter

Himself to give us our challenges. It's our custom that we tend not to use his name --in case that would draw his attention to us, God forbid! A crazy superstition, eh?" He chuckled and led me to the table.

I reached to unbutton my cuff, but he motioned me to sit.

"No tefillin, rabbi?"

He grinned. "Just once a day." He sat down and waited while I settled into my chair. "So, Lar--", Rabbi Friedler interrupted himself, "Do you know your Hebrew name?"

"Um, Reuven, why?"

"When I can, I prefer to use the Hebrew name, if it's okay. When a Jewish baby is given their name, we say it is the 'name by which you will be known amongst Israel'. And you're amongst Israel! Would it be all right if I called you 'Reuven'?"

I shrugged. I hadn't been called that since my childhood. "Sure."

He smiled broadly and rubbed his hands together. "Okay, then, Reb Reuven, what's the latest?"

I told him of the disclosure of The Book of Remembrances and Hakadosh Baruch Hu, and the conversation I'd had with Andy. He raised his eyebrows. "Very detailed, these dreams of yours." He thought for a moment. "And your friend Andy sounds very knowledgeable."

"Well, *he* seems to think I might actually be defending Cain."

"Hmmm. Could be. Remember, if your *kishkes* tell you that your friend Josh could not be on trial for Cain's crime, then you've got to pay attention to that."

"Okay, but I don't get it, Rabbi. How would defending the Biblical Cain help Josh?"

"Well, it *might* have no relationship at all. These dreams could be separate from your friend Josh altogether. Or," Rabbi Friedler considered, "it could be that the merit of your defending Cain will be applied to your friend's situation."

I shrugged. This "applying merit" idea sounded far-fetched.

"So here's the thing, Rabbi Friedler." I paused and leaned forward. "What am I supposed to *do*? I feel totally helpless in these dreams. It's crazy. I work in this court all the time, I'm in there a few times a week, and now, when I'm forced on leave, I dream about it and it terrifies me? I just don't get it. I feel like a flailing grasshopper in there."

"Interesting you should say that." Rabbi Friedler looked at me appraisingly. For an odd moment I was sure Rabbi Friedler was going to explain that the grasshopper was a reference to the 1970s Kung Fu show.

"When Moses sent the twelve spies into The Land to look it over, only two of them came back with a favorable report. The other ten spies said it would be impossible to conquer The Land, because the inhabitants were giants. Their exact words were..." Rabbi Friedler rocked his head back and forth while he murmured to himself. "'There we saw the Nefilim, the sons of the giant from among the Nefilim; we were like grasshoppers in our eyes, and we were so in their eyes'. You see? It was because the spies first felt like grasshoppers *in their own eyes* that they then said that the giants saw them that way as well. It was a case of --what do you call it?-- self-fulfilling prophecy. If I see myself as a grasshopper in my own eyes, then of course I think *you* see me as a grasshopper in *your* eyes, and then I *act* like a grasshopper, and everyone sees me acting like a grasshopper and so they treat me like a grasshopper and... on it goes!"

"So how do you break that cycle?"

"You remember that God runs the world. He didn't make you a grasshopper, Reb Reuven. He made you for a purpose, a human purpose. A unique and special human purpose that only you can fulfill. That's what Calaiv and Yehoshua knew. They were the two spies who brought back an encouraging report. 'We can do it!' they said, 'because God is with us. He has brought us here for a purpose. And He can do anything. If He wants us to go in and conquer The Land, then we can. So let's go do it!'" Rabbi Friedler dropped his enthusiastic hand back to the table. "But fear got the better of the people. They saw themselves as grasshoppers."

I nodded. "Okay, so I should remind myself that I'm there for a purpose."

Rabbi Friedler leaned in close and spoke intently. "Yes, Reb Reuven, you're there for a purpose. The Master of the Universe is sending you these dreams for a reason. He's giving you a challenge. And the Abishter only gives us challenges to serve a purpose. You may not know yet what that purpose is, but know that there *is* a purpose. And know that you are capable of meeting that challenge. You *can* succeed in that courtroom. You can!"

I mentally reviewed my court performance in the dreams so far. I saw no reason for Rabbi Friedler's confidence. I described my engrossed fascination with my hands.

"How can I keep from staring at my thumbs the whole time? It's like I'm hypnotized into a stupor by my two very ordinary thumbs that I've seen every day of my life."

Rabbi Friedler stretched out his own hands in front of him. He turned them slowly. "I wonder..." He trailed off, transfixed.

"I wonder how well we *do* see our thumbs every day." He looked at me. "We get used to things. We're surrounded by miracles on all sides-- 'The whole earth proclaims Your Glory', says the Psalmist. But we get so accustomed to Hashem's great miracles that we don't even see them any more. We forget the fantastic miracle of sight and get all bent out of shape because we have to clean our glasses when they get dirty! As I'm fond of saying, 'We live in a mansion and we complain bitterly when the doorbell is broken!'"

"So... what can I do..?"

"Well, hmmm." Rabbi Friedler bent his head and adjusted the large black yarmulke that covered it. "Maybe... if you spent a little time before you go to sleep trying to appreciate the miraculous blessing of your thumbs, perhaps you'll have less need to do it in your dreams?"

He sounded serious, so I put an expression of thoughtful consideration on my face.

"And of course, it couldn't hurt to say the bedtime

Shema and ask Hashem to help you be more effective in your courtroom dream."

"I suppose." In truth, I couldn't imagine doing any such thing.

Rabbi Friedler gave me a penetrating look. "And Reb Reuven--" He waited until I looked up at him. "Reb Reuven, you don't have to believe in Him to ask for His help."

22

At home, I sat in my chair and clicked through the cable channels. A late-night talk show was starting up. I grabbed a bowl of mini shredded wheat from the kitchen and settled in, but in short order the monologue was disappointing. I watched until the cereal was gone, powered off the TV, and set the bowl in the sink for tomorrow.

Even after brushing my teeth and changing for sleep I wasn't quite ready to call it a night. I stepped into my office and typed up legal notes on my computer. Why not? I labelled a manila folder "Cain/Josh Levin", and, as I tucked the printed pages into it, I took out a blue pen and wrote on the outside of the folder: "I have been placed here for a purpose".

I stared at my thumbs. I tried to conjure up the wondrous feeling in my dreams. But my thumbs stubbornly remained the humdrum, everyday digits they had always been.

Rabbi Friedler had said I didn't need to believe to ask for help. But how could you ask someone for something if you didn't even believe they existed?

I had nothing against people like Rabbi Friedler who found a belief in God helpful to them. It was a free country. But it wasn't for me. If everything in my life had been sent to me as a challenge from some all-powerful deity that could run the universe any way that He wanted, then He had a lot of explaining to do.

On the other hand, maybe the simple act of asking for help could actually make these dreams less nightmarish.

Religious fanatics could attribute it to God, but maybe it was simply psychology at work. It wasn't like it could hurt.

I said the six-word Shema prayer and muttered, "Please help" afterwards. It felt silly, but at least I'd done something. I headed to the bedroom.

I still had my folder of legal notes in my hand. On impulse, I stuck it under my pillow. I had seen that in a sci-fi movie once. I turned out the lights.

I am standing.
Right thumb pointing to left thumb. Two white moons. Symmetrical curves. Bookends to blue ink on cream folder, punctuation to a phrase.
"for a purpose".
A sharp clap of thunder.
"You may be seated."

The people on the bus go up and down, up and down, up and down.
For a purpose. Up and down for a purpose.
My knees bend and the chair takes my weight.
Creak, creak.
Up the creek, down the creek,
everywhere a creek, creek.
Up the creek without a paddle.
Paddle, paddle, fiddle faddle.
Hitch your wagon to the saddle.
For a purpose.
Thumb nails blush pink.
The miraculous thumbs slide apart.
"God has placed you here for a purpose."

I am sitting in a courtroom. The courtroom.
Defense counsel for Cain, the first murderer.
The Judge speaks, "Mr. Cohen, have you received the discovery disclosure from M. Sutton?"

He's asking you a question, and a question deserves an answer.

And an answer must be spoken.
Speak the speech, I pray you.
I can do this. I can do this.
"Yes, Your Honor."
The right hand opens the folder; the defense begins.
But this?
Can I say this out loud?
Can I say this to Him?
"Your Honor, we move to suppress the The Book of Remembrances."
"On what grounds?"
Okay. Here we go. Familiar ground. Familiar ground in alien territory.
"Your Honor, this book..."
> *The Book in which You record Your Judgements of life and death. The Book in which you record every act of every man.*
"...this book..."
> *--with which You run the world!*
> *For a purpose. For a purpose.*
"...has any human being ever seen this book?"
"Objection! Your Honour, irrelevant."
"We shall see, Monsieur Sutton." The Judge turns to me. "No human eye has seen The Book of Remembrances."
"Then how would it be possible to establish its authenticity, Your Honor?"
"Objection! Your Honour--" Monsieur Sutton splutters, at a loss for words. "Your Honour, if You declare it is so--"

"Your Honor, if the prosecution wants to introduce this book as evidence, they must clearly establish its authenticity. Forgive me, Your Honor, but to claim that God has given them the book would not make it admissible in any human courtroom. In this courtroom." I gesture with my right hand to include the entire space. I am careful not to look at my thumb; I am careful not to look around at the courtroom. My eyes are on The Judge. Unreadable.

"We move that The Book of Remembrances be disqualified."

The prosecutor is annoyed but silent; he has no refutation. The Judge looks at him. "M. Sutton?"

He droops. "Non, no argument."

The Judge nods.

"Very well." His tone is neutral, His posture impassive. "Motion granted. The Book of Remembrances is suppressed."

Yes! One down, one to go.

The bases are loaded as the Mighty Casey comes to bat.

Pride goeth before the fall.

Summer also goeth before the Fall.

Everything in its season.

To everything turn, turn, turn.

There is a season, turn, turn, turn.

And a time for every purpose under Heaven.

Purpose under Heaven.

Here for a purpose.

"Counselor?"
"Your Honor, we move to exclude the witness...
Hakadosh Baruch Hu."
"On what grounds?"
Coffee grounds.
Fair grounds.
Playgrounds.
Hopscotch and four-square.
Dodgeball, kickball, baseball.
Stealing home.
Safe at home.
Home free.
Cancer free.
For a purpose.
"Your Honor... it is not permitted for a judge --
any judge-- to be a witness at the same trial he is
adjudicating."
The Judge turns to the prosecutor. He is
kneading his hands together; he shakes his head
and mutters unintelligibly. He stands. He starts
to speak; he stops. The hands thrash and grip
each other forcefully, the head shakes violently.
The mustaches flap helplessly in the air. Wile E.
Coyote outsmarted by the Road Runner yet
again.
"M. Sutton?"
His palms fly upward, he sighs and sits down
with a thud. "I have nothing, Your Honour."
He looks defeated. Can it be that easy? It can't
be that easy.
The Judge faces the court recorder.

"The motion to suppress Hakadosh Baruch Hu is granted."

"Your Honour..."

The Judge turns back to M. Sutton, now standing at his table.

"Your Honour, we request an adjournment to reconsider zee case, assemble zee other evidence, consider zee other witnesses..."

He has nothing. He has nothing!

No admissible evidence!

It's over.

"Your Honor," I say as I stand, "the prosecution has no witnesses because they have no case. We move for an immediate dismissal."

The prosecutor's eyes blaze at me. "You..."

"You have nothing!" I say, turning to face him. "You may have a great case in the Heavenly Court--" I wave my right hand towards the heavens, "--but in this court you have no witnesses, no proof, no evidence of anything. You have no case. This court operates according to the laws and statutes of Hennepin County, and you cannot produce one shred of admissible evidence that Kayin ben Odom has committed any wrongdoing." I hold up my index finger, "Not one."

The prosecutor's eyes fly to The Judge, back to me.

"You're quite zee stickler, Mr. Cohen. Indeed, I am quite familiar with zee Hennepin County court system; I am there all zee time. But let me understand zat you will accept evidence in zees case if it is ruled admissible, yes? You will accept, as relevant and conclusive, zee incontrovertible evidence I intend to introduce zat Kayin ben Odom is guilty of zees crime -- clear evidence from a source zee court deems authoritative, yes?" The beady eyes drill into me. I sense a trap. He thinks he has something. But what? I review his words, but see nothing for him.

"If you can produce such evidence, surely. Bu--" I break off. Something is wrong. Horribly wrong.

M. Sutton looks expectantly at The Judge, who nods slowly. Reluctantly? What is going on?

An evil smile flashes triumphantly under the luxuriant mustache. I have fallen into his trap. Somehow, I have lost the case. Lost it before it has even begun. I am stunned.

"In light of today's developments, the prosecution is granted an additional day to disclose other competent evidence. This court stands adjourned."

The gavel thunders.

23

Suddenly awake, I abruptly sat up. I steadied my breathing.

Familiar scenery. Same bed. Same blinds. Same reassuring red lights proclaiming 4:16.

I was fine. Everything was all right.

Except for the fact that my life was now being ruled by a fantasy court case that took place in my dreams.

The sinking feeling in my stomach reminded me of how things had just ended. I had fallen into Monsieur Sutton's trap. He had appeared comical when the case seemed to be hopeless for him. But there was nothing funny about him when he was winning. There was a shrewdness and cunning that was unmistakable. And there was something vaguely familiar in that image of him that I could not quite place.

If I stayed awake, Monsieur Sutton would not be able to deliver his amended disclosure. Would a haloed deputy appear on my doorstep with huge white wings on his back and a black pistol on his belt, hauling me off to Hennepin County Jail where I would be locked up for contempt of dream court?

I showered and went into the kitchen. Over a bowl of Frosted Flakes, I reflected that things had gone much better in this dream. The fear and the helplessness were certainly less overwhelming. That was encouraging.

I opened my therapy notebook and started writing.

Maybe the calmer experience in court was due to applying my rational mind to "the case", as Andy had suggested. It could be strictly psychological.

I flashed on an image of my toughest law school professor, Professor Morton. He wagged his index finger at me from the front of classroom 325. "A good lawyer is rarely surprised in the courtroom because a good lawyer plans for contingencies. A good lawyer always has backup plans. Always. Preparation, preparation, preparation." Maybe my preparation had brought me peace of mind.

On the other hand, Rabbi Friedler would no doubt ascribe my success to the recitation of the Shema prayer before bedtime. Interesting how people could see the same event and interpret it so differently. Like the conflicting testimony of eyewitnesses. They often only saw what they already thought they would see.

And of course, maybe neither Andy nor Rabbi Friedler was right.

24

Outside the hospital, I parked in the covered ramp and sprinted across to the main entrance where a few folks huddled under the overhang to avoid the rain. Making my way through the dry sterile halls, I reflected that Josh usually biked fearlessly through the rain. He had smiled when I asked him about it one wet morning.

"Do other cyclists go out in this weather?"

"Not many. The casual riders don't want to get wet, and the serious bikers don't want to get their *bikes* wet. So that leaves the road to us crazies."

As I entered Josh's room, I imagined the other crazy bikers cycling through the rain this morning, perhaps wondering why Josh wasn't out there smiling in the downpour with them. They would have no clue he was here in this room, fighting for his life in the oncology ward.

"How are you doing, Josh?"

"Hey, man. The latest news is good: no biopsy, and no radiation. They're just going to slice open my head and take out a golf ball!" Josh smiled and made a circle with his thumb and forefinger, which he touched to his forehead and then flung outward with a flicking gesture. "Confucius say, 'Man with golf-size brain tumor... his thinking sub-par!'"

How he could joke about it, I didn't know.

"When's the surgery?"

"Depends on the doctor's schedule. Friday, or if he's golfing, Monday. They said Tuesday at the latest."

"I see Cindy brought in a 24-hour clock for you."

"Yes, a little piece of home amidst all the hospital tubes and machines."

For Josh, a 24-hour clock was a piece of home. We had argued about it once. In the locker room, after I had lost a close game, I had been ready to argue about anything. When he had said the time was "0700", I had rolled my eyes, but he had said, "It's much more efficient to use a single number."

"I wouldn't say it's more efficient," I countered. "After all, I only have to say *three* syllables to designate 10PM, whereas your way it takes *five* syllables: twen-ty-two hun-dred."

"Leave it to a lawyer," he had said. "I'll stick with numbers, you stick to words, and we'll make a great pair."

Staring at his clock reminded me of what I wanted to ask him.

"Say, does four sixteen mean anything to you?"

"I don't think so. I mean, it's a progression of squares, which is interesting. You have two numbers. Two times two is *four*, four times four is *sixteen*. What makes you ask, Larry?"

"Oh, I keep waking up from these dreams at exactly 4:16 in the morning. I thought it might mean something."

"Ah." His face collapsed in thought for a moment. Then he brightened. "You know, 4 hours and 16 minutes is actually 256 minutes, and 256 is sixteen times sixteen. So you've actually got three squares: 4, 16 and 256."

"I would never have thought of that."

Josh maneuvered to sip some water.

"You're still having these courtroom dreams?"

I described the latest developments.

"It must be kind of strange to be arguing before God, saying that God can't testify and that His book isn't admissible, yes?"

"I thought you didn't believe in God."

"I don't. I mean, there *is* a cohesive force to the world. It's one big interconnected entity that pulsates with life. But I don't think there's a god in the sky that would reach down and banish Adam and Eve for eating some fruit off the wrong tree or whatever. That's our anthropomorphic construction, putting a human face on something too big for us to understand."

We were interrupted by the quick strides of an energetic visitor entering the room. Josh greeted him and introduced us. "Larry, this is my friend and colleague Eric Slayton, programmer extraordinaire; Eric, meet my good friend and racquetball partner, Larry Cohen."

We shook hands. Eric was slender, with stringy blond hair that he wore down past his shoulders. He sported blue and white hightops, faded jeans and a red-checked flannel shirt unbuttoned over a stencilled yellow T-shirt. I looked more closely at the block lettering on his chest.

```
There are 10 kinds of people:
those who understand binary
and those who don't
```

I pointed at the shirt, "I don't get it."

Eric seemed happy enough to let me in on the secret. "When *you* read the shirt you see it saying 'there are ten kinds of people', but that's just your bias showing. One-zero is only ten in base ten. In base two, or 'binary', one-zero represents two. So looking at it through the eyes of someone who understands binary, it reads, 'There are two kinds of people in this world, those who understand binary and those who don't....'."

"I get it. Very cute."

I got up to go. "I'll leave you geeks to your zeroes and ones. Glad to hear the good news, Josh. Hang in there, man." I gave his shoulder a squeeze. "Nice meeting you, Eric."

In the hospital cafeteria, I collapsed into a chair with a banana and an apple and called Andy. He answered immediately.

"So, Counselor, how did court go last night?"

"On the one hand, it went very well. Both motions to strike were upheld and the prosecution was left empty-handed. In theory, he has no case."

"Well done, Counselor. And on the other hand? In practice?"

"I don't know. He's up to something. I felt like I fell into some kind of trap, but I still can't figure out what it was. He's got an extension for amended discovery."

"But you made it through unscathed. And your shrink?"

"I see him at 11:00. You know, there's something familiar about that prosecutor, like I've seen him before somewhere, but I just can't place him."

"So describe him."

"On the short side, with a large, thick mustache. Showy and dramatic, but underneath it he's very sharp, with piercing eyes. Oh, and he's French. Outrageous accent."

There was a pause. I imagined Andy pinching his lips in thought as he ran through his mental library of cultural icons. "It's Poirot."

"Who?"

"Hercule Poirot. Agatha Christie's great detective. The Belgian genius who is always underestimated until in the end he solves the mystery and nails his man. Or his woman."

"That's it! And they always mistake him for French because of his accent."

"So tell me about the judge."

"Impassive and hard to read. Wears a big black cloak with a hood that hangs over his face."

"Hmmm. That's tougher. The first thing that comes to mind is the Ghost of Christmas Future. You know, from A Christmas Carol. The Dickens story about Ebeneezer Scrooge. Better repent before Christmas, Larry."

There was a pause and a muffled sound. "Gotta go, Larry. Ciao."

25

I pulled up to Dr. Silverberger's office twenty minutes early, so I sat in my beamer.

Josh had looked good, enjoying the mental numerical gymnastics almost as much as his groaner puns. I visualized the warning smile that stole across his face two weeks ago.

"Larry, what did the Buddhist monk say to the hotdog vendor?"

"What?"

"'Make me *one* with everything!'"

He had continued mercilessly, "After the vendor presents him the hotdog, the monk hands him a twenty. He waits a full minute and then requests patiently, 'Change?!'. The hotdog vendor replies, 'Change must come from within!'"

I clicked on the oldies station, and Olivia Newton-John was crooning about unrequited love. I reclined the driver's seat to a more comfortable position as she sang, "Let me be there..."

The lone form stares up at me.

Evidence: The Book of Genesis
Witnesses: Moses ben Amram

26

"Dr. Silverberger, you've got to get these dreams to stop."

He lifted his eyebrows and tilted his chin slightly to one side. I tried again.

"Okay, you've got to help *me* get these dreams to stop."

"I take it you've been having this dream every night?"

"Yeah."

"And would you say they're getting more intense, staying the same, or lessening in intensity?"

"Well, it's funny. The 'intensity' as you call it *seems* to be decreasing. I mean, that first night it was so strange and I was paralyzed with fear. So the fear is less overwhelming now, but in the courtroom my mind often swirls with distracting word associations and it's hard to focus on the proceedings."

He nodded. "Often when we start working on an issue, there are initial fear reactions we have to overcome. And these new blocking thoughts could be your mind protecting you from a potentially overwhelming experience." He thought for a moment. "Or the word associations could contain related material, clues to help unlock the meaning. Do you see the same courtroom scene every night, or has that part changed in any way?"

"It's changed. There's been a progression. It's weird. I mean, it's like a real court case."

"So in the dream you described last time, it sounded like it was just you, alone, in a courtroom. And now..?"

"Well, in the first dream I only *noticed* myself. But I was just totally overwhelmed. I just stared down at my thumbs the whole time. Like I'd never seen thumbs before."

He nodded encouragement.

"But, really, I think the others were in the courtroom from the start. It's just that now I'm more able to function. I can see the other people more clearly and interact with them. Although the judge is weird. I mean, I can't see his face under his cloak's hood, but I sort of know what he's thinking as if I could read his expression, you know? Which is good because it's, well, it's progressing like a real court case. I mean, on the one hand I have no idea what's going on or why this is all happening, and on the other hand--" I shrugged, "it feels like a regular court case. In fact--" I looked over at the blinds that blocked the view from the parking lot. "In fact, I've actually been kind of 'preparing' the case during my waking hours. My friend Andy suggested it."

"And has that been helping?" He asked the question in an even tone, as if he had no opinion as to whether it was crazy to be spending real time in legal preparation for a fantasy court case unfolding in my dreams.

"Well, I think -- it's not hurting, anyway. And I also, um, said a little prayer before going to sleep. Rabbi Friedler said it might work."

"Mm-hmm."

"He said I didn't have to believe to ask for help -- which is good, because I don't 'believe', by the way-- and I figured it wouldn't do any harm or anything."

The doctor did not seem to have much to say about it

either way. His expression remained neutral.

"Any other changes to your routines? Any developments in relationships, or new activities?"

"Being off work is a little weird. I have all this time. I kinda feel like the wandering Kung Fu priest Josh mentioned... not really connected to anything, anyone." I shrugged. "I visit Josh in the hospital, I see Andy to talk over the, er, dreams, and I've been meeting with Rabbi Friedler, too. He has me put on tefillin" --I gestured with my right hand circling my left arm-- "and he sounds the shofar and then we sit down and talk about the latest. He's a funny guy, actually."

"How so?"

"Well, on the face of it he's a harmless old man with a child's joy and a child's simple view of the world. He sees God as running every detail of the world and he lives insulated in his community and is happy with his traditions and his beliefs. Which is all fine, of course. But-- how can I say it? He also sometimes seems very shrewd and knows how to draw a person in and get them to do exactly what he wants them to do." I told him about Andy's warning.

"How does it feel when you're with him?"

"Oh, I feel safe enough, but, well, I'm keeping an eye out."

Dr. Silverberger nodded as he looked at me. "So I'm hearing you describe a certain amount of concern with your words, but I notice a buoyant enthusiasm and warmth when you describe your time together."

"Well, he's fun to be with. Even the tefillin and the shofar stuff somehow seem cool. It's, it's something about his attitude, I think. His joy is contagious."

Dr. Silverberger was quiet, as if he was waiting for me to speak. Or maybe waiting for me to realize something that he'd already figured out.

I asked, "Do you think he's okay?"

"Well, without meeting him it's hard to say very much, but so far nothing you've said is overly concerning."

"Is it 'somewhat' concerning?"

Dr. Silverberger shifted in his chair. Then he smiled. "I was just wondering if this rabbi has become something of a father figure for you. Perhaps he's filling a certain role? That's neither good nor bad in and of itself. But I noticed when you reviewed your relationships last time and listed the people you talk to --and don't talk to-- you didn't mention your father..."

So here we were. The good doctor was pretty sharp, and didn't waste any time getting to the awkward moments.

"He died when I was eight," I said.

"I'm sorry." From the corner of my eye I saw him slowly nod in sympathy. "That must have been hard."

I hated when people said that. Especially with that empathetic look. Like they knew something about it and wanted to help me by showing how understanding they were. I didn't care how many courses on grief counseling this man had taken, he had no idea what it had been like to lose my dad to a heart attack. Alive one moment and dead the next.

"It's fine. You get used to it." One fewer chair at the dining room table. "I don't think I'm latching on to Rabbi

Friedler to fulfill some childhood need to have a father. He's just being helpful in a stressful situation."

"You know, Larry, having a father is not just something a child needs. We all need the kind of guidance and feedback and support that a father usually provides."

He nodded again.

I nodded back at him. A little taste of his own medicine.

"One of the things a strong father does for us is give us a reference point for expectations; he 'sets the bar', so to speak. Tells us when we've done enough and should take satisfaction in our efforts, even if we don't like the outcome we experienced. Or, on the other side, he tells us when we need to redouble our efforts, even though we feel like giving up. It's a comfort to be able to rely on a father for those things, to show us a middle path. Someone who's been there before, and who knows us inside and out. And loves us anyway." Dr. Silverberger smiled. "That's something we can all use." He paused as if considering whether he should say more. "My own father passed away two years ago, and I'm still not used to it. I still sometimes have that impulse to pick up the phone and call him."

I nodded. He had a point.

"So when a person loses their father at an early age, like you did, they generally seek out that kind of guidance and feedback from an older man in their life. Or sometimes from several different men. It's a normal and healthy thing to do." Dr. Silverberger measured my reaction to his words. "So it would make sense that you would use Rabbi Friedler in that capacity, if he's someone you trust."

"Well, maybe." I thought back over the male figures from my childhood. Not too many stood out actually. There was my sixth grade math and English teacher. He was cool. I remembered looking up to him. And Coach Hardy in high school, I supposed. Still, it didn't feel like they had had this kind of "father role" that Dr. Silverberger was describing. And then there was the disastrous "Uncle Paul" that my mother had almost married when I was twelve. None of them seemed to fit the bill.

"So if a person doesn't get guidance from a 'father figure' when they're little, are they just totally screwed?"

Dr. Silverberger chuckled. "I wouldn't say that. It's true that a son without a healthy father figure often struggles with feelings of inadequacy that can persist into adulthood. The absent father can take on mythic proportions, and it can seem impossible to attain his approval, no matter what level of success the son attains. He can work hard, become successful, and become the envy of many, but still feel inside like he's never good enough." He looked at me. "And some take the other path of withdrawing from the world because they can't figure out their role in it. They find themselves disconnecting from family and relationships because they don't know the rules and it's safer to just retreat from the world, rather than engage and risk being defeated." Dr. Silverberger leaned back. "But of course those are just generalizations. Every person's experience is unique."

"So why would this father stuff be coming up now, when he died over twenty years ago?"

"Sometimes unresolved issues come up when you have time to work on them; it's almost like the psyche decides to make use of the free time to get some work done. But often stress in the present day stirs up unresolved past issues. And with your recent breakup and your friend being seriously ill, it wouldn't be unusual for those stresses to trigger memories of past struggles with death or separation."

"So you think these courtroom dreams stem from unresolved childhood stuff around the death of my father?"

"They could be related. The possibility of a connection did cross my mind. The judge figure in your dream resembles the classic depiction of the grim reaper, for example, and the God witness could perhaps be the ultimate father figure. So it might be significant that this prosecutor tried to introduce a book of *remembrances* and the Heavenly Father witness in your dream, and you asked this death symbol to dismiss them both. That could symbolize an internal struggle: one part of you wants to revisit old memories and father issues, while another part feels that death ended both your remembrances and your father in your life."

Dr. Silverberger sat back and shook his head. "But that's just speculation -- the preliminary thoughts inside *my* head. I can tell that's not where *your* head's at. And you may be right; these dreams may have nothing to do with your father at all."

"But you think my spending time with Rabbi Friedler

does have some kind of father thing mixed up in it?"

"Well, it's true that the father-son relationship is a primal one, and when a son loses his father at a young age, we see that father-son dynamics often pervade other relationships in subtle, and in not-so-subtle, ways." Dr. Silverberger leaned forward and smiled. "Fathers have a way of showing up... in the most unexpected places."

There was another silence that became uncomfortable.

"So if these dreams *were* somehow connected to my father, what then?"

"Well, we would explore your memories and feelings surrounding your father's passing and see if the dreams point you to any unresolved conflicts."

"How would that help?"

"Going back over experiences and feelings and reprocessing them as an adult can be therapeutic. A child's mind can create distorted ways of seeing the world. Left unexamined, those views can influence our behaviors in a wide variety of situations and relationships."

"I just don't see how these dreams about defending Cain could possibly have anything to do with some old wounds left by my dear departed Dad."

"They might be unrelated."

"But you obviously think there's a connection. So what is it?"

Dr. Silverberger actually laughed. "You're nothing if not persistent. All right. The connection that popped into my mind --which I'm not wedded to, mind you-- is that the trial could reflect a child's feeling responsible for his father's death. So you're on trial--"

"But *I'm* not the one on trial here! It's *Cain.* Or maybe Josh."

"That's true." Dr. Silverberger nodded to himself slowly, and then with increasing speed. It was a gesture I was coming to think of as equivalent to a baseball pitcher's windup. The good doctor was building up to another lecture.

"You've probably never heard of Fritz Perls? Well, he was the father of Gestalt Therapy back in the 50s, and one of the dream analysis techniques he pioneered was the deconstruction of dreams by treating each person in the dream as representing a part of the dreamer's psyche. He would go so far as to have the dreamer face an open chair and start a dialogue with this part of themselves. They would then switch chairs to answer back from that part of their psyche. These conversations were incredibly powerful and healing for the patients. Some unbelievable outcomes. And often quite dramatic." Dr. Silverberger took a moment to reflect appreciatively on the man's accomplishments. "So for example, this prosecutor, this Poirot, could be seen as a self-critical or self-undermining part of your psyche. The judge could be your superego or inner moral compass. And so on."

"Interesting." Actually, it *was* interesting. "So then what about the missing defendant? If it's not Cain, why isn't some part of me showing up?"

"Well, it could be that if there *is* a part of you that feels guilty, but you may not be ready to face it yet. That could be a pretty intense encounter, after all."

Dr. Silverberger looked at his watch. "Ah, it looks like

our time is up for today."

"But what about tonight? What do I do about tonight?"

"Well, you could try journaling some conversations with the different people in the dream and see what that brings up." He considered. "If it's helping, keep saying the prayers, or 'preparing for the case'. If it's working, stick with it."

27

Rabbi Friedler was unreasonably happy to see me. Maybe I was the last person he needed to help to fulfill his good-deed quota for the day. In any event, we did the tefillin thing and the shofar sounding amid his joyful ministrations. It was beginning to feel more familiar, which was nice. Or worrisome, depending on how you looked at it.

"What is it about the blowing of the shofar that makes it so..."

"Special? Well, the sages say it's like the sound of a child crying out to his father, and so it awakens our hearts to cry out to *our* Father. It's a primal sound that bypasses the intellect" --Rabbi Friedler drew an energetic right hand around the crown of his head-- "and pierces our hearts." He thumped his chest and then smiled as he flowered his hand heavenward. "Opens us right up."

He put away the shofar and gestured to the long table. I sat and told him the developments in my dreams, including the latest disclosure form.

He nodded, impressed. "This is really quite something! It sounds like you're doing much better, yes?"

"Better? I don't know. I think I'm in trouble with this next set of witnesses. I mean, *Moses*. I assume that 'Moses ben Amram' is *Moses*, right?"

He nodded.

"And the *Book of Genesis*..!"

Rabbi Friedler laughed. "No, I meant it sounds like

you're doing better with the whole awe and wonder thing. The first dream you said you were too overwhelmed to understand what was going on, or even to hear the charges being read."

"Ah, yes, well that does seem to be a lot better." I debated how much I should say. "I tried saying the *Shema* like you suggested. And, um, I asked for help."

Rabbi Friedler beamed. "Wonderful."

Mrs. Friedler appeared with lunch: egg salad sandwiches, broccoli-raisin salad, and lemonade. Sruli appeared out of nowhere to join us. I followed the Friedlers to the kitchen for the ritual hand-washing, followed by the blessing over the meal.

Rabbi Friedler bit into his sandwich like a child having his first ice cream cone of the summer. "Delicious, Ma!"

The sandwiches were quite good; no doubt the egg salad was homemade, the tomatoes freshly sliced, the portions generous. "Ma" must have already eaten, because she retreated to the kitchen while the three of us had lunch around the table.

I looked over at Rabbi Friedler messily enjoying his sandwich, with egg salad falling off the sides back onto his plate, and occasionally onto the table or his lap. What was I expecting from this man? Was I looking for a replacement father?

"So," I asked, "what would Moses have to say about Cain? I don't get the connection."

Rabbi Friedler nodded enthusiastically. "I don't see a direct connection either, Reb Reuven. But if this dream court operates according to ways of the human world, the

Torah won't be able to speak on its own --although sometimes I'm certain it does!-- but in court I would expect you'd have someone to present it or something, yes? And if so, Moses would certainly be the man for the job!"

Sruli chimed in, "I'm no lawyer, but you have no case at all if the Torah is used as evidence. It's open-and-shut. Kayin murdered his brother Hevel; the Torah says so straight out. How can you argue against that?!"

Rabbi Friedler nodded. "You've certainly got a job on your hands. But then, Hashem wouldn't give you the case if there were nothing you could do."

"But, Ta, you've got it right there," Sruli turned his head up and to the left, murmuring some part of Scripture until he got to the part he wanted to quote. "*'Vayakam Kayin el Hevel achiv vayahargayhu.'* 'And Kayin rose up against Hevel his brother and murdered him.'" The translation was directed towards me.

"Enh." Ta sounded reluctant.

"But, Ta, Kayin planned it out. He tricked Hevel into giving him the land and then killed him with a sword so he could own the whole world. It's murder one, plain and simple!" He turned to me. "Sorry, Reb Reuven. There's just no place to start."

"But you see, Sruli, just because Kayin did actually murder Hevel, that doesn't mean that it can be proven in court. Right, Reb Reuven?"

I smiled. "Unfortunately, it's often true that the guilty go free. That's the price of ensuring that none of the innocent are convicted. For example, if a piece of evidence is not handled correctly, it may be ruled inadmissible in court, and then the jury never even hears of that piece of evidence. Even if it's the murder weapon found in the killer's house."

That got me thinking. Clearly there was no physical evidence left of the murder. Whatever sword Cain used would be long gone by now. But then, that might not stop M. Sutton from being able to produce it in dream court. But then he would have had to list it as evidence, and he hadn't. Which meant he was relying exclusively on the Book of Genesis. So if I could get that excluded, he would have no case. I would be home free.

This was beginning to look easy again. The Book of Genesis would never pass muster as an evidentiary source. From the court's perspective, it was just a book. A nice book, a popular book. Even a holy book. But at the end of day, just a book. Not evidence.

We finished the sandwiches. R. Friedler brought a napkin across his mustache, which looked like it would never be free of egg salad again. He nodded at Sruli, who picked up three miniature prayer books from a basket, handing one to his father, and one to me. I was relieved that when he opened it for me and found the blessing after meals, there was an English transliteration.

R. Friedler led the formal invitation to the bentching, a few responsive lines which echoed eerily to my childhood, and then we each murmured our prayers individually. Sruli was done in a flash and buried his head in an ancient book until R. Friedler and I finished.

Suddenly, in my mind, Professor Morton wagged his finger at me, "A good lawyer always has backup plans. Always."

In this nightmarish courtroom, I needed to be a good lawyer. So what if the Book of Genesis *was* admitted as evidence? What would I do? What was even possible if that happened? To prepare a contingency plan, I would need to know exactly what evidence was in the Torah.

I asked R. Friedler what the Torah said about Cain killing Abel.

"Well, let's take a look," exclaimed R. Friedler, animated at the prospect of studying Scripture with me. He motioned Sruli to the bookshelves and he returned with an old tome. He opened it to an early page filled with Hebrew from top to bottom and side to side, some in large print, some in small print; a sea of words and meaning. Rabbi Friedler found his place and started reading, first the Hebrew and then the translation. I was surprised; it was quite short.

"*Vayomer Kayin el Hevel achiv*...Kayin --that's Cain-- talked with Hevel his brother --that's Abel." R. Friedler, I realized, was translating freely on the fly. "*Vayehi beyosam basadeh*... and it was that they were in the field. *Vayakom Kayin el Hevel achiv vayahargeinu*... and Kayin rose up towards Hevel his brother and killed him."

Something wasn't quite adding up. I looked at R. Friedler. "What else does it say?"

"Well, that's it on the murder; then we move on..." R. Friedler scanned the text, "Hashem asks what happened, and Kayin says, 'Am I my brother's keeper?!'... Hashem says, 'The blood of your brother cries out to Me!'"

I was lost. Something was missing. "Wait a minute, wait a minute." I gestured to Sruli, "Where did you get the whole tricking him thing, using a sword, planning everything out?"

Sruli circled around R. Friedler to find his place in the text. "It's right there-- Rashi explains, quoting the Midrash--"

Rashi, Rashi. The name was familiar, but I couldn't quite place it. And I thought Midrash was stories for children, so--

Seeing my confused expression, R. Friedler explained. "The five books were written down by Moses, but to understand them, we need the oral Torah --also given at Mount Sinai. The oral Torah gives the context and fills in the details. For example, we are commanded at Sukkos to "take the fruit of a beautiful tree". How do we know it is the esrog and not an apple? The oral Torah. Hashem commands Moses to hammer out a menorah of gold, 'as I showed you'. But exactly what Hashem showed Moses isn't spelled out in the written Torah. We're commanded to wear tefillin, but the written Torah gives no description of what tefillin are. The Oral Torah was passed down from generation to generation and finally codified into the written Talmud." R. Friedler beamed as he caught his breath. He clasped his hands together, interlacing his fingers. "The written Torah requires the oral Torah, and the oral Torah requires the written Torah. They are two halves of the whole; neither can stand without the other. It's a match made in Heaven!"

As Sruli read through some of the Midrash, I realized there was no way to win the case if the Torah was accepted as evidence. Cain's motives and methods were detailed, and the murder was clearly premeditated. If this was admitted, my client was a goner. The case hinged on dismissing the Torah as evidence, an approach R. Friedler could not help with.

R. Friedler must have seen my head shake, because he grabbed my hand and encouraged me in an intense voice, "Remember, it is the merit of your *work* on this case that you have asked Hashem to apply on your friend's behalf. The real success is in the time and energy you invest. You may not have to win the case in the traditional sense. Your efforts are precious, and your study is holy in the eyes of the Abishter. May your friend be healed completely and quickly!"

"Amen!" Sruli chimed in, and I mumbled the same.

It felt like time to leave, so as Sruli headed for the front door I got up to follow him. Rabbi Friedler, however, had something else on his mind. He motioned me to sit down. "You know, Reb Reuven, if the Abishter made our challenges easy, success would be pretty hollow. We wouldn't really have accomplished anything significant. Nobody roots for a football team if they're the only team playing on the field; they may make a touchdown every play, but it's meaningless. They need the opposing team for the contest to be worthwhile.

"So for us to accomplish anything meaningful, the challenge has to be significant. And that means that there will be times when we get discouraged, doubt ourselves, feel like giving up. This is where the Other Side, sensing an opening, jumps out from the recesses where it has been crouching and tries to take advantage of the situation. He wants us to quit, so he attempts to convince us that it's futile, a waste of time. No way can we overcome the obstacles in front of us.

"But we *can* persevere, Reb Reuven; we can master those emotions and temptations. Not all at once in some grand battle, but step by step. Even the smallest baby steps are important when we move in the right direction. In fact, small steps are the best steps." Rabbi Friedler lifted his feet in demonstration, an old man taking baby steps. "And when we try, when we take even the smallest step, the Abishter is right there to help us, to give us the strength and the resources we need to succeed. Our job is to trust that He will show us the way when we can't see it for ourselves."

Rabbi Friedler scrutinized my face to see how I was taking his pep talk. I had to admit, he was pretty good at it. His confidence and determination were almost as contagious as his joyfulness.

"Don't worry," I said. "I'm not giving up on this court case just yet." I've got a friend in the hospital to whom I've made a commitment.

I stood up and Rabbi Friedler walked me to the door. I was suddenly aware of how much of his time I had been taking, and I felt awkward. Surely he had a lot of other responsibilities. It was one thing to talk with Dr. Silverberger for an hour at a time; that was how he made his living. The rabbi was spending hours with me for nothing. If he were a lawyer, the bill would be enormous.

"Say, um, Rabbi Friedler, do you, uh, have a standard hourly fee or anything? I feel like you've been very generous with your time."

"No, no," Rabbi Friedler chuckled. "In fact, in

Talmudic times rabbis were enjoined to have a profession, and *not* to make their money off the Torah, God forbid. The Torah is a gift from God to *all* Jews, and knowledge of it is not something for sale to the highest bidder!"

I could tell Rabbi Friedler was about to give the other side of the story.

"Of course, should you feel inclined at some point to make a contribution to the Slovodjaniner outpost here in the Twin Cities, we would happily accept your donation. But really, that is an entirely separate matter, not to be connected with your learning."

It sounded like splitting hairs, but Rabbi Friedler was clearly serious.

"There is, however, a big favor you could do for me that would bring me great joy..." Rabbi Friedler looked up with his crinkly smile. "Would you join us for a Shabbos dinner this Friday night?"

Suddenly all of Andy's dire predictions were about to be realized. Before I knew what had happened, I heard "I'd be delighted to!" usher forth from my lips. It was a moment I knew I would never hear the end of from Mr. I-told-you-so New Yorker.

28

Andy surprised me by arriving only eleven minutes late. He took his seat asking, "So what did your shrink say?"

"I tell him all this stuff, and instead of concrete suggestions of how to fix it, he suggests maybe it all has to do with things that happened decades ago."

"So what did he say?"

"This is a problem happening right here, right now. I'm not sleeping at night; I can't stay awake during the day. If I don't get this resolved before I go back to the office in two weeks, I'm in *big* trouble."

"Are you going to tell me what he said, Counselor?"

I shifted to a more comfortable position in the booth.

"He talked about how some shrink from the 50s used to interpret dreams by saying each person in the dream was part of the dreamer's psyche. Sounded like a stoner."

"Look, Larry, I know you don't want to hear it, but sometimes our problems of today really *are* rooted in troubles from our past." He caught the eye of the pimple-faced server at the next table and tapped his watch meaningfully. The server nodded and held up an index finger. "I've been thinking about your case, Counselor. You can get the case thrown out in a heartbeat."

"How so?"

"I've got a handful of ways. One: jurisdiction - the crime did not occur in Hennepin County, so the case should not be tried in the Hennepin County Court.

"Two: double jeopardy - Cain was already punished

for his crime, so he can't be tried again.

"Three: death - Cain died and therefore cannot be tried.

"Four: judicial disqualification - the judge was a participant in the events, and finally,

"Five: ex post facto - none of the laws of Hennepin County had been established." Andy paused for dramatic emphasis. "Murder wasn't against the law when Cain killed his brother!"

I applauded. Andy bowed slightly in his seat. Still, something about the approach didn't sit well with me.

"So I thought you'd be relieved, Counselor; why the long face?"

"It's hard to explain, but I just get the feeling..." I shook my head. "You know, Rabbi Friedler suggested that maybe I don't need to win the case, that just putting in a good effort might be enough. And now here you are with ideas on how to throw the case out..."

Our server came and took our drink order; as he left, Andy was caught with another idea.

"Hey, what about temporary insanity as a defense?"

I considered; Andy pressed.

"You have to admit, Counselor, Cain knew that God 'knows all and sees all', yet here he was murdering his brother right in front of the Almighty! Crazy! In fact, the Talmud says that a man only sins if his heart is filled with the 'spirit of folly'."

"That may be true, but I'd need a psych eval of Cain from a competent expert, and I can't see where that would come from, no matter how clever my subconscious is. Besides, it's hard to imagine this judge allowing me to amend the plea-- I already entered a plea of 'Not guilty'".

Andy shrugged. Our server arrived and placed our Heinekens in front of us on little napkins. He popped the tops and left. We clinked the bottles together in a toast.

"Anyway, enough about me already," I said. "What's up with you, Counselor?"

"Emergency deposition in Chicago; they've actually set it up for Saturday. I've got a flight to O'Hare Friday afternoon, hoping to get in early so I can squeeze in a dinner date with Ruth."

My head came up a little too quickly to meet Andy's laughing eyes.

"Did I say 'Ruth'? Sorry, I meant to say 'Gayle'."

"Very funny."

"Must have been, judging by the shocked outrage on your face. Hey, you could come down with me, you know; we could double date. You and Ruth, me and Gayle. How about it?"

"Thanks, but no thanks." Payback time. "I'll be busy Friday night having Shabbos dinner at Rabbi Friedler's house."

"What?!" And then Andy laughingly wagged his forefinger at me. "Very good, Counselor, you had me going there."

"Actually, I'm serious; I accepted his invitation this afternoon."

Andy spoke with a quiet intensity. "Look, Larry, this is not something to be careless about; this is no joke. These chassidic sects are dangerous."

He took a breath. "My second cousin Daniel ended up in their clutches midway through his junior year. It started off innocently enough; he put on tefillin a few times, started studying Torah weekly, a Shabbos meal or two. The next thing you know, he dropped out of Columbia and was going to live in their village in the hills outside Haifa. He had just turned twenty-one and had signed over his college trust fund money to them, given away all his 'secular' things, and was ready to get on the plane."

"Yeah? What happened?"

"Well, he had sent a letter dumping his old girlfriend --she wasn't Jewish-- and she called his dad, and then his dad called my dad --since my dad's a psychologist as well as his cousin-- and after some dramatic late night heroics, they brought him back home and my dad deprogrammed him. They lost a lot of money, but at least they got Danny back."

I thought about Rabbi Friedler. "And this was the Neeners?"

Andy grimaced. "It was actually the Lurtzinovers in that case, but, Larry, it's the same thing. They're all the same."

"Yeah, maybe." I let out my breath. I had never seen Andy like this. "Look, Andy. I'm sorry about your cousin, I really am. But you already warned me to be careful and, hey, I'm being careful. I'm paying attention, okay? So far Rabbi Friedler has been a standup guy. Sure, he's a religious fanatic. But-- look, he knows this Cain stuff and he's helpful. Or at least he's trying to be helpful. And he hasn't asked me for anything."

"Yet."

Andy waved down our server for the check.

"Andy, isn't there some middle ground between hating these Neeners and getting sucked into religious fanaticism?"

"In this case, my friend, that 'middle ground' is just a slippery slope."

29

Bedtime. As I brushed my teeth, I reflected on what I could expect. I knew M. Sutton had something in store. He was more clever than he let himself appear.

If he *did* get the Book of Genesis admitted as evidence, what then?

I needed to prepare the nuclear option. I went into my office and typed up the motions to dismiss, just in case. Preparation, preparation, preparation. I put them in the manila folder and laid them under my pillow.

I am standing.
Right thumb points to left thumb, left thumb points to right thumb.
You first; no you first. My good sir, I insist.
Two white miraculous moons. Beautiful, functional. Overly polite. Bookends.
"God has placed you here for a purpose."
The Judge enters, the gavel thunders. "This court is now in session."
We sit.
"Mr. Cohen, have you received the supplemental disclosure?"
"We have, Your Honor. "
Here we go. Round Two.
Return of the Jedi.
Return of the King.
Beware the ring,
beware death's sting,
beware of becoming the devil's plaything.
For a purpose.
I open the manila folder in front of me.
"Your Honor, we move to exclude the Book of Genesis."
"On what grounds?"

On the grounds that the Earth was not created in six days.
On the grounds that snakes cannot talk.
On the grounds that Adam and Eve were as silly as a nursery rhyme.
Jack and Jill went up the hill

to taste forbidden water.
Jack fell down and broke his crown
and Jill collapsed with laughter.

I love to laugh, ha ha ha ha,
  long and loud and clear
I love to laugh, ha ha ha ha,
  it's getting worse every year
Laughter is the best medicine.
Laughter will cure all that ails you
Except when what ails you is cancer.
For that, you need to win a court case.

"Your honor, the Book of Genesis constitutes hearsay."

M. Sutton rises. "Your Honour, zee rules of evidence provide that 'statements in ancient documents' are not considered hearsay."

"Your Honor, can the prosecution produce any evidence --evidence admissible in this court of law, that is-- that the words in the Book of Genesis are the words of God?"

"Your Honour, we do not introduce zee Book of Genesis as zee Word of God, but rather as a source of Truth."
Source of Truth? The distinction does not seem to help his cause.

"And Your Honour," he smiles under his mustaches, "zees court has already accepted zee Book of Genesis as a source of Truth."

I turn, staring at him. Is he serious? He tilts his head and nods at me with a perfunctory smile. Smile, smile, crocodile. How does your garden grow?

With a dramatic flourish of his hands, M. Sutton continues in a lecturing tone.

"Your Honour, zees court, zee Hennepin County Court of Minnesota, was established in 1858, with zee mission of dispensing Justice amongst zee citizens of Hennepin County. Justice, Your Honour, requires zee foundation of Truth."

He pauses; his words echo in the courtroom with dramatic effect.

"To ensure zat a witness testifying in zees court speaks only zee Truth, Your Honour, zee founders instituted zee ritual oath to 'tell zee Truth, zee whole Truth and nothing but zee Truth, so help me God' while placing his hand upon a book. And what book was chosen for zees ritual of Truth?"

Monsieur Sutton looks briefly around the courtroom, nodding to acknowledge that everyone knew there had been only one correct choice available to the court's founders.

"Zee Holy Bible, which begins with zee Book of Genesis!"

M. Sutton stabs the air with this forefinger.
"In so doing, Your Honour, we contend zat zees court established zee Book of Genesis to be an authoritative source of Truth."
Monsieur Sutton bows as if taking a curtain call.

"Your Honor, this court no longer requires witnesses to take an oath on the Bible."

"Your Honour, zee fact that in modern times zees court is gracious in not requiring each witness to take an oath on Zee Holy Bible does not reflect on zee court's commitment to zee authoritative Truth found therein. It reflects rather on zee low spiritual state of zee witnesses. A witness may choose not to enact zat portion of zee ritual. Zee court, however, has never wavered in its commitment to offering Zee Holy Bible for zee purpose."

"Your Honor, placing one's hand on a book to take an oath does not make that book an authoritative source of Truth."

"Your Honor, zees court does not allow a witness to swear upon zee Farmer's Almanac, or zee Complete Works of Shakespeare, or even zee latest edition of zee Oxford English Dictionary. If a witness swears on a book, zat book must be

Zee Holy Bible. We contend zee court has thereby established it as an authoritative source of Truth." He extends his right hand condescendingly towards me. "Can zee defense counsel provide a credible alternative explanation for zee court's choice of Zee Holy Bible in zee context of an oath of truthfulness?"

There is nothing to say. I shake my head. I look down. My thumbs point to each other. The manila folder sits open on the table. I close it slowly. "God has placed you here for a purpose."

"Your Honor, it is one thing to acknowledge that a book contains 'truth', it is quite another matter to submit that book as evidence in a criminal trial. The prosecution can cite no precedent in this court that establishes the Book of Genesis as an evidentiary source."

"Your Honour, we contend zat zee only reason Zee Holy Bible has not previously been submitted as evidence is zat no criminal case has yet been heard in zees court where it would have been appropriate."

I consider. I could object that some of the 'truths' contained in the Book of Genesis are at best metaphorical, but I know I am out of my depth; Monsieur Sutton must clearly be ready for such a tactic. He would run rings around me and I would end by looking ridiculous.

I leave it there. We both stand waiting for The Judge's ruling. He sits still as a rock. Silence.

"Motion denied. This court recognizes the Book of Genesis as a source of Truth; its words are therefore admissible as evidence."

Monsieur Sutton hides his smile behind a manicured hand. His case is won. His trap succeeded. The grasshopper is caught. The verdict is a foregone conclusion.

I look down at the manila file folder, pressed down by the right thumb. The miraculous thumb.

Professor Morton's voice echoes in my head. "No matter how solid your case, always prepare a fallback position."

"Anything else on discovery, counselor?"

I shake my head.

"Nothing further, Your Honor."

Let the Sutton gloat. Let him think he has won.

I open the folder.

The motions stare up at me.

The nuclear option.

"Your Honor--"

"Will counsel please approach the bench."

Monsieur Sutton and I make our way around our tables to stand in front of Him. The black hood inclines towards me.

"Mr. Cohen, you have some motions for dismissal?"

This is not good.

"Yes, Your Honor: lack of jurisdiction, double jeopardy, ex post facto, judicial disqualification and death of the defendant."

Monsieur Sutton opens his mouth, but is quelled by the slightest lifting of The Judge's right hand.

"Quite right." The Judge nods, thoughtful for a moment.

"Yes, you are quite right, Mr. Cohen; this case does not belong in this court. Under usual circumstances, it would be heard in The Heavenly Court, where these restrictions of time and place don't obtain. But--"

I am surprised to feel an almost paternal gaze resting upon me. I think I hear a softness in his voice as he continues, "but in response to your petition to plead the case, We arranged for the case to be heard in this court, where your legal skills and experience would be given full reign."

He pauses for a moment, perhaps looking for understanding in my face. When He resumes, His voice is formal again.

"So, Mr. Cohen, it seems to Me that you have three options here: One, you can file these motions to dismiss and then defend the case in The Heavenly Court--" From the corner of my eye I see M. Sutton's lips twitch on his otherwise wooden countenance.

"Two, you can file these motions and retire from the case altogether."

"Or three, you can continue to defend in this court without filing these motions."

"The choice is yours, Mr. Cohen. That is all." He dismisses us with a nod.

Walking slowly back, my thoughts race with each footfall. If I quit, I will have accomplished nothing. In this court I have at least managed to bar the Book of Remembrances and God Himself from the prosecution's case. It looks bleak, but how would I fare in The Heavenly Court, where I would have no idea how to even begin? Monsieur Sutton's bemusement at the prospect may have been a feint, but obviously God Himself had determined I would do best in this court, which was why I was here. For a purpose.

Monsieur Sutton and I resume our respective places at the same moment and turn towards The Judge.

"Mr. Cohen--?"

For a purpose.

"No motions, Your Honor."

He nods and turns to the prosecutor. "Monsieur Sutton, are you ready to present your case?"

"We are ready and willing, Your Honour."

"To move us along, shall we dispense with opening statements and closing arguments, gentlemen?"

M. Sutton and I nod. "Very well. Trial commences tomorrow. This court stands adjourned."

The gavel thunders.

30

Awake. Jarring, but my head was steady. The room did not spin; the hardwood floor looked like a man could walk on it. The clock read 4:16. I was going to be okay.

But the case was hopeless. There was no way of defending Cain in any court, not if the Bible was admissible as evidence. It was impossible. And that had to mean there was no heavenly message here, no divine involvement, because God, if He existed at all, wouldn't give me a hopeless case.

Therefore this whole courtroom dream had to be coded symbolism from my subconscious that I couldn't decipher. And that Dr. Silverberger couldn't decipher, either-- or wouldn't explain to me, even if he could figure it out. I shook my head.

The good doctor had suggested that I actually talk with these dream characters. Engage them in dialogue as if they were real.

I reached doubtfully for my notebook on the bedside table.

Dear Monsieur Sutton, who looks like Hercule Poirot for no reason I can understand, why are you here? Why are you tormenting me?

I put down my pen and looked around the bedroom, daring him to materialize and explain himself. No ethereal visitors appeared. And then, oddly, an answer blossomed in my mind, "I am zee catalyst for zee change."

I wrote a response: *What change?*

"Zee change you seek, but of course. You are stuck, my friend; you keep running away from zee problems."

What problems?

"But of course you know zee problems."

Look, this is totally unhelpful. If you're trying to be a 'catalyst for change', don't be coy. I already have Dr. Silverberger for that. You want me to change? Describe the problems; give me some answers.

"You must use zee little grey cells, yes? My friend, *my* job is to push you to work; *your* job is to *do* zee work. It would be zee foolishness to present zee solutions from zee outside, voilà, like zee hôtdog from zee street vendor. No, no. Zee change, she must come from within."

How can I work on 'zee problems' if I can't even identify what they are?

"Ah, you must play zee detective, yes? Since you run from even zee tiny shadow of a problem, zee most simple investigative technique will suffice. Simply observe what you run away from, my friend, and there you will find zee problem. Remember: anger, she masks zee fear. And fear is a finger pointing to a problem in zee heart."

I do not run away from problems.

"Mais oui, it keeps you safe. Safe in your cave, hidden away from humanity. My friend, you are so alone zat you *pay* someone to listen to you. And from even him you run away! Is zat a sign of someone with no problems?"

What would you know about human problems? You're some figment of my imagination based on a character in a book.

"Let me guess, my friend: I am stupid. I am so stupid

zat now you make angry and decide to run."

I am not angry, and no figment of my imagination is going to push me around.

I put the pen down. "M. Sutton Poirot" was more blunt than Dr. Silverberger, which was refreshing, but 'hiding in a cave'?

Sure I had broken it off with Mary when she had become hysterically irrational and tried to guilt me into marrying her, but up until then we had shared a real relationship. And Josh and I were close. And even Andy and I had our moments.

And while I hadn't spoken to my sister since she got married, that was natural; she was busy with her new life. And my mother-- who could be close to that woman? She was so locked up in her own little world...

I looked at the clock. 5:14. The diner would be open by the time I walked there for breakfast.

31

Rabbi Friedler smiled as he let me in. After donning tefillin and hearing the shofar, I stated my mission.

"I need to know exactly what evidence the Torah gives that Cain murdered Abel; what is the precise wording of the text?"

Rabbi Friedler nodded and moved to the large bookshelf nearest the table. "How's your Hebrew?"

"Um, pretty much non-existent. I mean, I learned the basics when I was a kid, but that was over twenty years ago."

R. Friedler pulled out two books, each from a different place, and set one of them down in front of me, finding the page he wanted me to see. I was relieved to see English on the left-side page. Then I glanced over at the right-side Hebrew words.

"Actually, I still remember the sounds for most of the letters, and a *vav* before a word means 'and', right?"

I saw Rabbi Friedler smile and nod as he sat down opposite me. "Very good; very good." He scanned through his Hebrew-only text to find where the Cain story started. Then he leaned over and placed a knobby finger at the beginning of the Hebrew verse on my right-hand page and pointed out the corresponding place in the English translation.

"Okay, let's start at the first mention of Kayin. I'll read each *pasuk* in Hebrew, and then you read the translation in English, okay? And then we'll see what the commentators have to say."

"Um, okay."

"*V'haodom yada es Chava ishtoe vatahar vatailed es Kayin vatomair kanesee eesh es Hashem.*" He motioned to me.

"'*Now the man?*'" I looked up and he nodded. "*Now the man had known his wife Eve, and she conceived and bore Cain saying, 'I have acquired a man with Hashem.*'"

"Chava says, 'I have acquired...' which in Hebrew is '*kaneesee*'. This is why she names him 'Kayin'; '*kaneesee*' and 'Kayin' stem from the same grammatical root. We see in the Torah that the name of a person gives a clue to their essence: who they are, and what they struggle with, or what their mission is."

"So what does 'Kayin' mean exactly?"

Rabbi Friedler squinted a little. "I would say, 'possession' or 'acquisition'."

I looked back to the text. I didn't see how Cain's main struggle was with possession or acquisition. But I did know that you couldn't convict a man in Hennepin County court for having a possessive nature.

"*And additionally she bore his brother Abel; Abel became a shepherd and Cain became a tiller of the ground.*"

"Here Rashi comments that Hevel became a shepherd because he feared Hashem's curse against the ground. You remember that after Adam's sin of eating the forbidden fruit, God cursed the ground. Let's see..." Rabbi Friedler skimmed some other columns of small print. "Another commentator says that Hevel chose a profession that allowed him to spend his time in solitude contemplating spiritual matters, like Abraham, Isaac,

Jacob, Moses and David did."

"What, so Cain's being a 'tiller of the ground' is somehow evidence of spiritual inferiority?!"

"Some of the sages see it that way." Rabbi Friedler continued.

"And it came to be, after some days, Cain brought a mincha offering to Hashem from the fruit of the ground."

"This was the first mincha offering; we see later in The Holy Temple that the mincha sacrifice was brought twice daily; it was Kayin that brought the first one."

"And Abel brought --he, too-- from the firstborn of his sheep and from their choicest. Hashem turned to Abel and to his offering."

"So here Ibn Ezra comments on the contrast between the description of their offerings. You see that Kayin brought *'from the fruit of the ground'*, but Hevel brought *'from the firstborn of his sheep and from their choicest'*. So Hevel went to the trouble of bringing the best he had, whereas Kayin simply brought what he could easily give up. That is why Hashem turned to Hevel's offering, but not Kayin's."

"Isn't that reading a lot into the phrasing? Maybe Cain also brought his choicest 'fruit of the ground'."

"Well," Rabbi Friedler explained, "we have a principle that when God created the Torah, He did so with a perfection that was meticulous down to the smallest detail. So every space, every letter, every seemingly 'extra' or 'missing' word or phrase-- they are all there intentionally to teach us something. Since the Torah goes out of its way to tell us that Hevel brought his choicest, but is silent about how Kayin selected his fruit, the sages pick up on that and infer a message."

This was beginning to feel tedious. Clearly the commentators, having decided that Cain was guilty, had gone back through the verses leading up to the killing and read into them all kinds of evil motivations and sinister character defects. It was totally biased hearsay. But that was good. It meant that I could get it thrown out if M. Sutton tried to introduce it. I scanned ahead briefly in the English; we were almost to the part I needed to hear about.

At that moment, Mrs. Friedler emerged from the kitchen carrying a tray laden with lemonade and banana bread. Rabbi Friedler held up a slice and carefully recited a blessing over it. I responded 'Amen', and he repeated the procedure with the lemonade.

The food was delicious --no doubt homemade-- and we enjoyed it wholeheartedly. After a few slices, Rabbi Friedler brushed away some crumbs and found his place.

He pointed towards my book. "Verse six."

"And towards Cain and towards his sacrifice Hashem did not turn, and this angered Cain greatly and his face fell."

"And Hashem said to Kayin, 'Why are you angered, and why has your face fallen?" I held up my palm and shook my head. "I don't get that. Cain came up with this great sacrifice idea and brought an offering to God, and then his younger brother came along and outdid him by bringing something supposedly better, and then God turned to Abel and not to Cain--! I'd be pretty ticked off, too! It seems obvious why Cain's 'face fell'; he was

disappointed and felt cheated." Another point occurred to me. "Isn't God supposed to know all and see all? Why would He have to ask Cain why he's angry? Even if it weren't obvious, shouldn't God know without having to ask?"

Rabbi Friedler nodded vigorously. "A good question! And all the more so when God later asks Kayin, 'Where is your brother?'. Surely God knows what happened to Hevel?

"Of course, this started with Kayin's father, Odom, back in Gan Eden. After Chava and Odom eat the forbidden fruit, God famously asks Odom, 'Where are you?'. Surely God knew where they were! No one can hide from the Almighty!" Rabbi Friedler reflected on his own words. "Although sometimes we seem to imitate Jonah and run away from Him!"

"So what's the answer? Why does God ask the questions when He already knows the answer?"

"Well, clearly God is not asking the question in order to gain information. So that must mean He is asking the question for our sake, for us to reflect on what we have done, and on our current situation. If we look back at Odom's question, for example," Rabbi Friedler flipped back a few pages and ran his finger down the smaller print. "We see that the Midrash Aggadah explains that the question was a way of introducing a dialogue, rather than suddenly imposing a punishment. The Vilna Gaon suggests that the question was more spiritual, 'Consider well how you have fallen from your exalted status!'" He flipped back to our section on Kayin. "Here, we see Rashi explaining that God asks, 'Where is Hevel your brother?'

to give Kayin a chance to confess and repent." Rabbi Friedler looked up. "And you notice that God asks, 'Where is Hevel *your brother?*' Why would He include 'your brother' there?"

Rabbi Friedler had a point; it wasn't like there were so many strangers wandering around named 'Hevel' that Cain was going to misunderstand the question.

"So you're saying God included '*your brother*' to get Cain to think about what he had just done?"

"Exactly! The entire question was for Kayin's benefit, to give him an opportunity for *teshuvah* -- repentance!" Rabbi Friedler eyes sparkled. "Ah, but we have skipped over two crucial verses! Verse seven...*"

I dutifully translated, "*But surely if you improve, it will be forgiven, but if you do not improve, sin crouches in the opening. Towards you is its desire, but you can master it.*"

"Here is the essence of what Hashem is trying to teach Kayin! Ramban explains that He is teaching us as well: Man can always repent, and God will forgive us! The problem is not our imperfections, that's part of being human. Our problems begin when, instead of improving, we give in to pessimism and stop trying. Discouragement is the Sutton's primary weapon!"

Rabbi Friedler glanced up at me from his text. "You know, this is the perfect text to be studying now, right before Rosh Hashana, the day of judgement!"

He continued, "And here we are! The murderous verse where Kayin does the deed! Verse eight...*"

"*And Kayin spoke with Hevel, his brother. And it was that they were in the field and Kayin rose up against his brother and murdered him.*" I re-read the translation. Something wasn't quite right. "But yesterday when you were translating, you said Cain had 'killed' Abel. Here it's written that Cain 'murdered' him. Why the discrepancy?"

R. Friedler smiled and wagged an index finger. "I can see why you're a good lawyer." He pointed at my book. "The Pebble translation does tend to incorporate the commentaries and the Midrashim, so it's understandable they would use 'murder' here as the English for '*vayahargayhu*'." R. Friedler squinted his left eye as he looked up at the ceiling. "I suppose, the most literal translation might be 'struck him with a mortal blow'."

"Wow, that's much better! 'Struck him a mortal blow.' From that by itself, there are potentially all kinds of extenuating circumstances. And I take it there were no witnesses?"

"None except God Himself!"

No wonder M. Sutton had wanted to call God to the stand! The only eyewitness to the world's first murder!

That meant that the only evidence M. Sutton had at his disposal was from the commentators. The big question was whether those interpretations were considered part of the Book of Genesis that had been admitted as evidence. Clearly Rabbi Friedler considered the rabbis' explanations to be part and parcel of the whole Torah, but maybe there was a way to dismiss them.

And suddenly the whole idea seemed silly. Spending my time studying these old books at the Friedlers when Josh was languishing in the hospital. Mounting a legal defense of a biblical crime in my dreams wasn't going to shrink a tumor or help a surgeon operate.

The best use of my "vaykay" was probably spending more time having fun, as Dr. Silverberger had suggested. Getting involved in activities where I lost track of time and forgot about these dreams altogether.

Rabbi Friedler sensed that I had reached a threshold. He reached out his hand to congratulate me on some fine Torah learning.

"And may the merit of your learning be applied on your friend's behalf. May he have a complete and speedy recovery!"

32

At Hidden Falls, a small waterfall nestled into the steep Mississippi riverbank, I set out my lunch in a miniature picnic. The crisp fall air felt good in the warm sun, and the running water was hypnotic.

Dr. Silverberger thought I might feel guilty about my father dying. I supposed it was possible. Who could know what was hidden deeply in their subconscious? But it didn't feel right. The man just dropped dead a week before his 31st birthday, walking home from synagogue one Saturday morning. Even if I had been with him, there would have been nothing I could do; I was eight.

Apparently one of the men he was walking with had run into the nearest house and called 911, and someone else had run to let my mother know. She had taken my sister with her to the hospital, sending our neighbor, Mrs. Goldstein, to the playground to collect me, where I and my friends had been playing on the jungle-gym. Mrs. Goldstein had sat with me at the house, and my mother had returned more quickly than anyone had expected; my father had been dead on arrival.

So was I feeling guilty? Hardly. If anything, I felt some resentment at him for dying when I was so young. Running out on the family. Of course that was almost as stupid as feeling guilty. As if my father had chosen to die so young.

The good doctor had suggested I focus on getting support, connecting with people I knew well. Not many of those were available at the moment.

I could call my mom. She would go ga-ga with delight

that I was calling, and then be totally unhelpful, but I could still do it. You never knew; she might be empathetic. Miracles could happen.

I dialed my cell as the gurgling water made its way home to the river.

"Hello?"

"Hi, Mom."

"Oh, Larry! How wonderful! So nice to hear from you! How are you? Is everything alright?"

"Just fine, Mom; just fine. How are things in Chicago?"

"Well, you know how things go. The cantor sang Lecha Dodi to a different tune last Friday night and everyone was talking about it at the Kiddush. Most people liked it, but you know old Mrs. Hammerstein always wants things the same old way, no matter what. So she gave an earful to young Rabbi Wolf, the poor dear. I do wonder how he puts up with her, but I guess that's his job.

"Speaking of which, he did ask me if you were still seeing that young woman..?"

"Her name is 'Mary', Mom, and no, I'm not seeing her; we broke up weeks ago."

"Oh, well, I'm sure he'll be relieved to hear that! Rabbi Wolf said that almost half of Reform Jews today marry outside the faith, and very few of their grandchildren remain Jewish at all. You remember the Buxbaums, in the house on the other side of Mrs. Goldstein? Their daughter married a Catholic boy and now they moved to Texas to be near the grandchildren. Texas! You know how many Jews there are in Texas?!"

"Four hundred and sixteen?"

"Probably fewer, what with everyone wearing boots and cowboy hats. Well, on the positive side, a lovely Russian couple moved into their house; Stravinsky-- no, Kazinski! They made a good impression on Mrs. Goldstein. They're planning on building a Sukkah for the first time in years, because their youngest is visiting. He apparently has become religious, and I guess some of their other kids are dabbling a little. Anyway, they invited me to their open house Sukkah party in two weeks. It's the same day as your birthday, and so, well, maybe you could come and we could have a little birthday celebration? And I know Mrs. Goldstein would love to see you, too."

"I'll see if I can get the time off, Mom; otherwise, it would be hard to get there and back on a short weekend."

"They work you so hard. It's just not right to keep a boy from his mother."

33—

At the hospital, Josh was getting bathed, so Cindy and I went down the hall to the family visiting area.

Cindy said, "The surgery is scheduled for Tuesday." She looked a little sleep-deprived, but happy about the news.

"That's great. How are you holding up?"

"My family is close by and they're a big support, and the community from our church has just been great. We're getting a lot of prayer coverage." She looked at me. "Do you pray, Larry? I mean, if it's not too personal a question."

"No, it's fine to ask. But prayer isn't really my thing."

"But you come from a religious family, right?"

"Well, my mom grew up Reform --that's on the liberal end of the spectrum-- and my dad's family was Conservative, which is kind of in the middle. But each had grandparents who were more traditional. They met at a Hillel House in Chicago, exploring their more orthodox roots."

"So how did you grow up?"

"We were quite observant until my dad, um, died." Cindy nodded; Josh must have told her. "I was eight. Shortly after that my mom went back to Reform, and... well, that's how it went until I went away to college."

"So prayer wasn't part of Reform?"

"Well sure, but not how you mean it. I mean, we went to synagogue on Friday nights, and we said prayers there, and sang the songs and stuff. But— I don't know. It never felt like praying *to* someone, you know? Not like anyone was actually talking one-on-one to God."

Cindy shook her head slowly. "I just can't imagine making it through this without leaning on Him; without taking refuge in His comfort and strength."

34__

I arrived at the Rock Bottom Brewery a little early, figuring I'd eat something before Andy arrived with the gang. They would be coming after work to shoot a few rounds of pool and have a beer or two before heading home. Rock Bottom was a good place to do that. They had four pool tables on the first floor and a full menu. I ordered the Bacon Chicken Mac 'N' Cheese and a Kolsch beer.

Andy entered with Brad and Peter, and they made their way over. Brad was a tall blond leading man, and Peter was thin and dark, with an easy laugh. Andy knew them from college theater, and when he moved to Minneapolis, he established monthly pool gatherings at Rock Bottom so they could stay in touch. Like me, there were sometimes one or two other friends that joined in, but the core group was the "three musketeers" as they called themselves. After a few beers they sometimes started singing show tunes. So far, the management hadn't thrown them out.

We paired up for "distraction" eight-ball, Andy and I against Brad and Peter. Distracting the opponents while they were trying to shoot was part of the game for them.

As Peter racked the balls, it occurred to me that there were four players and sixteen balls, counting the cue ball.

"Say, Andy, does four-sixteen mean anything to you?"

"It's the day you start expecting something back!"

"How's that?"

"It's my father's joke. He was born on April 16th, the day after taxes are due. He says from January first until

April fifteenth, it's all one way: you're paying taxes to Uncle Sam. On 4/16, you start expecting something back. That's a Republican psychologist's idea of humor."

We watched Brad take the first shot.

"How's the big case? Have you gotten Cain acquitted yet?"

"I've got some trouble, but I can fill you in on the technical legal details another time."

Peter had overheard us. "What's that about Cain?"

"Larry's been dreaming he's defending Cain --you know, Cain and Abel from the Bible."

"Really?"

"Yup." I took a swig of Kolsch and looked around the bar. Mostly pairs sharing tables, leaning their heads towards each other and minding their own business.

At my turn, I banked the three into the corner, Brad and Peter started singing a parody of a number from The Music Man, waving their hands and dancing in mock choreography.

"Oh, we got trouble, right here in the Twin Cities. With a capital 'T' and that rhymes with 'C' and that stands for Cain!"

I sank the one-ball, followed by the four-ball and the seven-ball; take that, fellas. But then I missed the potentially game-winning shot, a tough slice on the eight-ball.

As I took up my spot next to Andy, he said, "Nice run, Larry." And then, "Seriously, how is the case; did I give you enough to get it thrown out?"

I told him the Bible had been accepted as evidence because it was a "Book of Truth" used for swearing in witnesses.

"What?!" Andy exclaimed. "I can't believe it. That's a *Christian* Bible! You can't be serious."

"I hadn't thought of that."

"Oh my goodness. I can't believe you fell for that!" Andy shook his head and muttered, "What a mess."

He sank the eight-ball, giving us the win, as I stood there feeling like a loser.

35—

At home, I prepared for bed.

I wondered if Cain had felt like a grasshopper when God had rejected his mincha offering. Or maybe later when he was banished from his family forever.

Before turning out the light it occurred to me that I hadn't recited the Shema prayer the previous night. I said the six words and turned out the light, mentally preparing for the worst. And as I closed my eyes, I whispered, "Please send me some help, Father."

I am standing. We are all standing.
The Judge sits, the gavel sounds.
"This court is now in session. You may be seated."
I sit. We all sit.
Simon says, "Put your hand on your head."
I put my hand on my head.
Simon says, "Put your hand on your tummy."
I put my hand on my tummy.
"Put your hand on your nose."
But I am not fooled.
Can you pat your head and rub your tummy at the same time?
Mrs. Goldstein smiles her admiration.

"M. Sutton?"
"Thank you, Your Honour." M. Sutton stands and announces, "We call Moshe Rabbeinu."
The courtroom stands in anticipation. Suddenly radiating from the witness box, larger than life, is a bearded giant in a plain woolen cloak, a staff in his right hand. I stare in disbelief. It cannot be. I blink my eyes twice in quick succession.
Charlton Heston?
The bailiff swears him in.a
"Please state your name for the record."
"Moses ben Amram"
"Do you affirm to tell the truth, the whole truth and nothing but the truth?"
"I do."

"You may be seated."

M. Sutton rises and approaches the witness, one hand smoothing his luxuriant mustaches.

"You are zee one and only Moshe Rabbeinu, who received Zee Holy Torah on Mount Sinai from God Almighty?"

"I am."

"You led zee Jews through zee Wilderness for forty years, teaching them Zee Holy Torah?"

"I did."

"When zee Children of Israel had questions about zee meaning of Zee Holy Torah, they came to you for answers and clarifications, did they not?"

"They did."

"You were able to answer most of their questions without assistance?"

He hesitates, but answers, "I was."

"And when you knew not zee answers, you sought and received clarification and additional revelations from Zee Book's Author?"

"I did."

M. Sutton turns to The Judge.

"Your Honour, we offer Moses ben Amram as an expert witness in Zee Holy Torah."

The Judge turns towards me and I shake my head in a small negation. No point in trying to disqualify him. I have a sinking feeling in my stomach. We're going down, down, down.

M. Sutton licks his lips delicately and proceeds with his expert.

"Moshe Rabeinu, are you familiar with zee parshah of Bereishis?"
A smile hovers around Moses' lips.
"I am."

This here's _my_ book you talkin' 'bout,
Your own ugly self, so short and stout,
_I_ wrote it, dude.
so don't be rude.
The five books of who?
It sure ain't you!
It's Moses, man, get the name down right.
I was up on the mountaintop day and night.
Ask me a question, I'll give you a clue.
Cuz that's The Good Book, man, obey or you're through!

I shake my head vigorously to silence the growing hip-hop beat.
No rapping. No trapping.
Don't get caught napping.
A trial is hap'ning.
For a purpose.

M. Sutton opens an old Hebrew book in front of Moses.
"Is zees text from Sefer Bereishis of Zee Holy Torah?"
Moses carefully scans the page in front of him.
"It is."
"Let zee record show zat zee witness has

identified Exhibit A as a portion of the Book of Genesis." M. Sutton is uncharacteristically stiff. Surely his case is virtually won with Moses on the stand and the Book of Genesis admitted for evidence. Why is he so tense?

"Would you please read it into zee court's record?"

A frown darkens Moses' face as he stares down at the book. His eyes flit to The Judge and he lifts his brows in a question. Is the Judge smiling faintly; does He shrug? M. Sutton's taut face and darting eyes betray his perplexity. Moses rises. He is a big man. I hear the shuffling sounds of the courtroom rising to their feet behind me. I stand. Moses walks around an apprehensive M. Sutton to stand in the center of the court facing The Judge. He raises his staff. There is an awed silence as the words of The Torah suddenly appear in the air above, three large columns of wrought Hebrew letters on ancient parchment, dominating the courtroom. He points his staff at the first column of words and begins. Chanting.

His voice fills a completely silent courtroom. It rises and falls in the ancient phrases of the Torah chant. I am mesmerized. The words come pouring out from the depths of his heart. He lovingly pronounces each letter and vowel, an old, old song sung to him in the cradle, or even the womb. The story of his family, his tribe, his God. A song worn smooth from constant repetition and daily study. His life's work.

I make out the names "Kayin" and "Hevel" but I understand nothing else, save the deep regret in Moses' voice as he retells this tragic chapter of his forebears' history.

And suddenly it flips: an optical illusion, a reversal of images. The Torah so large in front of me is no longer superimposed over the courtroom that has disappeared behind it. Instead, the courtroom appears peeled away, like the drawing of a thin curtain, to reveal the ancient Holy Torah always lurking, hidden, just beneath the surface.

The text shimmers and dances, rippling black letters in the open air. Glittering and swirling, like black flame. Even the white spaces between the holy letters squirm and undulate to Moses' song. The words envelope me. I waver and sway with them. Swept away.

And suddenly the Torah is gone; the room is quiet once more. Moses lowers his staff and returns to the witness box. I sit slowly, stupefied.

There ain't no sound,
what just went down
with awe all around
Moshe Rabbeinu, he ain't no clown
be careful, Sutton, don't make him frown
cuz he gonna turn you upside-down

take you on your last trip through downtown
You don't mess with Moses,
or you sleep with roses
Six feet deep
Permanent sleep.
Ain't gonna lie,
You sin, you die.
Peace.

M. Sutton moves to regain the spotlight; his voice holds a mixture of satisfaction and relief, "Thank you, Moshe Rabbeinu."
M. Sutton retrieves a paper from his briefcase. He places it with exactness in front of Moses.
"Please to read zees English translation for zee record."
Moses scans the sheet for a few moments and stares squarely down at the little pear-shaped man in front of him.
"No."
M. Sutton's jaw drops in disbelief. He looks quickly to The Judge. Moses continues matter-of-factly, "I am here to tell the truth, the whole truth and nothing but the truth. And this translation, Monsieur Sutton, is most certainly not the whole truth."
M. Sutton is amazed. His mouth hangs open and he hesitates, frozen, a deer caught in headlights. Then he nods resolutely, a quick recovery.
"Very well."
He walks quickly back to the prosecution table

and picks up a second copy of the translation.
"Please to listen carefully," he instructs Moses.

Moses don't like the dude so much
Cuz M. Sutton, boy outta touch
Tryin' to damage some of the Yidden,
Serpent say they did some thing forbidden,
Can't get past Moshe, cuz nothing is hidden
He'll take your 'staches right off your face
He'll show you who's who, put you down in
your place
Smashing your smirk with tablets of stone
You're busted, kid, take your bad self home.

Moses is a hostile witness!
No wonder M. Sutton is so tense!
The hills are alive with the sound of music!
Hope springs eternal!
M. Sutton clears his throat. He holds up his
paper, a king's messenger announcing a
proclamation:
And it was, after some days, Kayin brought of the fruit
of the earth an offering to God. And Hevel brought, he
too, from the first-born of his flock, from their choicest.
And God turned to Hevel and to his offering. And to
Kayin and his offering He did not turn, and Kayin was
very angry and his face fell. And God said to Kayin,
"Why are you angry and why has your face fallen?
Surely if you improve-- forgiveness; but if you do not
improve, sin crouches at the opening and towards you is
its desire -- you can rule over it."

M. Sutton pauses for air, and his eyes dart around the courtroom.

Can't beat that. Can't beat that.

Satisfied, he resumes:

And Kayin spoke with his brother Hevel, and it happened they were in the field, and Kayin rose up against Hevel, his brother and smote him."

M. Sutton eyes me over the top of his paper with a curling lip. I have no case. The evidence is conclusive. I am finished. I am in trouble. I need help. Lots of help. Please.

"You'll see how he does go on, though, doesn't he?" whispers a voice at my right elbow.

Startled, I turn to see an old black cowboy hat on a white-bearded man in a dusty suit. He is leaning forward to see past me, surveying M. Sutton intently.

"Rabbi Friedler?!" But the antiquated hat sits differently on his head, the features familiar but somehow wrong, and the beard too long and smooth.

He is Rabbi Friedler, but he's not Rabbi Friedler.

"Father," he confides from the corner of his mouth.

Excellent! "Thanks for coming, Rabbi Friedler, um, Senior?" I stammer in a low voice.

"The name means nothing," he murmurs.

M. Sutton clears his throat and continues.

"And God said to Kayin, "Where is Hevel your brother?" and he said, "I do not know; am I my brother's keeper?"

And He said, "What have you done? The voice of your brother's blood cries to Me from the earth. And now-- you are cursed from the land that opened its mouth to take the blood of your brother from your hand."
When you work the earth, she will no longer give her strength to you; a traveler and a nomad you will be in the land."
And Kayin said to God, "My sin is too great to be borne. Behold, you have banished me today from the face of the earth and from Your face I will be hidden; and I will be a traveler and a nomad in the land, and it will be that those who encounter me will smite me."
And God said to him, 'Therefore, whoever smites Kayin before seven generations are sustained—!' and God put on Kayin a sign so that he would be spared by all that encounter him. And Kayin left from before God."

M. Sutton whirls and is suddenly standing combatively in front of the witness box, left hand on hip, right hand pointing at the great man.

"A rather abrupt transition, don't you think?" suggests the hushed Rabbi Friedler, Sr.

"Moshe Rabbeinu, will you confirm zat zee translation I just read into zee court record accurately conveys, for zee purposes of zees trial, zee essential facts of zee section of Bereishis you read from Zee Holy Torah?"

Moses' mouth twists in a light grimace. He considers thoughtfully. He takes his time. M. Sutton cannot rush him. But at last he finds no room for equivocation. M. Sutton has worded his question well.

Reluctantly, "Yes, it does."

"Merci!"

M. Sutton turns victoriously on his heel and walks back to his table. A contemptuous little smile forms beneath his radiant mustaches. In deadly slow motion, he lifts his eyes awfully towards me. He stares in cruel exultation. He is undaunted by the sudden appearance of Rabbi Friedler, Sr.; his eyes are on me alone. Without the slightest hesitation, he flourishes his left hand towards the witness stand.

"Voilà tout. Your witness."

What is there to say? Where is the weakness in the testimony? What opening do I have? I had hoped for inspiration. None is forthcoming. I look to Rabbi Friedler, Sr., who now stands up. My hopes rise with him, but he simply says, "No questions at this time, Your Honor." He sits back down, directing me a single confident nod of his head.

At the threshold of my hearing, M. Sutton murmurs quietly, "I thought not."

The Judge intones, "M. Sutton?"

M. Sutton rises and faces The Judge. He inhales dramatically, and pulls his small round frame to its full height. "The prosecution," he declares triumphantly, "rests, Your Honour."

The Judge nods.

"Very well."

He turns to R. Friedler, Sr. "The court welcomes you, sir." He glances at me and then back to Rabbi Friedler, Sr. "The defense will proceed when we reconvene on Yom Sheni. This court stands adjourned."

I look the question to the Rabbi.

Behind a cupped hand, he whispers, "Monday!"

The gavel thunders.

36

The tefillin ritual with Rabbi Friedler was beginning to feel familiar and comfortable. The shofar blasts were still both soothing and jarring at the same time. Both were over before I could think much more about them.

"How did court go?" Rabbi Friedler asked, beaming with interest.

I described the scene of Moses' sudden appearance and the reading of the Torah.

"What I wouldn't give to hear Moshe Rabbeinu leyning!" he cried enthusiastically. "What a treat! What a blessing!"

I related my startled reaction at seeing Charlton Heston reprising his role from *The Ten Commandments*. "If these dreams are, well, for real-- I mean, if God is *really*, um, sponsoring this trial and conducting these dreams, then why Charlton Heston for Moses? Doesn't that strike you as kind of weird?"

As soon as the words left my mouth, I knew Rabbi Friedler would remind me that nothing happens in this world except by Divine Will. Instead, he surprised me.

"Would you say that God has a body?"

"You mean a flesh-and-bones, human-type body?"

"Yes, exactly. Would you say that God has a human body?"

"No-o."

He nodded vigorously at the expected answer. "Exactly. And yet the Torah speaks of God leading us out of Egypt 'with an outstretched arm' and 'a powerful hand'." He looked at me expectantly, like a child asking a riddle.

"I don't see what you're getting at, Rabbi."

"You see, the Torah speaks to us in the language we understand. The rabbis comment that God so much wants us to engage with Him, that He speaks our language, even at the risk of fundamental theological misunderstandings!"

"So...?"

"The Torah speaks to us on so many levels simultaneously." He gestured with his hands to indicate many horizontal levels. "The simple meaning we often understand immediately --or we think we do-- although even with Rashi's help..." He shook his head as if remembering being mistaken too many times. "The deeper levels reveal themselves over a lifetime of study. And God reveals different things to each of us at different times, according to our needs. The Torah speaks to the little child, the young man, the simple peasant and the sainted scholar -- all with the same words, all at the same time!

"So," he stabbed the air with a triumphant finger, "even though God doesn't have a literal arm, even a child understands the meaning of being taken out of Egypt with 'an outstretched arm'. It resonates with our experience and allows us some limited ability to understand the actions of an Infinite and Awesome God in this finite world of ours."

"So you think God was bringing Moses to me in the guise of Charlton Heston because I can somehow understand *him* as Moses better than I would if the *real* Moses appeared?"

"Something like that." Rabbi Friedler smiled, "The images you see in your dreams help you to receive God's message. They are not meant to be 'real' representations. Of course, you could also understand it as 'the most accessible symbol for Moses available from your subconscious.' Both explanations say the same thing."

"But why would your father appear in my dream? Why would he be the most accessible symbol from my subconscious?" I told him the part where Rabbi Friedler, Sr. had appeared.

Rabbi Friedler laughed. "You got me there! Maybe that question is better directed to your psychologist!"

"Speaking of which..."

"Yes?"

"Well, my therapist thinks I may be turning you into my father." I said it in a joking tone, but Rabbi Friedler considered it carefully.

"Well, the sages do compare the teacher-student relationship to the father-son relationship in many places. It can be an enduring bond. And family is an important source of strength." He looked at me thoughtfully. "However I can be of help, Reb Reuven, you just let me know. You're always welcome here."

I stared down at the table and bit my lip until I could return Rabbi Friedler's soft gaze.

"Thank you, Rabbi."

3.7

The next morning, in his office, Dr. Silverberger seemed slightly distracted. He said something about us possibly being interrupted, and then asked me how I was. He nodded as I told him about the conversation with Poirot.

Then I told him about calling my mom. He asked how that went, and when I revealed that no miraculous intervention had caused empathy to flow from a well that had long run dry, he asked about other family members.

"Would you consider being in touch with your sister? Do you have any uncles or male cousins?"

"My father did have a younger brother, but the last time I saw him was at my bar mitzvah umpteen years ago. He's orthodox. We don't have a lot in common. Anyway, on what pretext would I write to him?"

Dr. Silverberger smiled. "You don't need a reason to be in touch with him; he's your uncle, your family. I expect he would be happy to hear from you."

"Even after all this time? I'm practically a stranger to him."

"Especially after all this time! He probably wonders what kind of man you've grown to be, and would be interested in hearing what your life is like these days."

Dr. Silverberger's cell phone rang. He peeked at the number and grimaced slightly.

"Sorry, Larry, I'm going to need to answer this; excuse me a minute."

I started to stand up, but he waved me back into my chair and swiveled away from me towards his desk.

"This is Dr. Silverberger." I could hear some indistinct noises on the other end of the phone. Dr. Silverberger stood up. He said something to me about staying where I was and disappeared out the door. His empty chair stared at me, still slowly rotating.

I looked around the suddenly bare room, the abandoned desk. Unbelievable. *Unbelievable!*

How could he do that? It was totally unprofessional. He couldn't just walk out on me. I wasn't some throwaway doll. I was paying him to provide a service and he was obligated to provide that service. Who did he think he was?

I paced back and forth. The room felt like it was shrinking. I jerked the door open. The hallway was empty; he was nowhere in sight. Vanished just like that.

I walked to the reception area. Where was he?

I dropped into a chair and dialed Andy.

"What's up, Larry?"

"Has your father ever left a patient in the middle of a session?"

"Not to my knowledge. What's going on?"

"This psychologist just walked out on me!"

"Did he explain why he was leaving, or say when he'd be back?"

"Look, I don't know what the heck he said, he just stood up, mumbled something, and was gone!"

"How long has it been since he walked out?"

"I don't know. What, I'm supposed to keep track of his time now?"

"Well--" Andy sounded suddenly distracted, as if someone had just set something on his desk, "I suggest you check it out with him. Maybe there was a good reason. Say, Larry, I gotta go; let me know how it turns out, okay?"

I turned off the phone. This was stupid. The whole situation was stupid. Maybe I should just go home.

An echo sounded in my mind. *Let me guess, my friend: everyone is so stupid zat now you make angry and run away.*

Great. Voices in my head telling me what to do. Just when I actually needed a doctor, he had run out on me.

I made my way back down the hall.

As I poked my head through the door of his office, Dr. Silverberger looked up from a file folder, "Oh, good, there you are! Sorry for that interruption. For a moment there, I was worried I had lost you."

"Um, no." I came in and sat back down. "Just needed a bathroom break."

Dr. Silverberger looked at me for a long moment. It was suddenly clear to me that there was exactly one men's bathroom on the floor and he had just been in it. And why was I lying to this man, anyway? *He* was the one who owed *me* an explanation, not the other way around!

"I apologize for the disruption, Larry. That was an emergency from a new client and I had to help her call 9-1-1." Dr. Silverberger continued to look at me carefully. "What was it like for you while you were waiting?"

He didn't fool me. I wasn't some naive little kid he could fool with some patronizing fake sympathy. He could try that on his more gullible patients. The chair he sat in was supported by a single column which spread out into an asterisk near the floor, and under each branch was a plastic castor. He could roll around in any direction he wanted to, forward one minute, backward the next. Sidewise at a moment's notice. Maximum flexibility and maneuverability. Meanwhile, I was stuck in my chair.

I shook my head, "It was fine. I just wasn't sure how long you'd be gone, or if-- you know." I wiped my eye with my right forefinger.

"You know, Larry, sometimes feelings can be triggered--"

"Look, let's not make a big deal out of it, okay? We got interrupted, but now we're back, right? Okay, so let's get back to what we were talking about!"

Dr. Silverberger regarded me for several slow seconds before nodding deliberately.

"All right, Larry; let's see-- I think we were talking about family?"

38

The nurse at the oncology station told me Josh was sleeping and suggested I come back later. In the waiting area, I pulled out my cell. No texts. An email from my mom forwarding some article she had seen online. On impulse, I dialed her number.

"So nice to hear from you twice in one week! Won't Gila be jealous when I tell her!"

"Say, Mom, what can you tell me about my uncle?"

"Oh, your father's younger brother Nathan. Teaches economics, if I remember; I haven't heard from him in-- well it must be years now! He lives in Sacramento. Came to your bar mitzvah, but since then, not a word! But I suppose he's busy with his family. Had a lovely wife and three small kids. Yes, the boy and the twin girls, probably teenagers now!"

"Do you have an email address or phone number for him?"

"Well, I doubt he's still at the same address, even if I could find it after all this time. But it's so strange that you would ask all of a sudden like this. Not that there's anything wrong with being in touch with family, of course!" My mother paused to see if I would answer the question she was trying to ask without asking. The silence lasted longer than her restraint. "Is everything all right, Larry?"

"It's all good, Mom, just wondering."

I logged on to the guest WiFi and googled "Nathan Cohen economics California". It was easy to pick out the professor of economics at the University of California,

Sacramento. The staff directory there listed his email address and a picture. His face was open and inviting, as I supposed all the professor's pictures were. But the smile was genuine and he had my father's eyes, the ones that used to stare out at me from the picture my mom kept on her bedside table. After school, when she was still away at work, I would sneak into her room sometimes just to look at it. A man and a woman, happy and in love, optimistically facing the world together. Professor Nathan Cohen's face looked out at the world with that same trust.

I clicked the email link. Suddenly I had an open email window.

What should I say? Dear Uncle Nathan, to whom I haven't spoken in almost sixteen years, how's it going, buddy? Heard any good jokes lately? Oh, and by the way, I'm so isolated and lonely that I'm seeing a shrink, I might be going crazy, and could you please be my father-figure for the next few months or the rest of my life?

The mouse hovered over the close button.

Zee small steps, they are zee best steps.

Dear Uncle Nate,
It's been a long, long time, but for some reason I started thinking about you lately and I thought I would be in touch, just to connect and catch up.
The brief story for me is that I'm living here in St. Paul, working as a criminal prosecutor for Hennepin County,

staying in shape with workouts and
racquetball, regularly playing bridge
(didn't you used to play?) and otherwise
keeping out of mischief. I'm still
single, although of course my mother has
great hopes for me. :)

How are things for you, and how are
your wife and kids? They must be in their
early twenties by now!

Anyway, I hope things are going well in
your life.

Your nephew,
Larry

Zee family, she is an important source of strength.
Before I could out-think myself, I clicked 'Send'.

In the Middle

39—

What to wear? That was the question of the moment. Of course I knew to wear "Shabbos best"; my father used to have a special section of his closet set aside for his fancy Sabbath clothes. Every Friday he would bring his dressy suit and freshly laundered shirt on their hangers into the doorway of my room, and I would grab my little suit and shirt, and rush to meet him. Hand in hand, we would walk down the hallway to the pink-tiled bathroom and wash up for Shabbos together. He would even pat a little of his aftershave on each of my young cheeks. Then we would set off to the synagogue together, brilliantly dressed and smelling of Old Spice.

Walking my hand along my hanging dress shirts, I selected a traditional starched white one, just back from the cleaners. With my charcoal trial suit and a thin black tie, I would at least be showing the proper respect. I had a fleeting thought of Hevel, choosing the best of his flocks for his Mincha offering. Two could play at that game.

R. Friedler's synagogue sat atop a hill on Edgecumbe Road. The U-shaped drive had a steep pitch and was lined with cars, which would no doubt be parked there until Saturday night, when the Sabbath restrictions would expire. I found a spot at the end of the drive and walked up the hill towards the front door. It had been many years since I had set foot in a sanctuary, and that had been a Reform synagogue. Hard to remember what the Orthodox experience had been like so many years before that. I had a hazy memory of leaning into my father on a cushioned bench, wrapped within his prayer shawl, feeling his warmth as he murmured his prayers. But who knew what these Neeners did inside their big stone building? I shrugged. Only one way to find out.

I pulled open the front door, and found myself in a corridor running from a staircase heading up on my right, to a doorway on the left that led further into the building. A small bulletin board confronted me with a confusing patchwork of postings in various languages.

As I pondered my choices, three loud young boys burst past me, running from the stairs to the inner doorway. I looked around. I had expected a greeter to say "Shabbat Shalom" while directing me where to sit. My old synagogue back home had always had someone doing that.

I made my way up the stairs. As I gained the top landing, I saw double doors at the end of the hall, and, through their glass openings, a congregation gathered in the sanctuary. As I drew closer and peered in from the side, I could see elegantly dressed men and boys seated in chairs, what looked like large family groups, or a few men gathered in twos and threes. Most of the men were wearing the same style of European hat and long black dress jackets, which shimmered in the light. They looked like princes from the 1800s, conversing easily in their small groups, although a few appeared to be reciting prayers, swaying and holding various well-worn books in their hands. There was a small raised platform in the center of the room, no doubt where they read the Torah during services, but which was now occupied by small well-dressed children playing. The whole scene felt chaotic and foreign.

"Reb Reuven! Good Shabbos!" I turned to find Sruli rushing towards me from my right. He shook my hand, offered me a head covering from a basket of yarmulkes -- which I belatedly realized everyone was wearing on their heads-- and found me a blue prayerbook with Hebrew and English running side by side.

Apparently I had missed Mincha, but was "just in time" for the Sabbath evening prayers which would be starting "any minute now".

He drew me inside to sit between him and Rabbi Friedler, who greeted me with a sincere smile, a hearty handshake and a firm nod, all the while murmuring prayers under his breath. I took my seat and looked around. I was relieved to see that the younger men wore suits much like mine, and the boys had white dress shirts and black pants, one or two with cute little vests. In the back rows I spied some visitors like me, and a few kids that looked like college students, dressed in cheap blazers and polyester slacks. As I turned back around, I noticed Rabbi Friedler's hat was different from the others; definitely a cowboy hat, now that I saw it up close.

From a lectern in the front, facing the wall, a tall thin figure with a beautiful baritone sang a lyrical motif. Most of the congregation responded in kind. A brief shuffling ensued as conversations broke off, groups reformed, prayer books were opened, and the Friday evening service began. Sruli found my page and pointed out a hanging wooden display in the left corner, which showed the current page in a number chart that some nearby kid kept up-to-date as the service progressed.

We started off with a series of Psalms. The leader chanted the first and last lines in Hebrew, and everyone murmured or sang out the intervening words. Or sometimes the congregation sang the entire Psalm together. I read the English; the Hebrew went by too quickly for me to keep up. Periodically I glanced furtively up at the page numbers to see where we were.

The leader finished the last Psalm with a musical flourish, and the congregation rose and started singing "L'cha Dodi", which I recognized from the long-lost day school assemblies that crowned the week every Friday afternoon. I turned two pages. There it was: "Welcome the Sabbath bride". The tune was lively and vaguely familiar, like I might have heard it long ago from a distance. The upbeat melody invited participation, but the words were hard to follow in the Hebrew, even though the simple tune made it easy to hum along. By the fifth repetition, however, I noticed that the seven-word chorus between the verses was the same every time, and I joined tentatively with the singing.

Suddenly everyone turned to face the rear. I nodded as I remembered: on the last verse, you turn to welcome the Sabbath Queen. Then we all turned back and the song was over.

Or rather, the words of the song were complete. The crowd continued singing in joyous celebration, and the tune kept going, wordlessly, as the volume swelled. Soon a ring had formed around the raised dais in the center of the room, and the men were dancing exuberantly. Fathers hoisted boys on their shoulders, teenagers jumped up and down as they went around in a circle. Several peripheral stars formed, with men locking their right arms together and twirling to the music. R. Friedler clapped his hands, loudly bellowing the tune. Sruli motioned me to join him; I shrugged. I saw that some of the college kids were just as confused as I was, and they were just walking along, swept up in the crowd.

Just when it seemed like the singing was winding down, some enthusiastic youth would whoop up energetically and suddenly the pace would pick up, the momentum would be regained, and the dancing would continue at an even livelier tempo. With no words, and the tune repeating mercilessly, I had no excuse to hold back. I joined in.

And there I was, hollering and picking up my legs to move around in the packed circle with everyone else. We kept going around and around and around. Sruli smiled in shared delight. Little kids laughed from atop their fathers' shoulders. Old men with long beards shuffled along enthusiastically.

And then, finally, the singing trailed off, and the dancers moved towards their chairs. We retook our seats.

From the midsts of the congregation a few scattered men stood, and suddenly the mourners' Kaddish rang out. From joy to sorrow in a heartbeat. "*Yisgadal v'yisgadash shemei rabah.*" These were the words they had said in my childhood house, so long ago, breaking the numbing silence that had descended on my family like a shroud. All week long they had come and said these words, and all week long I had mumbled "Amen", as

Uncle Nate had instructed me. "It will help your *Tatti* in Heaven", he had whispered. I did as I was told, but secretly I had held back, mumbling the word incoherently, hoping that if they kicked him out of heaven, maybe he would have to come back here to earth, here to our house, here to wipe away my mother's tears and coax a smile back to her silent, ashen face. Only he could do that.

I was startled from my reverie by a trumpeting "*Borchuuuu*" prayer call from the leader. The congregation bowed and responded in kind. Then we all sat. I looked up for the page number as the murmuring commenced. As I found my place, we were suddenly saying the familiar Shema prayer I had been saying with Rabbi Friedler when donning tefillin. I joined in, pleased to know at least one prayer.

After several minutes more, the congregation rose and the leader pronounced another Kaddish. To my right, Rabbi Friedler took three small steps backwards and three small steps forward, bowing ritually and beginning to sway. Sruli pointed out the prayerbook's section for "the silent Amidah", and then took his own three steps back and forth. I copied his steps and read the instructions. "Take a moment to remember that you are standing before the Throne of the Lord Almighty," it said. "Your Creator, who gives you every breath you take, including the one you are enjoying at this very moment."
I read the English. "Blessed are you, our God and God of our fathers, God of Abraham, God of Isaac, God of Jacob..." It was interesting how this central prayer started with the mention of fathers, as if having a father

were somehow required before one could pray to God. If so, I was out of luck.

The prayer leader chanted more prayers, and after another mourners' Kaddish, there was suddenly a familiar prayer in a tune I knew. My mouth started automatically singing the words "*Aleinu l'shabeyach la-adon ha-kol*". I was back in third grade at the morning prayer assembly, and this was the last prayer we did, every morning.

After just a few lines, the singing suddenly stopped. In unison, the congregation recited some Hebrew phrase I had never heard before. The entire assembly spoke the words together, ending with "Hevel v'Larry"! My spine tingled and a shiver shook my body. "Hevel and Larry"--? I looked around wildly. The *Aleinu* prayer had resumed, but I was too stunned to join in. What was this? Nobody was looking at me; they were acting as if nothing unusual had happened at all, as if they said something about Hevel and Larry every Friday night.

Rabbi Friedler had a lot of explaining to do.

40

At the end of the service, Rabbi Friedler stood up and made some announcements to the minority of congregants who paid attention to him. The rest were talking amongst themselves in animated voices. I turned to Sruli.

"What was *that*?"

"What was what?"

"That last prayer-- that's the *'Aleinu'*, right?"

Sruli nodded, surprised, "You recognized it!"

"Well, yes, but--"

Rabbi Friedler interrupted me to introduce some other men who would be joining us for dinner. The first, looking like a younger version of Rabbi Friedler, was Rabbi Shlomo Vashkin, visiting from North Dakota with his twin boys, Menachem-something and Tzvi-something-else. They each shook my hand with the same, "Nice to meet you, Good Shabbos!" They were followed by Dovid, a short, muscular Israeli man, who crushed my hand when he shook it. His four-year-old son, sporting the same brown curly hair, was too shy to say anything, but his name was apparently Alon, which Dovid pronounced ah-LOAN in a thick clipped accent. If Alon had ever shaken his father's hand, it would explain his reticence to ever shake anyone's hand again.

While Dovid and Rabbi Shlomo carried on in Hebrew, Sruli herded us through the crowded hallways and towards the doors; Rabbi Friedler lagged behind, constantly interrupted by jovial men wishing him "Good Shabbos!" or exchanging jokes in a language I assumed was Yiddish.

We spilled out into the horseshoe drive, conversations and laughter filling the cool night air around us. As we started walking towards the Friedlers house, Rabbi Friedler and Sruli started singing a tune with no words. Rabbi Shlomo and his twins joined in immediately: "Da-da da-da dum-dum, da-da da-da dum-dum..." Oddly, I recognized it immediately, but I could not believe Rabbi Friedler would know the tune, let alone sing it on Shabbos. It was the theme song from Chitty Chitty Bang Bang, an old, old musical that was one of the few secular DVDs my mother and father watched with us when we were younger. We used to sing along, cheering the old race car on, all scrunched together on the couch. My father sat next to me; my mother to his left, and Jessi squirmed in my mom's lap. Dick Van Dyke was the whimsical inventor with a young son and daughter, and they went on fairy tale adventures in that old magical car with a lovely woman they had all just met. The car was named "Chitty Chitty Bang Bang" after the noises it made.

Except Rabbi Friedler's tune had apparently changed after the first line or so, and it wasn't the movie theme song at all. It was probably an old wordless tune from somewhere in Eastern Europe. Rabbi Friedler's tune repeated itself in small sections, and I found it easy to hum along. Even Dovid seemed to pick it up.

When the voices wound down, I asked Rabbi Friedler where the tune originated. He said it was a wordless melody, or "niggun", attributed to Reb Shlomo de Geller, so named because of his yellow beard.

"It sounds just like a tune I know from my childhood that went like this--" But it was a mistake to start humming the theme to Chitty Chitty Bang Bang, because after the first four notes the kids thought I was launching into a reprise of Shlomo de Geller's niggun, and off we went again, singing his tune over and over again.

Rabbi Friedler knocked on his own front door and then opened it. The smell of fresh-baked bread embraced us. A little girl raced towards us and jumped up into Dovid's strong arms. He twirled her around and kissed her, saying "Shabbat Shalom" in his Israeli accent. She was followed by a woman slightly taller than Dovid, introduced as his wife, Moran. Then Sruli brought forth two college students named Skye and Dan, who tried to look comfortable as they shifted from one foot to another.

R. Friedler ushered us inside, and my eyes widened seeing the complete transformation of our weekday study hall. Tonight we walked into an older era, a formal supper in a Victorian parlor. Candlestick chandeliers hung from the ceiling; oil lamps shone over the mantelpiece. Light sparkled off the silver candlesticks on the table and the many Kiddush cups at various places. Fine china and old silver place settings were carefully spaced atop a lace tablecloth, in front of wooden chairs adorned with doilies over their tall upright backs. A side table glowed with many candles, blessed by the ladies doubtless congregating in the kitchen with last-minute preparations.

R. Friedler ducked into the kitchen and reemerged a

moment later, saying it was time to sing Shalom Aleichem, a song greeting special Shabbos angels. He invited us to join him in stepping outside, as the mystics of Safed had in olden times, and he immediately launched into a lively rendition of a song I found I remembered fondly. He was almost dancing down his walk, staring towards the heavens, as if welcoming the angels descending towards his home.

As he started into the second verse, up the driveway came a tall, well-dressed man, who pumped R. Friedler's and R. Shlomo's hands and immediately joined in the chorus. He looked like Santa Claus come to life. He had bright red cheeks above his bushy white beard and a jolly manner that engaged R. Shlomo's kids, who yelped with delight when they saw him. He hoisted Menachem on his shoulders, and R. Shlomo picked up his other boy, Tzvi.

R. Friedler turned and we all started making our way back towards the front door, singing all the while. Santa Claus walked upright as if to enter the house with Menachem on his shoulders, and pretended confusion as to why he was not fitting through the doorway. Several times he tried to enter, as Menachem's hands smacked the bricks above the portal with delight. Finally he backed up several steps and brought Menachem through a forward somersault and down to the ground. R. Shlomo repeated the procedure with Tzvi and we finished the song, pouring into the dining room amidst peals of young laughter.

Mrs. Friedler appeared from the kitchen, welcoming everyone in turn and indicating where they should sit. R. Friedler introduced the next song, "Aishes Chayil", as

King Solomon's ode to the 'woman of valor', describing Jewish women in relation to their husbands, and, metaphorically, the Children of Israel in relation to God. R. Friedler led the song of adoration, smiling at Mrs. Friedler, who stood just inside the kitchen door.

And then, towards the end of the song, I heard it again! Hevel's name sounded out clear as a bell, in a phrase something like "*v'Hevel hayofee*". I looked around at the men. Nobody thought it out of place that Cain's dead brother was suddenly mentioned in King Solomon's praise of women.

I turned it over in my mind as R. Friedler blessed his children one by one. Apparently he had two teenage daughters in the kitchen who came out to be blessed as well. I saw R. Shlomo bless his children, and Dovid blessing his little princess. Had my father blessed me like that? I had a dim idea that he had, both hands covering my head like a holy crown. He had murmured the ancient words and sealed the blessing with a warm kiss on my forehead. "Good Shabbos, my little Reuven."

R. Friedler filled his silver cup with wine to overflowing and proclaimed that he would have everybody in mind for Kiddush. Next to him was a tray of small silver shot glasses, and a matching empty pitcher. He lifted the silver cup and placed it carefully into his right palm. Glancing at the side table of candles, he chanted the portion of Scripture describing the first day of rest. He raised the cup in the manner of a toast, and everyone responded "*L'chaim*". He continued on through the Hebrew Kiddush, swaying to the words, absently splashing wine on his plate. Everyone responded

"Amen!", once near the beginning, and then again at the end. He drank some of the wine, and then filled short glasses that Sruli brought to each guest.

"Is there any challah in the house?" Rabbi Friedler asked in an exaggerated tone as he looked around, wide-eyed. The twins giggled and pointed to the covered cutting board in front of R. Friedler's plate. R. Friedler looked all around the table in comical fashion, feigning confusion, in what was clearly a weekly ritual. "Underneath, underneath!", chanted the boys. R. Friedler bent over at the waist, lifted the edge of the tablecloth and appeared to search under the table. While he was doing this, Menachem whisked off the challah cover, revealing two homemade braided loaves. As R. Friedler emerged from the lace, both Menachem and Tzvi pointed excitedly, "There, there!".

R. Friedler's eyebrows raised high at the miracle of the bread's appearance. "Challah! This changes everything! Let's wash!" To the rest of us, he explained that there were two sinks in the kitchen where we could wash, and another off the entryway, in the back hallway.

As everyone rose to their feet, R. Friedler pulled me aside.

"Reb Reuven, you're a Kohen, right?"

"Um, yes."

"Well, we have a tradition here at the Friedlers. You know that when the Second Temple was destroyed, the rabbis established the home as a Temple-in-miniature. The Shabbos table is our altar, and the two loaves of challah our offering to Hashem!"

"Okay..."

"So, the first time we have a Kohen for a Shabbos meal, we ask him to make the motzi blessing over the bread, the offering to Hashem. Just as you would have done the service of the offering in The Holy Temple. Would you be willing to do that?" R. Friedler asked. "It's just exactly ten words, and there's a card with the words, both in Hebrew and in the English transliteration."

"Well--"

"'*Baruch atah Hashem, elokeinu melech haolam, hamotzi lechem meen haaretz.*' That's all it is."

I shrugged. Somehow I could not say no to this man. "Sure."

"Wonderful! Thank you so much!"

We turned and joined the kitchen line for washing. As we gathered behind Skye, he turned and asked what the missing bread routine was all about. R. Friedler explained, "Whereas usually we would just make a *motzi* blessing over the bread for a weekday meal, on Shabbos we first make a special Kiddush over wine to celebrate the special holiness of the day. So we cover the challah so as not to embarrass it. After all, we are asking it to take second seat, as it were, and that's a hard thing to do in a crowd. Especially when you're used to being first."

Santa Claus turned around and said heartily, "I have always suspected that the real reason there's a cover over the challah is to protect it from the Rabbi's wine as he makes Kiddush!" He made a cascading fountain gesture with both hands. Nodding to me, he introduced himself as Jonathan Livnitz, extending his right hand for a firm shake.

As the line advanced to the sink, I watched Santa

Livnitz wash, and then Skye, who read the laminated instructions and carefully pronounced the blessing after awkwardly rinsing each hand three times from the two-handled cup. I stepped up and repeated the procedure, hoping to appear more graceful.

After drying my hands, I returned to the table, uncertain exactly where to stand. R. Friedler joined me a moment later and nodded at the laminated card next to the challahs at the head of the table. Above the blessing were instructions. R. Friedler had conveniently left out this ritualistic part. Now I was on the spot. I stepped forward towards the cutting board, reading the directives on my right.

Lift the loaves, one in each hand, and turn them to press the bottoms together. Check.

Transfer them to your left hand and, with your right hand, draw the knife lightly across both loaves. Check.

Find a spot on the right challah where you will make the first cut, and use the knife to make a small knick, then set the knife down. Check.

Using two hands, lift both challahs and pronounce the blessing below.

As I lifted the warm bread, I imagined I was in The Holy Temple offering up a holy sacrifice to God Almighty, as some ancient ancestor of mine would have done. Would God accept my offering, the offering of a Kohen who had cast off the ways of his ancestors? A Jew who could hardly even pronounce the blessing?

And then, I saw myself from overhead, from somewhere high above the ceiling. What was I doing here? A pretender, an intruder in a world dedicated to serving God, engaging in fantasies of grandiosity. How ludicrous.

I looked at the bread in my hands. Over the top of the challah loaves, in the warm glow of the candlelight, the radiant smiles of the enchanted children melted my heart. Impostor or not, they expected a blessing from the descendant of Aaron the High Priest.

I pronounced the words to a chorus of "Amen!", and carved up the bread.

41

From the kitchen came an endless stream of salads and fish dishes. Herring, gefilte fish, salmon, lettuce salad, pasta salad, egg salad, tabouli, hummus, and other bowls of brightly colored sauces and vegetables whose names I could only guess. As the dishes were passed around, R. Friedler announced he was inviting each guest to state their name along with something we were thankful for from the past week. He started with himself.

"Moshe Friedler, and I am thankful for the good news of a new grandson, born Thursday morning in Jerusalem!" The crowd responded with hearty shouts of "Mazal Tov" and clapping. He gestured to me with his right hand.

"Larry Cohen", I started. "Something I'm thankful for?"

Rabbi Friedler nodded encouragingly. "Some weeks are harder than others for identifying blessings! Take your time."

I felt the seconds ticking by, everybody's eyes on me. Finally, I thought of Josh. "I have a friend in the hospital," I said, "and this week things are looking up for him."

"May he have a refuah shlema," said Santa beside me. "Jonathan Livnitz. I'm thankful for my lovely wife Lucy--" he gestured towards a short woman disappearing into the kitchen, "and my son was visiting this week from California."

"Skye Blufeld, from Berkeley. I'm pre-law at the U and I'm thankful for midterms being over!"

It continued around the table, Rabbi Friedler giving each guest his full attention to hear their name and their gratitude. When it came to Rabbi Shlomo's kids, Menachem Mendel said he was thankful for his father and his mother. Tzvi Shimon quickly said he was thankful for his father and his mother, and then, glancing at his brother, added that he was also thankful for God in Heaven.

When the circuit was complete, Rabbi Friedler remarked, "What wonderful blessings! May Hashem continue to bless us in revealed abundance!". There was a chorus of "Amen", and the table talk broke up into smaller conversations.

I turned to Rabbi Friedler. "Can I ask you a question?"

"Certainly! I love questions. In fact, a good question is better than a good answer!"

"Something odd happened during the *Aleinu* prayer at the synagogue..."

"Oh?"

"How come nobody noticed? Right in the middle of the prayer, didn't everyone stop and say something in Hebrew about 'Hevel v'Larry'?"

Rabbi Friedler looked up to the ceiling, squinting his right eye. Then he smiled. "Yes, I guess we did!"

"And then during that King Solomon song, towards the end, there it was again *'v'Hevel hayofee'* or something."

Rabbi Feller shook his head, smiling broadly. "I had never put that together, but there it is also. 'Hevel' in both places!"

"So you say it every week that way? What does it mean? Why would Hevel's name be in the prayers like that?"

"Well, the name means 'nothing'--"

My jaw dropped and I stared numbly at him. Déjà vu.

"That's what your father said to me."

It was Rabbi Friedler's turn to stare.

"In my dream," I explained, "I thought he was referring to my calling him 'Rabbi Friedler, Sr.', but that's exactly what he said. 'The name means nothing'."

"Very interesting; very interesting." Rabbi Friedler loaded some dark purple substance onto his gefilte fish and passed the bowl to his right. "After dinner we can get more into the specific passages if you'd like, and consider what this might mean. But in the meantime--" R. Friedler turned to me with a forkful of decorated fish in midair and a crinkly smile on his face. "In the meantime, perhaps you should reflect on anything else you remember my father said to you in your dreams."

42

As Mrs. Friedler's helpers cleared the fish plates and forks, Mrs. Friedler herself served the matzoh ball soup. Two large doughy spheres beckoned in a chicken broth with small bits of spices, carrot slices and chicken pieces. The aroma brought me back to Passover in my mother's kitchen; she fed me and my sister a bowl of soup before the seder so we wouldn't be too tired and cranky as the evening wore on before the meal. The same delicious smell. Rabbi Friedler took a taste and grinned up at his wife. "Excellent, my dear." She answered his smile and returned to the kitchen.

"Let's sing a song!" insisted Menachem. Rabbi Shlomo started in with an old song I recognized from summer camp: "*Dovid, Melech Yisroel, chai, chai, v'kayam...*" Dovid joined in, too, with his kids clapping along. Skye and Dan surprised me by doing hand gestures in time with the tune, and Sruli copied them clumsily, trying to learn.

As everyone began to eat the soup, there came a natural quiet, and R. Friedler invited R. Shlomo to speak on the Torah portion of the week.

"This week, we have the double portion of *Neetzavim-Vayailech*," began Rabbi Shlomo earnestly. He explained the name of a portion, like the name of a person, captures its essence. "But *'Netzavim'* means 'we are standing', and *'Vayailech'* means 'and he went'. How do we resolve this seeming contradiction?"

Rabbi Shlomo looked around the table, asking us to consider the question.

"The Rebbe suggests that one way of resolving this tension is to consider the time of year these parshiyot fall. This month of Elul, leading up to Rosh Hashana, we do *teshuvah*, repentance. Rosh Hashanah, as you know, is the new year, but it is also the Day of Judgement. So on Rosh Hashanah, we are standing in court before the Judge of Judges. That's *Neetzavim*, 'we are standing'.

"Once we know before Whom we stand we must then complete our *teshuvah* by *Vayailech*, going towards Him!" Rabbi Shlomo smiled at his listeners. "May it be His Will that we all do complete *teshuvah* before Rosh Hashana; may we go towards Him with all our hearts; and may He accept our repentance and reward us with the coming of the Moshiach, speedily and in our day!"

"Amen!" responded R. Friedler, "and *yesher koach*."

Dan spoke up, "So the names of the *parsha* imply that we stand before God and go towards Him?"

Rabbi Shlomo nodded, "Exactly. As King David says in Psalms, 'I place Him before me always.' '*Sheeveesee Hashem l'negdee samid*'."

Dan must have learned some Hebrew because he remarked, "That's interesting, because doesn't the word '*neged*' mean 'opposite' or 'opposing'. So placing Hashem before me always means having Him oppose me always?"

Jonathan Livnitz said, "Yes, exactly! Opposing, but for a purpose, not just to be contrary. Just like we have opposable thumbs. We say that the thumb 'opposes' the other fingers, but they're all part of the same hand. They work together. '*Neged*' doesn't necessarily mean antagonistic opposition, right Rabbi?"

The question had been directed to R. Friedler, but R.

Shlomo jumped in. "In traditional Torah study, you have a study partner that challenges your thinking, in a sense opposing you. He makes you clarify your arguments and your interpretations, ultimately arriving at a deeper understanding. You're studying business at the U, right?" Dan nodded. "So you're learning that your economic competition makes you work harder, right? And in law--", he turned to Skye, "the system of justice has opposing sides in order to get at the truth. Even the Adversary that Hashem sends 'opposes' us, but it's ultimately for our own good!"

Jonathan said, "In the Garden of Eden, Hashem saw that it was 'not good for Odom to be on his own', so he created 'ezer k'negdo', a helpmate opposite him. The woman that completes a man makes him whole, and the word 'k'negdo' is also from 'opposing' or 'opposite him', right Rabbi?"

R. Friedler nodded. "I have often thought it ironic that skeptics think believers cling to religion out of emotional weakness, a need for some grandfather in the sky to reassure us that everything will be okay. Some think that believing in God is some self-absorbed way of escaping the harsh realities of a cold, cruel world. But I have found over the years that a close relationship with Hashem is quite challenging. And while I know that the difficulties He places before me are ultimately for my own good, and everything He does stems from the deepest love and concern for me to become the best I can be... it can be hard to see that in the moments of struggle. The Master of the Universe does not coddle us, and sometimes it can even feel like He is opposing us." R.

Friedler took a sip of water. "But it's important to remember that when he does give us correction, it is out of His love for us. As the *pasuk* says, *v'yadata eem levavecha kee ka'ashair yeyasair eesh es b'noi Hashem elokecha m'yasreka.* 'And you shall know with your heart that Hashem your God disciplines you just as a man disciplines his son.'"

Rabbi Friedler looked around the table. "It is only when we deeply embrace that knowing, when we are *certain* that His presence and His love are behind His often-mysterious ways of guiding us, that we can say, with King David, 'Your rod and Your staff, they comfort me.'"

43—

The soup course was followed by entrees, which included chicken, brisket, some kugel noodle dishes, some kind of vegan "macaroni and cheese", which the twins loved, breaded eggplant, and sides of butternut squash, broccoli salad, couscous... was there no end to the food?

There was more singing, more talking about the parsha and Rosh Hashana, and a Rebbe story in Hebrew from Dovid (dutifully translated by Rabbi Friedler afterwards). Finally, with his little girl showing signs of dozing off, Dovid asked if we could bentch so they could get her home to bed. Sruli passed out the prayer pamphlets and those who had taken off hats or jackets put them back on. Rabbi Friedler asked if I wanted to lead the formal invitational call and response, but I declined the honor. There were only so many Kohen duties I felt capable of assuming in one evening.

Rabbi Friedler washed his fingers and lips from a small contraption, a combination water pitcher and bowl, and then passed it along to me, with an accompanying hand towel. After the last man had used it, Mrs. Friedler removed it from the table, and we sang through the entire set of prayers with gusto, the twins banging on the table to keep rhythm.

Afterwards, Dovid and Moran carried their sleeping angel to the door and said their goodbyes. Rabbi Friedler walked outside with them, while Mrs. Friedler brought out dessert. The twins squealed when they saw strawberry sorbet among the delicacies. I could appreciate their enthusiasm, even though I no longer shared it.

It was at Joey's ten-year-old birthday party that I had tasted my last ice cream cone. Or tried to taste my cone. We were a small crowd at the local Baskin Robbins store. I was just about to take my first bite of my favorite ice cream when a stranger's kid had stepped backwards into me, sending me and my cone sprawling.

Tears welled up in my eyes as I saw the tile floor streaked with my beloved pink bubblegum flavor. "Hey, Tyler, look at this blubbering baby!" said the kid.

I stuffed my tears and my pride down my throat and ran out of the store to get air. The kid's father emerged a minute later offering me a replacement cone, but I just shook my head.

Joey asked what happened, but I said it didn't matter; I said I didn't like ice cream that much anyway.

And from then on, I actually hadn't liked it.

"Reb Reuven, would you like some sorbet?" asked Sruli, no doubt seeing my gaze. Dr. Silverberger would probably suggest that I try some to have a "corrective experience" or something, but over the years I had grown accustomed to the flavor of chocolate, so I decided on the fudge brownies instead. They looked quite tasty.

Sruli handled the serving up of the sorbet, as we passed trays of brownies, cakes and cookies along with fruit salad and a multi-sectioned dish of various hard candies. Mrs. Friedler brought out mugs for coffee, tea and hot chocolate, and a few hot water butlers, encouraging us to make our choices and mix our own.

Rabbi Friedler turned to me and reintroduced the

topic of Hevel.

"So, Reb Reuven, you mentioned hearing the name Hevel come up twice tonight. You see, there's a sentence that some communities recite in the *Aleinu*, that others don't. It goes, '*Shehem mishtachaveem l'hevel v'lareek*'." He emphasized the final 'k' sound. "I can see where it might sound like 'Hevel v'Larry' when the congregation says it together. The *Aleinu* prayer is speaking of our obligation as Jews to praise the Master of all things, and this little variation comments that other tribes of the earth bow down to nothing, whereas we bow down to Hashem. The word for 'nothing' there is '*hevel*', as you noticed.

"And in the *Aishes Chayil*, we speak of the wonderful qualities of a woman of valor, and towards the end we observe--", he squinted at the ceiling in recollecting the exact phrasing, "-- '*sheker hachain, v'hevel hayofee*'. 'Charm is false, and beauty is nothing'. Because the true essence of a woman is revealed in her service of God, which is what makes a holy Jewish home out of the otherwise empty space contained within four walls!" Rabbi Friedler looked fondly down towards the end of the table, where his wife was just sitting down.

"So these mentions of Hevel are just part of the prayers? The word '*hevel*' means 'nothing', and I just happened to notice it because of these dreams?" I shook my head slowly in disappointment. "It wasn't 'Larry', but '*lareek*'; I just misheard it. It was all just a mistake."

"Well, I wouldn't necessarily come to that conclusion. Perhaps Hashem was trying to draw your attention to the meaning of the name 'Hevel'. You said that in your dreams my father had told you the name meant 'nothing' as well, yes?"

"Yes. But what's the significance? Why would it matter that Hevel's name means 'nothing'?"

A voice to my left intruded; apparently Jonathan had turned his attention our way. "That's interesting, Rabbi. If a person's name signifies their essence, I would have expected Hevel to have a name meaning 'pure' or 'spiritual'; wasn't he on a higher level than Kayin, who was only interested in worldly possessions?"

"I think the majority view is that Hevel means 'nothing' in the esoteric sense of being able to see that this world is nothing, and Hevel therefore was attached to nothing in this world, being on such a high spiritual level. But if I'm not mistaken, there was another view... Sruli, would you please bring me the Maharal's Drasha for Shabbos haGadol?"

Sruli dutifully returned with a thick volume, which Rabbi Friedler paged through to find the passage he recalled. "Ah, yes, here we are. According to the Maharal, Hevel really was a nothing. He just copied his brother without having any innovation of his own. The Maharal notices the language 'And Hevel, he, too, brought', and suggests that the seemingly extraneous 'he, too' implies that Hevel's motivation was simply to be like his brother, or to outdo him, rather than to serve God in his own unique way."

"But Rabbi," object Jonathan to R. Friedler, "if Hevel were just copying his older brother like that, why would God turn to Hevel's offering and not to Kayin's?!"

"An excellent question!" Rabbi Friedler exclaimed,

singling out Jonathan with his crooked finger. "Why indeed?!"

By this time we had attracted the attention of Rabbi Shlomo and the college kids. Dan suggested, "Maybe God was trying to teach Cain humility?"

"Possibly," considered Rabbi Friedler, "possibly."

Rabbi Shlomo said, "I like that idea of turning away from Kayin's mincha to offer him a lesson in humility, but why would Hashem accept the sacrifice from Hevel if he was just copying his brother? It would be giving Hevel the wrong message, encouraging him in the wrong direction. Why not reject Hevel's mincha, too, if it was just offered out of sibling rivalry?"

"Amazing!" exclaimed Jonathan. Everyone turned to him to hear his thoughts. "Don't you see?! Usually we think of Kayin as the jealous brother, and here the Maharal is suggesting that the jealous one was Hevel all along! Amazing!"

"But if Hevel was the jealous one," objected Rabbi Shlomo, "again, why would Hashem accept his mincha?"

"Perhaps," said R. Friedler slowly, "that was the best Hevel could do. If Hevel was really the 'nothing' that the Maharal suggests, maybe he had done his best by copying his brother. Perhaps that was the highest level he could achieve. That would explain why Hashem would accept his mincha offering."

"That would also explain the next verses, where Hashem asks Kayin what's wrong", suggested Sruli. "Hashem basically says, 'What's the problem, Kayin; why are you so down? All you have to do is improve and everything will be fine!' Hevel had done his best, but

Hashem is telling Kayin to do better."

I tried to imagine what it would be like for Cain to have his pesky younger brother's offering accepted instead of his own. No wonder he had gotten angry.

Rabbi Friedler nodded. "That fits in nicely with the Rebbe's emphasis that our experiences are always about the individual's relationship with Hashem. Hevel has done his best in the relationship, and so Hashem turns to him and accepts his offering. Kayin is still able to do better in the relationship, so Hashem challenges him to raise his level." Rabbi Friedler had another thought. "This different way of looking at Hevel and Kayin comes to us at a perfect time --thank you, Reb Reuven. This is the time when we reflect deeply on our own personal relationship with Hashem and look for improvements we can make for the new year. May we consider in what ways Hashem is asking us to improve, and may we take those steps and draw closer to Him in the coming year."

44

An hour later, when the conversation finally wound down, R. Friedler walked me to the door. He surprised me by continuing with me outside, down his walkway, and down the block. "It was a great pleasure to have you join us, Reb Reuven; thank you for elevating our table with your blessing, your singing and your great questions!"

"Thanks for having me, Rabbi."

"Perhaps you'd like to join us for lunch tomorrow, after the morning services?"

I was unprepared for the question. Alarm bells went off in my head. *It's a slippery slope*, Andy had warned.

"Thanks for the invitation, Rabbi, but I'm not sure what my plans are..."

"No problem, Reb Reuven; no problem." Rabbi Friedler patted my shoulder. "Just know that you're welcome. Services start at the shul around 9:30, and we'll probably be gathering here around 12:30, God willing; we'd be happy to see you at either, or both."

I thanked him again. He wished me a good Shabbos and turned back towards his house.

I reflected on the Shabbos dinner as I walked. Soon I spied my M3 in the synagogue drive, beckoning to me. But it occurred to me that I could walk home. It was close enough. That was what a Neener would do. It was what Rabbi Friedler would do. It was even what my father would have done, if he were here with me, holding my hand.

But he wasn't here. It was just me. I got in the car and

started the engine. I looked both ways, ensuring there was no traffic or passersby, and pulled out onto Edgecumbe Road. I hoped no one would ask Rabbi Friedler why someone was driving a beamer away from the synagogue on Friday night, in violation of the Sabbath.

45—

I slept like a baby. No dreams, no nightmares, no stress. When I awoke, sunlight was streaming through my bedroom windows, and birds were chirping outside. I luxuriated in my flannel sheets. There was nowhere I needed to go, nowhere I needed to be.

Time off was a good thing. So was a good night's sleep after the crazy dreams of the past week. Rabbi Friedler might praise the Sabbath as a day of rest for religious reasons, but I would celebrate simply feeling well-rested.

I glanced at the clock. 11:16. Now that was a good night's sleep! An extra seven hours did a body good.

It occurred to me that I could still go to the Friedlers for their afternoon meal. He had explicitly said I'd be welcome there even if I didn't go to the synagogue. In fact, now that I thought about it, Skye and Dan hadn't gone to the Friday night services, but they had shown up for dinner last night.

And then it hit me: I still had no idea how to counter Moses' testimony, and Monday was fast approaching.

Which brought up the question of what "Monday" meant. Did it mean another court dream Monday *night*, or did it mean court would be in session early Monday *morning*? Did the dreams occur before or after midnight? It felt like they happened right before I woke up, but dreams could be funny that way.

My cell phone rang. It was Andy calling from Chicago during a break from his deposition. I asked him about his case, but he wanted to hear about me. I told him about the evening at the Friedlers. To my surprise, his only comment was on Rabbi Friedler's choice of hats. "Most peculiar, Counselor. The Slovodjaniner Rebbe wore a Barselino, so his followers always wear Barselinos. Anyway, how's the case?"

"Well, we were in recess last night, but pretty conclusive evidence presented by Moses the night before. But there was something odd there, too. I don't know why, but Moses seemed like a hostile witness."

"Of course he was! He'd leap at the chance to help Cain."

"Why would Moses want to help Cain?"

"Because Moses was a murderer, too."

"What?"

"You don't know the story? Moses was a prince in Pharaoh's palace, and he's out walking around one day and he sees an Egyptian beating up one of the Jewish slaves. So Moses feels his brother's pain, looks both ways to be sure no one sees him, and takes out the Egyptian."

"Kills him?"

"Dead as a doornail, Counselor. Clearly premeditated; murder one. That's why Moses had to leave Egypt. Pharaoh, lord and master of Egypt, found out that Moses had murdered an Egyptian, so of course Pharaoh came after him. Moses fled to Midian and became a shepherd for forty years. Didn't they teach you anything in that day school you went to?"

"Well, I knew Moses was a shepherd..."

"He went from being a prince in Pharaoh's palace to being a shepherd in the fields of Midyan, and it wasn't a witness relocation program. Moses was a fugitive murderer. It's no wonder he takes Cain's side of things. Everybody likes to praise Moses as a saint, but that's not the way it went down. Cain might have been the first murderer, but Moses tried to perfect the art."

"You're sure about this?"

"Of course I'm sure! Ask your dinner pal, Rabbi Friedler."

46

I parked a block away and walked to the Friedlers. Call it hypocrisy, but I just couldn't bring myself to drive up to his house on the Sabbath.

There was a cover over the doorbell, so I knocked. Sruli answered and ushered me inside, saying my timing was perfect and I had arrived just in time for Kiddush.

As I entered the dining room, Rabbi Friedler smiled in greeting and set his overflowing silver wine cup into his right palm and pronounced a short blessing. Everyone answered, "Amen" and rose to wash.

Rabbi Friedler greeted me warmly as we got in line. I noticed the crowd was smaller, but otherwise mostly the same as last night. Santa Claus and his wife were in attendance, as were Sruli and his sisters, Rabbi Shlomo, his wife and the twins. We washed and assembled in the dining room, where Rabbi Friedler held up the challah loaves for a blessing. I was relieved that he hadn't asked me to preside over it this time.

Lunch seemed less formal than yesterday's dinner, and the women lingered at the table more often. Over the salad course, Mrs. Friedler asked her husband to recap the sermon from the synagogue, which led me to think that she hadn't gone to services either. Then it occurred to me that she might have been asking for my benefit, without wanting to embarrass me. In any event, he readily agreed and asked Sruli to bring him a Chumash.

Rabbi Friedler pointed out several different occurrences of the word 'hayom' or 'today'.

"The Rebbe tells us that the word *'hayom'* is to

remind us that we are standing before Hashem *this* day, *today*! This isn't just an event that happened thousands of years ago. *This very day*, this very moment, we are standing before Hashem, accepting His covenant. *This very day* Moshe Rabeinu is warning us not to stray in our hearts, but to return to Hashem. And *this very day* is our opportunity to return to Him, no matter how far we have strayed." Rabbi Friedler allowed his gesturing right hand to return to his lap. He looked around at the gathered assembly and turned a few pages. "The double parsha ends with Moshe reassuring us in *Vayailech*, 'Even if your exiles are at the end of the heavens, the Lord, your God, will gather you from there, and He will take you from there.' No matter how far we have strayed, even to a distant shore, Hashem promises us that eventually, 'you will return to the Lord your God, with all your heart and with all your soul, and you will listen to His voice.' So there is hope for all us sinners!" Rabbi Friedler lifted his silver wine cup for a toast. "May we all return to Hashem, *this very day*, in this season of repentance, and may He bring us a favorable judgement on Rosh Hashanah! *L'Chaim!*".

"*L'Chaim!*" the group answered.

Mrs. Friedler and Mrs. Livnitz rose to bring out the next course. Cold cuts, brisket from last night, and a savory stew which I recognized as *cholent*, the uniquely Jewish dish served at Shabbos lunch from a crock pot, where it had been simmering all night. Meat, potatoes, beans and barley.

As a child, it had always been a favorite of mine, although my sister insisted it was 'an acquired taste', and she certainly had never acquired it. I guessed that Mrs. Friedler's cholent would be outstanding, and it was. Of course, she probably had been perfecting her recipe for the past fifty years.

As the food was passed around, and more side dishes appeared from the kitchen, I tried to think of how to broach the subject of Moses' character and motivations. I was sure Rabbi Friedler would have a different answer than Andy's.

I turned to R. Friedler, "So Moses was speaking for the entire double *parsha*?"

Rabbi Friedler nodded as he passed me the sliced turkey. "Moses wants to be sure that we understand our covenant with Hashem, because he knows his time on this earth is nearly over, and he won't be there in the flesh to guide us. So he speaks not just for this double *parsha*, but for the entire book of *Devarim*, to remind us and inspire us to cleave to Hashem, even after he is gone. That's part of what makes him the greatest prophet the Jewish people have ever known."

"You know, that reminds me of a question I have..."

"Mmm?"

I lowered my voice in an effort not to be overheard. "When Moses was being sworn in as a witness, you know, in my dream--" I saw Rabbi Friedler nod. "I noticed that he was asked 'to tell the truth, the whole truth, and nothing but the truth', but the court clerk didn't say, 'so help you God', and Moses didn't add it, either. As the greatest prophet of the Jewish people, and a man so in tune with his relationship to God, why wouldn't he add that phrase? I would think Moses, of all people, would say, 'So help me God' as a matter of course."

Rabbi Friedler agreed, "You would think so, and it's a good question!" Rabbi Friedler ladled more *cholent* onto his plate. "I think I know an answer. As a general practice, we Jews don't swear by God's name, not even in court."

"Why is that?"

"Well, because swearing falsely by God's Name is a very serious sin. A violation of one of the Ten Commandments, in fact. So we wouldn't want to have a practice of requiring witnesses to swear in God's Name because if one of them were tempted to lie in court, the resulting profaning of God's Name would be a very serious violation. So as a general rule we don't allow anyone --unless Jewish law demands it-- to make an oath using God's Name."

"But isn't perjury a sin in its own right? Wouldn't they already be sinning if they lied in court?"

Rabbi Friedler smiled. "Indeed! Bearing false witness against your fellow is certainly a sin! But even if a Jew does perjure himself, we still want to help him avoid sinning a second time by swearing falsely by God's Name. Even though he's a sinner, we're still commanded to love him as we love ourselves, so we try and help guard him against himself. Hashem loves the sinner, and He wants us to love the sinner, too, and help him repent. Which is a good thing, because we're all sinners, you know!"

Jonathan Livnitz laughed heartily, "Isn't that the truth, Rabbi! I can't imagine the state of the world if God gave up on us after our first mistake!"

Rabbi Friedler continued, "When we sin, Hashem weeps for us as a father weeps over a wayward son, a river of a thousand tears. And when we return, His rejoicing is unbounded; He celebrates with the joy of a thousand smiling embraces."

"Thanks, Rabbi; thanks very much." I helped myself to more *cholent* and passed it along to Jonathan. "I had been hoping the answer might explain why Moses seems to be a hostile witness."

Rabbi Friedler explained to Jonathan, "You see, Reb Yonatan, Reb Reuven is defending Cain in his dreams, and the prosecutor, you know who, called Moshe Rabeinu to the stand to give testimony."

"Incredible!" exclaimed Jonathan. "You must be quite special to merit such dreams! Moshe Rabeinu on the witness stand! But of course he would be a hostile witness if it were the Adversary. Don't you think Moshe Rabeinu would try to thwart the Sutton wherever possible, Rabbi?"

Rabbi Friedler considered. "Yes, I would think so. We know that Moshe is a faithful defender of the Children of Israel before Hashem. Even after the sin of the golden calf, even after the rebellion of Korach, even after all the murmurings and complainings, he's still willing to fall on his face before Hashem to save one of the congregation. Moshe is the ultimate shepherd of his flock."

Sruli said, "But, Ta, Kayin wasn't part of Moshe's flock. Kayin wasn't even Jewish!"

Rabbi Friedler raised his bushy eyebrows. "Very true, very true! Well, perhaps Reb Yonatan is correct; perhaps Moshe Rabeinu is simply trying to obstruct the

Adversary on general principle."

I could see that R. Friedler wasn't going to go near the topic Andy had raised without prompting. I asked, "Rabbi, I know Moses was a shepherd, but why did he leave Egypt?"

"Oh, that's a great story, demonstrating again the faithfulness of Moshe Rabeinu to his people. Moshe saw one of his people in distress, an Israelite being beaten by an Egyptian taskmaster. He was so enraged by the sight that he rose up and killed the Egyptian on the spot. When Pharoah heard what had happened, he came after Moshe to kill him, so Moshe fled to Midian, where he became a shepherd. Taking care of a wandering flock for forty years was good practice for becoming the leader of such a stubborn and stiff-necked people!" He gestured towards his chest, "Us!"

"So that's actually something that Moses and Cain have in common," I suggested. "They both killed someone and had to leave their home because of it." I held my breath, anticipating Rabbi Friedler's censure.

Rabbi Friedler surprised me by considering the comparison for several moments before responding. He stroked his beard slowly. "An interesting parallel, indeed. They did both kill a man, and both were forced into exile, leaving their homes and their families. In fact, when they left, each of them were afraid of being killed themselves." Rabbi Friedler raised his forefinger. "But," he wagged his finger and nodded, "there are also significant differences. For example, Moshe Rabeinu killed an Egyptian to protect his people, his tribe, whereas Kayin killed his own brother, *within* his tribe, for his own gain. Moshe feared being killed by Pharoah, because Pharoah presided unchallenged over the morally bankrupt system of slavery. Kayin, on the other hand, feared being killed by anyone whom he encountered because of the injustice he himself had perpetrated against his brother."

"This is wonderful, just wonderful, Rabbi!" exclaimed Jonathan, his white beard waving as he nodded his head enthusiastically. "I have never heard a comparison between Moshe and Kayin before!" He turned to me. "You inspire the most original discussions, Reb Reuven!"

"There is another crucial difference between them as well," continued Rabbi Friedler. "Kayin goes out from before Hashem, and never returns, whereas Moshe Rabeinu flees from Pharaoh and his court, but eventually Moshe Rabeinu comes back to confront Pharaoh, and to insist that Pharoah let the people go." Rabbi Friedler nodded to himself. "I've often reflected that in parsha Bo, Hashem instructs Moshe to 'come to Pharaoh', rather than 'go to Pharaoh'. It's an odd phrasing, and the commentators take notice.

"He says, 'come to Pharoah', come to the palace of the one who tried to kill you. It's as if Hashem is telling Moshe that the way to get closer to Hashem is to confront his deepest fear, and in the facing of that fear, he will draw near to his Creator. 'Come to Me, Moshe, I am here, right next to Pharoah, the source of your fear!'"

"That's the strongest religious defense of psychotherapy I've ever heard, Rabbi," remarked Jonathan.

The Friedler daughters began clearing the table and

Mrs. Friedler and Mrs. Livnitz started bringing out the sweets. Rabbi Friedler started a niggun, and the men joined in singing loudly. They wound down as the desserts were passed around. Jonathan excused himself to the restroom, and Sruli moved over into his seat.

"Say, Ta, I was reading more commentaries on Kayin and Hevel last night, and the Vilna Gaon suggests something interesting about Kayin."

"Mmm?"

"After Hashem rebukes Kayin, Kayin talks to Hevel in the field. The Vilna Gaon focuses on the Torah's language of 'vayomer' instead of 'vayedaber' to suggest Kayin spoke to him gently and sincerely." Sruli offered his father the book, opened to the passage he was quoting.

"Interesting, interesting," murmured Rabbi Friedler as he read the commentary. "Coming as it does right after his conversation with Hashem, you might even think that Kayin was seeking Hevel's advice about how to improve his mincha offering! Now that is certainly a fresh look at Kayin!"

"If Hevel was really a 'nothing', as the Maharal suggests, then I can understand why Kayin might have risen up to kill him. Hevel probably responded like this," grinned Sruli. He stuck his thumbs in his ears and wagged his fingers, taunting, " 'na-na-na-na na-na'!"

Rabbi Shlomo looked up and laughed from the floor near the far end of the table, where he was playing with his twins. "Speaking of playing nicely together, it's not often you hear a Neener chassid quoting the Vilna Gaon!" R. Shlomo remarked.

"I learned it from my father," rejoined Sruli. "If he

thinks it might bring us closer to Hashem, he'll quote anybody!"

Jonathan returned and asked Rabbi Friedler if we could bentch because there was a class he wanted to attend at the shul.

After the group prayers were sung, Rabbi Friedler accompanied me to the door. This time Sruli walked me down towards the street.

"When is your next court date for Kayin?" he asked. "Or do you know?"

"Apparently Monday," I answered. "That is what 'Yom Sheni' means, right?"

"Absolutely." he confirmed. "I guess it makes sense you wouldn't start on Yom Rishon, Sunday. That would mean you'd have to prepare on Shabbos."

We took a few more steps down the street.

"Do you know what your defense strategy will be?"

"I'm not really sure yet. These Shabbos conversations have given me a lot to think about, but I have some time, I guess."

"Not as much as you might think," warned Sruli, "Yom Sheni begins Sunday at sundown, so you basically have just a day and a half."

47

Josh tried smiling when he saw me, but his face lacked its characteristic lightness.

I put some cheer into my voice. "How are you, Buddha-man?"

"I've been thinking."

Josh fell silent. I waited. He didn't move. He just lay there, his eyes staring out at the distance. For a horrifying moment, I thought he might have had a seizure. Then he continued as if there had been no pause.

"You see, Grasshopper, life is a funny thing. We take it so much for granted that we don't realize how precious it is. Each and every breath." He inhaled and exhaled slowly, as if to demonstrate. "And then, in a heartbeat, when it may be taken away, we grasp at it with a fierceness..." He pulled his right hand into a fist.

I nodded. I blinked my eyes a few times. *Don't die, Josh.*

He looked out the window. "It's ironic. In Buddhist teachings, we're told that if you're going to mourn someone's death, you should do so at their birth. Because that's when you know they're going to die. As soon as they're born." His lips twisted in a grimace that was probably an attempt to smile. "Nobody gets out of this alive, Grasshopper."

I wanted to shake him. I wanted to shout, *You're not dead yet, Josh! You can beat this!* But I couldn't. I couldn't say anything.

Josh shook his head slowly. "It's so hard to see the people you love suffer."

"You sound," I heard myself say, "as if you're ready to... go."

Josh's gaze darted to my face. His right forefinger uncurled, pointing at me in emphasis. His head turned to face me directly; his lips parted, and his words reverberated as if someone were slowing down the soundtrack of the movie that was my life.

"Take it from me, Larry, a father of young children is never ready to go."

48

Over pork ribs at the Cleveland Wok, I considered my defense. The question was, if I called Moses to the stand, would he allow me to consider the Written Torah without the Oral Torah? It hardly seemed plausible; these were the five books of Moses, after all-- his life's work. He would hardly allow them to be understood differently than the tradition allowed. But whom else could I call?

I could try calling Cain himself to testify, but that was always a dangerous strategy. You had to really rehearse the witness well, train them not to introduce any extraneous evidence for the prosecution to use in cross-examination. The best defendants gave simple declarative answers on the witness stand, but few could do it well. They get too emotional.

And how would Cain show up in court? He might still be angry at his brother. He might still be angry at God. Or maybe the years of wandering would have softened his heart.

That was one of the strange things about this dream court. In real life, I would have an opportunity to interview the witnesses beforehand and know what their testimony would be. Practice with them, if necessary. Over and over, Professor Morton had drilled into us, "Never, never, never ask a question of a witness in the courtroom unless you already know what their answer will be!"

For the same reason, I couldn't imagine trying to call Abel to the stand. It would certainly be a unique strategy, though, calling the murder victim to the stand to testify at his murderer's trial. It would almost be worth doing just for the novelty. Certainly M. Sutton would never expect it. But Abel would be unpredictable, and probably hostile as well; he would hardly want to clear his brother.

I wrote in my journal to capture my thoughts.

Who are you Moses? What motivates you?

Charlton Heston's voice answered my question. *I am Moses ben Amram, faithful servant of God, who brought the Children of Israel out of Egypt to serve God in the Wilderness. My life is dedicated to God. Who are you, Reb Reuven, and what motivates you?*

I laughed out loud. I'm the one asking the questions here, buddy. I'm the lawyer; I ask the questions.

I will answer your questions, if you will answer mine.

Tough guy, eh? Of course he was. Here was a man who had gone up against Pharoah, who had led a cantankerous and rebellious people through the desert for forty years, who had even argued with God Himself. I thought I was going to intimidate him? It wasn't going to happen.

Especially since he is just a figment of your imagination, Larry Cohen.

Who are you, Reb Reuven, and what motivates you?

I'm Larry Cohen, or Reuven ben Michael Aba, if you prefer. What motivates me? That's a good question. Well, I guess I got into law to make the world a better place. That's what motivates me.

A laudable goal. May you have great success. Next question?

Why are you hostile to M. Sutton?

I have spent my life trying to bring stubborn Jews closer to God Almighty, and M. Sutton has spent his life driving them away. We are naturally on opposite sides. He has his job to do, and I have mine.

So tell me, Reb Reuven, why are you hostile to the traditions of your forefathers?

Look, it's my life; I live it the way I see fit.

It's your life, but it's a life that He gives you. He has also given you an instruction manual for how to get the most out of that life. It is a book called the Torah. A good book. You might want to look at it occasionally.

Speaking of the Torah... I need to know where you stand. I have a defense to conduct in the courtroom. My next question is: Will you give me a chance to consider the Torah in a different light?

My job is to help you draw closer to the traditions of your forefathers. To the extent that your exploration of the Torah brings you closer, I will help you in whatever way I can. If it takes you in the other direction, I will oppose you.

Okay.

It was ambiguous, but probably the best I could hope for.

My next question, Reb Reuven, is: will you give yourself a chance to consider the Torah in a different light?

You are not an easy man to work with, Moses.

You are not an easy man to work with, either, Reb Reuven.

Fair enough.

Will you give yourself a chance to consider the Torah in a different light?

What does that mean, exactly?

It means opening yourself up. It means being true to your truest self, hearkening to your soul. Listening to that still, small voice. Allowing yourself to want to return, Reb Reuven, and allowing yourself to take some baby steps towards the traditions of your forefathers.

What if I don't want to return? What if it's not for me?

Taste, and see what is good.

I considered. Baby steps. It sounded reasonable. Sort of. I wasn't promising to turn into Rabbi Friedler. The slope didn't seem that slippery.

Okay, but no promises.

No promises.

49

I awoke mid-morning and spent the day at the library with my laptop typing up notes, looking up references, and auditioning courtroom strategies in my head.

I checked in with Andy.

He said, "All you need to do is show a plausible alternative to dismiss murder one."

"I know. But if the Midrash is accepted, I don't see where I stand a chance. His motivation is there, and his clear intention to murder his brother; the Midrash paints the picture as if it were videotaped. I can't even raise dominion and control issues since the text explicitly states Cain killed him with a sword."

"With the Torah admitted, it will be hard to dismiss the Midrash." He quoted some sage on how important the Midrash is. "Well, good luck with it."

That night, as I prepared to go to bed, I said the Shema and asked for help. I also made an explicit resolution to follow through on my promise to Moses to 'give myself a chance to consider the Torah in a different light'. All I could think was, Josh had better be thankful if any of this actually worked.

I am standing in the courtroom.

I stare down at the manila folder containing my notes.

Between my opposing thumbs, "God has placed you here for a purpose."

A purpose, on purpose.

Does His purpose include a cooperative key witness for the defense?

The Judge sits, the gavel sounds.

"This court is now in session. You may be seated."

We sit.

"Mr. Cohen?"

I rise behind my table.

Will this work? Will he just materialize for me, the way he did for M. Sutton? I resolve to sound confident despite my doubts.

The power of positive thinking.

The power of a grasshopper shrinking.

The power of a blind man blinking.

The power of the Titanic sinking.

In the ocean.

By a porpoise.

For a purpose.

"Your Honor, we recall Moses ben Amram to the stand."

Instantly, he appears upright at the witness box, staff in hand. M. Sutton rises with the courtroom. The clerk swears him in. As he sits, *everyone sits. Here we go. Off to the races.*

Ready, set, go! Joey and I charge away from the starting line, racing around the blacktop as the gang roots us on. Joey is undefeated so far, but I am sure I can beat him. At the first corner, I slow down slightly, leaning into the turn, no stepping on the asphalt. Joey takes a wider arc, maintaining his speed, but falling behind a step. Accelerating down the straightaway, I gain a step on him. I still lead turning the far corner, but I know Joey always bursts to win at the end. I push hard, but still only have two steps on him. Rounding the last corner, I hear Joey's footfalls pulling up beside me. I dig deep for the final leg. I can do this; I know I can. I push my knees higher for a longer stride.

I step forward towards the witness box with my manila folder.

"Moses, when you appeared as a witness for the prosecution, you read verses from the Torah, from the parshah of Bereishis, is that correct?"

"That is correct."

"Those verses described--" I glance down at my notes, "the offerings of Kayin and his brother Hevel, God's response to those offerings, Kayin's conversations with God, Kayin's smoting of Hevel, and the subsequent punishment; is that correct?"

"That is correct."

I rest my hand on the railing of the witness box and look up at him. This man, this fearless leader, this most humble of all men, is larger than life, even sitting. Everything depends on his willingness to consider this text in a different light. Will he?

His wise eyes return my gaze. I speak deliberately, "Moses, does the Torah state, explicitly, in any of the words you read, Kayin's exact intention when he 'rose and smote' his brother?"

My careful manner does not escape Moses' attention. He regards me thoughtfully as he weighs the question. He nods his head slowly.

"The text I read does not explicitly state Kayin's intention."

So far so good. I let out my breath.

If a small smile flickered at the corner of Moses' mouth, it disappears before anyone else sees it.

"Moses, drawing on your expert knowledge of the plain meaning of the words of the Torah up until this point, is there any evidence that Kayin understood that death is even possible?"

"Yes."

I look my astonishment.

"The kid that Hevel offered from his flocks experienced death."

I nod. Never, never, never ask a question unless you already know what the answer will be. I turn away. I breathe in. I breathe out. Slow down, Mr. Cohen, slow down. Take the turn *without stepping on the blacktop. You can do this. You know you can.*

I turn back to my witness, bumping into a small child who spills his ice cream cone. "Oh, no!" he cries, "Hey, Mister! You knocked over my cone! You knocked over my cone!"
"It's all right; it's all right. I'll get you another one--" I turn around. The ice cream vendor holds up a perfectly shaped replacement cone in his hand. "But it will cost you, Larry; it will cost you."
"I'll pay the price!" Can he not hear the child crying? "How much?"
"The cone is free, but you have to really want it."
"I want it, I want it!" I reach out my hand. My father places the cone in my grasp and, clutching it, I turn to face the child, but the child is no longer there. Somehow, he was never there.
"It's for you!" cries the vendor as he fades into nothingness behind me.
I look down at my hand; it holds the manila folder of my notes.

I look up to see Moses regarding me, patiently awaiting my next question. I step back to regain my train of thought.

Forget the cone, Cohen.
Forget the crying, it's Kayin.

Kayin.
Kayin and death.
Kayin did not know death was possible. That's
right. I regain myself and address my witness.
I look at Moses. Will he be willing to draw the
fine line I need him to? Or will he oppose me, for
a purpose?
Never, never, never-- but sometimes you have to
ask anyway. If you want it with all your heart,
you ask anyway.

"Thank you, Moses. Again, drawing on your
expert knowledge of the plain meaning of the
words of the Torah up until this point, is there
any evidence that Kayin understood that
human death is possible?"
M. Sutton is on his feet, spluttering. "Objection,
Your Honour, zees is outrageous! Where is zee
Truth here? Counsel is twisting zee obvious
meaning of zee testimony!"
"On the contrary, Your Honor, the witness is
simply confining his remarks to the obvious
meaning of the text."
"Overruled."
Moses looks at me, is there the hint of a twinkle
in his eyes?

Twinkle, twinkle little star; how I wonder where

you are. He's up there in Heaven, little Reuven. Mrs. Goldstein smiles down reassuringly.

Moses replies, "No, there is no evidence in the plain meaning of the words of The Holy Torah that Kayin understood that human death was possible."
Yes! From the corner of my eye there is motion at the prosecution's table. M. Sutton is biting his lower lip and shaking his head slowly. His case is disintegrating before his eyes. But is there also impatience in his grimace?

And now for the clincher, the last leg. "So if I were to suggest to this court that Kayin struck his brother in a sudden burst of anger, without any intention of killing him, would you, an expert in the Torah, be able to refute that supposition using only the plain meaning of the words of the Torah that you read for the prosecution?"
The case hangs in the balance. But Moses is not a man to rush. He silently reviews the Torah up to that point. He weighs the meaning of each word. After deliberating thoughtfully for several long moments, he is ready to respond.
"No, I would not be able to refute that supposition using only the plain meaning of the words of The Holy Torah."
I stand and walk slowly to the center of the courtroom, as if taking in the implications of

Moses' testimony. I nod, as if to myself.
I turn back to the witness stand.

"In sum, then, you, Moses ben Amram --an expert authority on the Torah-- cannot disprove the possibility, using only the evidence submitted by prosecution to this court, that Hevel's death was an accident!"
Moses raises his eyebrows slightly, but then slowly nods. "Using only the evidence submitted by the prosecution, I could not disprove that possibility."
"Thank you. No further questions."
Wonderful. Superb. If this survives Sutton's cross-examination, the best he can hope for is involuntary manslaughter. I turn and grin at R. Friedler, who smiles back at me with pride and shakes my hand as I regain my seat at the table. "Well done, Reb Reuven; well done."
Take that, Sutton.

M. Sutton jumps up quickly and hurls an accusing finger at the witness box, "Moshe Rabbeinu, can you deny zat Kayin lured his brother out into zee field, where no one could see them, and, when Hevel turned heez back, rose up and killed him?"
I rise, "Objection! Hearsay, Your Honor. Moses was not a direct witness of the event."
"Sustained."
M. Sutton tries again. "Moses, are you familiar

with zee Midrash which states zat Kayin lured--"

"Objection, Your Honor! The Midrash has not been established as an authoritative source of Truth."

"Your Honour, zee Book of Genesis was accepted by zee Court as a source of Truth, and admitted as zee evidence. Zee Book of Genesis includes both zee Written Torah and zee Oral Torah. As zee Rambam says, 'One who ignores zee Midrash is a fool!'"

Rabbi Friedler beckons me with an urgent hand, and whispers in my ear.

I straighten. "Your Honor, in the same breath the Rambam also said that one who takes the words of the Midrash literally is a fool." I glance at M. Sutton and back to The Judge. "Regardless of the importance and validity of the Midrash, Your Honor, it has not been established as admissible evidence in this court. The Bible that M. Sutton so ably introduced as a 'Book of Truth' does not contain a single word of Midrash. Moreover, the Midrash was not introduced by the witness in direct."

"Sustained. The Midrash has not been established as a Source of Truth in this court. M. Sutton, please confine your cross-examination to the testimony given by the witness."

M. Sutton nods and looks over his notes.

"Moshe Rabbeinu, you testified zat Kayin had already seen death, but you then suggested he might not have known Hevel could die, or even zat Kayin might not recognize Hevel had been killed. How do you explain zat discrepancy?"

"It is true that Kayin had seen Hevel's animal offering die," Moses answers readily, as if he had anticipated the question. "But God is immortal and there is no evidence --in the plain meaning of the verses-- to suggest Kayin thought human beings, created in the image of God, could be killed."

M. Sutton frowns at his table. He clasps and unclasps his hands behind his back. He considers his options. He has none.

I have won! I have won!

As I cross the chalk finish line, Micah raises my hand in victory, declaring me the winner amidst the cheering onlookers. I do my little winner's dance. A victory worth celebrating. Put all your might into that last leg, and don't look back. That's how you do it. You just have to want it with all your heart and with all your soul. Joey stretches out his hand to shake mine. "Good race."

M. Sutton brings his right hand forward and caresses his mustaches. He nods. Then he shakes his head dismissively.

"Non, no further questions."

M. Sutton raises his eyes to the bench. "Your Honour, if it will help move us along, we are repared to concede zat zee plain meaning of zee written words of Zee Holy Torah, Exhibit A, do eave open zee possibility zat Kayin killed Heve ccidentally." He raises a cautionary hand "But in so doing, Your Honour, we request zee lefense focus on zee primary crime at issue in zees case."

What?

Mrs. Goldstein doesn't know what to say, what to say. She shakes her head sadly and says nothing, nothing. She pats my forearm with her aged right hand. She moves her left arm to encircle my sagging shoulders. There, there, it will be alright.

"Counsel will please approach the bench." I walk towards The Judge trying to make sense of M. Sutton's remarks. M. Sutton approaches quickly, but with concern in his eyes.

"M. Sutton," The Judge addresses him, slowly ifting a warning forefinger, "let Me caution you that such an admission may be prejudicial to other proceedings. Proceedings outside this courtroom."

M. Sutton's eyes widen momentarily. He squints, calculating. His jaw sets. His left hand lismisses the complication.

"No matter, Your Honour."

"Very well." The gavel echoes twice in quick uccession. The Judge turns to me. I am hopeful of an explanation. "Mr. Cohen, please refocus your defense accordingly. That is all."

As we turn back to our respective tables, I rapidly review. I have rebutted his evidence. His case is in tatters. He has proved nothing, or very little. He is left with involuntary manslaughter, at best. And now he dismisses the killing as an irrelevant side issue? The Judge agrees? Refocus? I crowd down next to R. Friedler.

"What is going on here?" I whisper urgently. "What's it all about?"

R. Friedler regards me with sparkling eyes. "It's about what it's always about."

"What is that supposed to mean?!"

He beams back at me and smiles. Like a clever child. Infuriating. What's the point of popping up here if you're not going to help when I need you most?

R. Friedler nods slowly as if he heard the question.

"Fathers--" Dr. Silverberger explains, suddenly occupying the rabbi's chair.

"have a tendency," continues Coach Hardy.

"to show up," lectures Professor Morton.

"in the most unexpected," observes Mr. Hansen.

"places," finishes R. Friedler.

I am dizzy. I look up from the metamorphosing R. Friedler to the waiting Judge.

Victory was in hand, but now I stand at a loss. From triumph to confusion in a heartbeat,

heartbeat. *My world is turning upside-down.*
Chitty Chitty Bang Bang crashing down from
the sky. What is going on? Moses' testimony is
irrelevant? Refocus on what?
The grasshopper is confused.
I need time.
I need time.

The grandfather clock chimes one o'clock.
My mother's face is white with shock.
Tick, tock.
Tick, tock.
Hickory dickory dock, the mouse ran up the
clock,
the clock struck one,
his ticker stopped,
he ran out of time on the spot.

"Please, sir, may I have some more?"
The ragged orphan holds up his bowl in
outstretched hands.
"MORE?!"
"Please, sir, just a little more time?"

Parsley, sage, rosemary, and thyme.
Your parsley: you dipped,
    in tears, at the seder,
Your sage: father figure,
    you learned from at cheder,
Your Mary: could've married,
    but you ran, 'cause you feared her,

Your thyme's running out,
        and the judgement draws nearer.

Please, sir.
More?!
Just a little more time.
For a purpose.

"Your Honor, in view of this, er, new development in the case, we move for a continuance of three days' time to reconstitute our defense."
M. Sutton protests. "Your Honour, zee continuance will not alter zee facts. We see no reason to waste more of zees court's time. Nothing has changed. Nothing will change. Zee defense simply has no case to present."
"Motion denied." The Judge turns to me. "Mr. Cohen, you have until tomorrow. Please be prepared. This court stands adjourned."

The gavel thunders.

5O

Awake. Heart steady. Morning. 4:16. Yom Sheni. Monday.

I was in my bedroom, on my bed. I was confused. What was the meaning?

416 had to be a clue. It couldn't just mean nothing, waking up each day at the exact same minute.

M. Sutton had dismissed the homicide as irrelevant; it didn't matter that Kayin had murdered his brother. Apparently Hevel meant nothing to this court. Which reminded me that R. Friedler, Sr., had implied that from the beginning. "The name means nothing." He had given me that hint immediately. Hevel, in life, might have actually *been* a nothing, but Hevel's significance in this dream court case was also apparently nothing. In death, as in life, Hevel was clearly nothing. But I had missed that clue.

Which reminded me that the real-life R. Friedler had suggested that I reflect on anything else his father might have said in my dreams.

I cast my mind back to Thursday night's dream, where Rabbi Friedler, Sr. had put in his first appearance. He had initially attracted my attention with a critical remark about M. Sutton; in the midst of M. Sutton reading the English version of the prosecution's evidence, Rabbi Friedler had mocked him, saying the prosecutor was running on at the mouth. Then, after introducing himself as Rabbi Friedler's father, he had responded to my whispered stammering of "Rabbi Friedler, Sr." with "The name means nothing." At the time, I thought he was being polite, but in retrospect I saw the deeper meaning to his words. I would have to carefully remember the precise phrasing of his other remarks in that dream.

After M. Sutton had finished with his English translation, and was asking Moses to comment as an expert, Rabbi Friedler had also cast some aspersion on his bad manners. Something about making an awkward transition. And then, at the end of Moses' testimony, R. Friedler had stood up on my behalf and said, "No questions at this time." At the very end, he had explained to me that "Yom Sheni" had meant "Monday."

Nothing in any of those interactions hinted at a hidden, deeper meaning, but I decided to make a list of them, in order, and see if I could recall the exact wording of each one. After adding the few words R. Friedler had said in this morning's dream, I ended up with this list.

Thursday night's dream:
- Critical of M. Sutton: "how he does run on"
- Introducing himself: "(I'm his) father"
- "The name means nothing"
- Critical of M. Sutton: "abrupt transition"
- To the judge: "no questions at this time"
- Explaining *Yom Sheni*: "Monday"

Sunday night's dream:
- After Moses' testimony: "Well done"
- "It's about what it's always about"
- "Fathers have a tendency to show up in the most unexpected places"

It was surely no coincidence that the dreams were coming to a head the night before Josh's surgery. I had to get to the bottom of what the case was all about, and then prepare the defense, all within eighteen hours or so.

I had an appointment to see Dr. Silverberger at 10:30; the only one who would be available earlier would be Rabbi Friedler.

I went online to check the time for the morning minyan... 6:45. Probably best to get there before the service ended, to make sure I caught him. Or, better, to attend the service itself. That would certainly fulfill my resolution to Moses "to be open to the traditions of my forefathers," and it would help ensure I caught Rabbi Friedler at the earliest possible moment.

There was still hope for this case.

51

I arrived at the synagogue ten minutes before the service, and followed a taciturn bearded man through the front door. He surprised me by heading left, towards the doors through which the unruly boys had disappeared Friday night.

The doors opened onto a short hallway, at the end of which was a smaller room, a modest sanctuary for the weekday services. I snagged a head covering from the basket by the door, and looked around for Sruli to help me find a prayerbook. He was nowhere to be seen. The room held a dozen bearded men in prayer shawls, most already in tefillin, but a few still putting them on. One had a teenage boy with him, and was instructing him how to wrap them on his arm.

R. Friedler stepped forward from a wooden stand near the front, enrobed in his prayer shawl and already murmuring his morning blessings. He smiled deeply and handed me a blue siddur, opened to the appropriate page. Then he brought me a pair of tefillin, nodding at an empty chair on his right. As I took out the tefillin, I spied the taciturn man to R. Friedler's left, and Rabbi Shlomo at the leader's lectern in the front. The latter was adjusting his prayer shawl in preparation for starting the service. As I finished affixing the phylacteries, Rabbi Shlomo's voice rang out, "*Hodu ladonoi keeroo vishmo...*".

I sat down and looked at the prayerbook. *Offer praise to the Lord, proclaim His Name; make His deeds known among the nations...*

After fifteen minutes of various Psalms, there was a Kaddish, some kind of responsive call to prayer, and shortly thereafter, the Shema. Following on the heels of the Shema came the silent standing prayer, followed by its repetition by the leader. Then, suddenly, they were taking out the Torah. I had not expected that on a weekday. The congregation rose in respect, and various responsive prayers were sung out. As the scrolls were paraded towards a small central podium, R. Friedler's quiet prayer neighbor was suddenly at my side.

"What's your name?" he asked.

"Larry Cohen."

"Your Hebrew name?"

"Oh. Reuven ben Michael Aba." I pronounced my father's name the way he had, "Mee-cha-ail".

Before I could ask him his name, he had moved to the podium, helping arrange the plush Torah cover on a chair, while Rabbi Shlomo checked that the scrolls were rolled to the correct place.

Suddenly, my name was called out in an oddly familiar way, "*Yaamod* Reuven ben Michael Aba ha-Kohen." Rabbi Friedler slid his prayer shawl around me and beckoned me up to the Torah scrolls. It felt like my bar mitzvah all over again.

Rabbi Shlomo instructed me to touch the fringe of the shawl to specific places in the scroll, and kiss it. I pronounced the indicated blessing, and then Rabbi Shlomo was chanting the Hebrew, just as Moses had in my dream. Except this chanting was over in about ten seconds. I touched the shawl to the parchment again, kissed it, and read the after-blessing. As I stepped to the side, several men put out their hands with a Yiddish exclamation, and Rabbi Friedler beamed.

I noticed Sruli near the doorway, swaying in silent devotion next to an older, squat fellow doing the same.

Two other men were called up, and Rabbi Shlomo finished the reading. Rabbi Friedler reclaimed his shawl from me as the Torah was carried ceremoniously back to its ark. As everyone retook their seats, I reflected on the honor of the aliyah I had just received. I hadn't heard my father's Hebrew name spoken aloud since my bar mitzvah, some eighteen years ago. Somehow hearing his name in this traditional setting had brought his presence closer to me; I could almost feel him sitting beside me.

The service wound up swiftly, ending in the *Aleinu*, this time murmured quietly. I studied the Hebrew words carefully. There it was, "*shehem mishtachavim l'hevel v'lareek.*" Just as Rabbi Friedler had explained. I sounded the words out slowly a few times.

Rabbi Friedler motioned me to stand, and Rabbi Shlomo sounded the shofar. The sounds of a child crying out to his Father.

Across the way, my eyes caught Sruli leaving, the shorter man herding him out the door. Noticing my glance, he pointed emphatically at me as he made a sound resembling a sneeze. He repeated the gesture and the sound, and then he was out the door, gone.

52

I turned to find Rabbi Friedler packing his prayer shawl away.

"Great to have you in shul this morning, Reb Reuven. *Yesher koach* on your aliyah!"

"Thanks, Rabbi. Say, if you have time... there was a strange turn in the court case last night, and I was wondering if you could help me unravel it..?"

Rabbi Friedler hesitated, the first time I had seen him do so in response to a request for his time.

"Perhaps this is *bashert*," suggested R. Friedler, "Yiddish for 'meant to be'. Sruli is helping out Rabbi Gruen in Rochester today, so I need a hand taking our *cheder* donations to a homeless shelter downtown. It's mostly clothes; nothing too heavy. Care to help out? We can talk on the way."

"Sure."

As R. Friedler gathered his things, I asked, "What does that mean, '*Yesher koach*'?"

"Ah, sorry. Our way of saying, 'Way to go!' or 'Well done!'. I suppose the most literal translation would take the form of a blessing: 'May your strength be straight!'"

As we left the building, Rabbi Friedler nodded towards his car, an old red Subaru wagon, covered more with rust than paint. He ducked into the driver's seat and leaned over to open the passenger door for me from the inside; apparently the exterior latch mechanism was broken. He turned the key and coaxed it to life, murmuring either words of encouragement or a prayer to God Almighty to start the thing. The engine finally caught. As he pulled down the horseshoe drive, R. Friedler kept his eyes on the road but asked me, "So, what's the latest development with the case, Reb Reuven?"

"Well, it's very confusing. It feels like I'm missing something fundamental, something basic. And because of that, my defense totally misses the mark."

"Hmm." R. Friedler considered. "If that's the case, then I suggest going back to the very beginning and reviewing each of your conclusions about these dreams; each conclusion, at every step along the way."

"Okay. Where do we start?"

"Good question!"

The *cheder* was just a few blocks away, a small building that housed the Neener school. We went in the door and down the stairs to a small office. There were roughly twenty boxes of various sizes and shapes, filled with clothes, toiletries, and toys. None of them were especially heavy, but the stairs slowed us down. Finally, we set the last boxes in the Subaru and we were on the road again.

"So I guess the first conclusion was about the court itself, the venue."

"Ah, yes. When you first told me of these dreams, you weren't sure exactly what courtroom it was. You concluded it was your workplace, the Hennepin County Court, right? Could it be a different court?"

I thought about it. The physical arrangement was court 14B; the layout, the decor, it all fit. The rules of evidence and procedure seemed to back that up, and the presence of the bailiff, the court reporter and the clerk.

"It certainly looked and felt like a human court, and all the evidence points to Hennepin County Court." I reviewed the earlier dreams in my mind, what I could remember of them. "M. Sutton used the history of the court to admit the Bible. It's definitely my courtroom."

"Okay. What came next?"

I thought back. "The charges. My friend Andy had convinced me that I must have heard the charges, if only in my subconscious, and then I remembered something that sounded like 'bendawma'. At first I thought it was the 'crime of crying, "bendawma"', and then Sruli realized it was the 'crime of Kayin ben Odom', remember?"

"Ah, yes, I remember that day. He's really quite something, that boy."

"Yes. It makes me wonder what he had to tell me this morning."

"He had something to tell you?"

"Well, it seemed that way. On his way out, he pointed at me from across the room, and sneezed at me or something."

The bushy eyebrows rose. "Sneezed at you?"

"Well, that's what it sounded like from where I was sitting. Maybe he said, 'issue' or 'tissue'? I should probably just ask him. Can you give me his cell phone number?"

"Ah, that won't help you contact Sruli today. R. Gruen has a 'no cell phone' policy when the boys are helping him; he wants their full attention on the mitzvah they're doing. But I would expect Sruli back at the shul for Mincha/Maariv at sunset, God willing. Or you could stop by the house later in the evening, if you'd like."

"Okay, we'll see how the day plays out. I'm not sure how much time it will take to put this defense together."

"Where were we? Ah, yes, you had discovered it was the 'crime of Kayin ben Odom'."

"Right. So I think the next conclusion was figuring out who was on trial. I had originally assumed that I was defending Josh, that he was one being charged. In my initial petition --or prayer request, or whatever it was in the hospital that day-- I had asked to use my legal skills to alleviate Josh's suffering. So it made sense that he would be the one I was defending."

R. Friedler nodded, and I continued.

"But when it became clear that it was the 'crime of Kayin', I didn't see how it could be Josh; it just didn't fit him." I turned to Rabbi Friedler. "I remember you told me to trust my— *kishkes*."

"*Kishkes*. Your gut feeling."

"Right. If there was no way Josh could be guilty of the 'crime of Kayin', it had to be-- wait a minute! The court would never put Kayin on trial for 'the *crime* of Kayin' because that phrasing would presume he was guilty of a crime from the start! To charge Kayin with 'murder in the first degree' would be one thing, but to charge him with 'the crime of Kayin' would violate due process. It can't be Kayin; it has to be Josh after all!"

"Ah, but you had ruled Josh out because you said he couldn't be guilty of jealousy or murder, right?"

"Right. So if it's actually Josh on trial, that would have to mean--", I looked at Rabbi Friedler with dawning comprehension. Together we finished, "The 'crime of

Kayin' is neither jealousy nor murder!"

"It fits!" I realized. "It explains M. Sutton's courtroom strategy. Back in one of the early dreams, it felt like I had fallen into a trap of M. Sutton's, but at the time, I didn't know what it was. But now it's clear! He had no evidence to convict Josh, and that was why he had wanted me to accept evidence from an authoritative source *that Kayin was guilty of the crime.*"

"I don't follow you, Reb Reuven."

"I had just gotten both the Book of Remembrances and God Himself dismissed, and M. Sutton had no case. So M. Sutton hoped to admit evidence that *Kayin* had committed the crime, because he knew that without the Book of Remembrances or God on the stand, he wouldn't be able to prove that *Josh* was guilty. The trap I fell into was accepting evidence about *Kayin*, when it was *Josh* who was accused of the crime."

"I see. The Sutton took advantage of your confusion."

"Exactly. Now we just need to figure out what this 'crime of Kayin' really was, and maybe I can mount a defense for Josh."

Rabbi Friedler parked his rust bucket on the street, and we walked through the doors of the shelter.

An ample, dark-skinned woman welcomed us with an open smile. She had a matter-of-fact directness that somehow reminded me of my old kindergarten teacher. She directed us to take our things to the "sorting room", a place R. Friedler had clearly made deposits many times previously.

Outside, we unloaded the donations to the strains of a hearty "Joy to the World", sung by a homeless beggar across the street. The shelter probably had rules against panhandling by their doorway, but they couldn't control the airwaves across the street.

"Oh, that's Arthur," remarked Rabbi Friedler, seeing my glance. "What a beautiful voice!"

We carried in the last of the boxes and made our goodbyes. On the way out, Rabbi Friedler surprised me by crossing the street instead of returning to his car.

As we approached the other curb, I heard Arthur counseling the passersby, "Don't let nobody mess with your joy today!" "Keep shining those lovely smiles, ladies!" His thin frame was all skin and bones; his worn clothes seemed as old as his grizzled grey hair. He looked like he hadn't eaten in days, but when he saw Rabbi Friedler, he broke into a large toothless smile.

"Good morning, my holy brother!"

"Good morning, Arthur! How are you on this fine day?"

"Well, the Lord woke up this old sack of bones this morning, so that makes it another blessed day!"

"Amen to that! Let me introduce my friend." Rabbi Friedler gestured towards me. "Reb Reuven, meet Arthur. Arthur, my friend Larry Cohen."

As we shook hands, Rabbi Friedler stooped to drop some change in an old coffee can set out to the side for exactly that purpose.

Arthur turned to thank him. "God bless you, Rabbi. God bless you."

"And may God bless you, too, Arthur."

I considered. When I saw beggars in downtown Minneapolis --usually on my way to or from work-- I just went on my way. I couldn't save the world, and many of these people were victims of their own bad choices in life. But today I decided to follow R. Friedler's example. When in Rome, and all that.

As I slipped behind Rabbi Friedler towards the coffee can, my eye caught the cardboard sign behind it, its red lettering proclaiming a surprising sentiment for an emaciated, homeless man.

```
Therefore we do not lose heart.
Though outwardly we are wasting away,
yet inwardly we are being renewed
day by day.


           2 Corinthians
```

As I dropped my dollar in the can, my eyes peered over the rim to rest on the bottom right corner of the sign, previously obscured. There, in red block numerals, I beheld:

```
                 4:16
```

I froze. Then, numbly, I pointed. There it was, in real life, on a dirty sidewalk, hiding behind an old coffee can, set out by a homeless man in broad daylight. The numbers I had seen after waking from each and every dream. And there was the message, attached to those numbers. "Do not lose heart."

I turned to Rabbi Friedler, who, having said his goodbye to Arthur, turned to see me gaping.

Arthur had already moved away and was exhorting

several passersby to "Praise the Lord!". He launched into what sounded like an old Negro spiritual.

Rabbi Friedler nodded in appreciation of the sign, and steered me around to cross the street to his car. "Very interesting," he said. "Very interesting."

As we headed down West 7th, back towards my car at the shul, R. Friedler appeared deep in thought. I said, "Isn't that amazing? 'Don't lose heart'!"

"Definitely most interesting," responded Rabbi Friedler slowly. "There are many places in the Tanach -- the Jewish Bible-- which express the same sentiment. Moses' exhortation to Yehoshua comes to mind, where he says, *chazak ve'ematz*, 'Be strong and courageous', for example. Or in Shoftim: *Al yairach levavchem, al teeroo v'al tachpezoo* -- 'Don't be faint in your heart, do not fear, do not panic' before going to battle." Rabbi Friedler lifted a hand towards the windshield. "And King David says in Psalms, *Lo eera rah, kee Atah eemadi:* 'I will fear no evil, for You are with me!'"

R. Friedler seemed more puzzled than astonished at this overt revelation of God's Hand. "What's the problem? Wasn't that a sign from On High?"

"Certainly, certainly," confirmed R. Friedler in a distracted voice. The light ahead turned red, and R. Friedler came to a full stop. He turned to face me.

"But my question, Reb Reuven, is this: with all the Hebrew Tanach available to Him, why would The Almighty use the Christian Scriptures to send a Jew such a message?!"

53—

We sat staring at each other in silence. Finally, the light turned green and Rabbi Friedler resumed driving.

We were each still turning the question over in our minds when we arrived back at the shul where my M3 awaited.

I still had not solved the riddle of what the dream court considered 'the crime of Kayin' to have been. If I could nail down what Josh's transgression was, I would still have time to visit him in the hospital and work up a defense before nightfall. But where would I find the answer? Who could tell me the 'crime of Kayin'? And then it struck me.

"Say, Rabbi Friedler..?"

"Hmm?"

"What does chapter four, verse sixteen of the Book of Genesis say?"

R. Friedler's brow clouded. "That's a good question, Reb Reuven; I have no idea!" Seeing my crestfallen face, he explained, "Chapter and verse numbers were actually a Christian innovation. For Jews, time-honored tradition divides the Torah into the weekly sections or *parshiyos*, and from there into *aliyot*, a portion for each of the seven men called up for an *aliyah*. That's how we study them-- one *aliyah* each day of the week. So I can tell you that the story of Kayin and Hevel falls out on Wednesday, in the fourth *aliyah* of the *parsha* of Bereishis, but I'm not sure where the Christian divisions of chapter four or verse sixteen land."

"But aren't the chapter and verse numbers printed in

the Chumash?"

"Yes they are! It was a great innovation, and we use those numbers, too, when we want to single out a particular verse. We just don't memorize them the way many Christians do. But let's go look it up!" Rabbi Friedler motioned enthusiastically towards my car. "Follow me home, Reb Reuven. Follow me home, like Yitzhak Yenkel, and let's see what treasure we can find in that Torah God gave us!"

54

Rabbi Friedler knocked on his front door and opened it. He announced "We're home!" as we spilled into the living room to find a Chumash.

Rabbi Friedler handed me the Pebble edition, and flipped open his own all-Hebrew volume, searching for chapter four. I was still fumbling to find Genesis as he started announcing.

"Chapter four is where the story begins...

"Kayin is jealous in verse five...

"Kills Hevel in verse eight...

"And that's it." Rabbi Friedler's voice sagged with disappointment. "We have the punishment, which goes through to verse fifteen, and then verse sixteen is just Kayin heading out to live in the land of Nod."

I shook my head; it didn't make sense.

"Are you sure?"

Rabbi Friedler came around to show me, finding the passage with ease in the Pebble version.

"Here's where Kayin kills Hevel." With his right hand, he pointed to the spot in the Hebrew. With his left hand, he moved his finger along the English translation. "Kayin's actions start here and the text runs on to... here, but you see how verse sixteen is all the way down here--?" He shrugged his shoulders. "It was a great idea, though, Reb Reuven.'

"Wait, wait. That's so funny how you just put that: 'the text runs on'. Your father said --what was the exact phrasing?-- 'You will see how he does run on.' Yes, that's what he said!"

Rabbi Friedler cocked his head and squinted his eyes, looking for my meaning.

I explained, "In Thursday's dream, M. Sutton was reading an English translation of this exact text into the record. Your father, appearing at my elbow, said, 'You'll see how he does run on.' I thought he was just insulting the Sutton, but maybe he was delivering another clue. Why did M. Sutton continue on past Kayin's actions? If the 'crime of Kayin' was murder or jealousy, he should have stopped right there in the text. Instead, he kept going. He 'ran on'!"

Rabbi Friedler nodded slowly, "Hmm. So where did he 'run on' to; where did he stop?"

I read in the English translation. "Here! Verse sixteen! Chapter four, verse sixteen!"

"Well, that certainly is interesting!" Rabbi Friedler raised his eyebrows. "But I'm not sure where that gets us. The *pasuk* is still quite ordinary; nothing criminal is mentioned at all."

I sighed. So close, and yet so far. Everything had pointed to this verse, Arthur's 4:16, M. Sutton leaving off at 4:16, always waking up at 4:16. And yet, here it was, a dead end; a brick wall. Nothing. *Cain went forth from before God; and he settled in the land of Nod, east of Eden.* Big deal.

Except... Arthur's 4:16 had said, "Don't lose heart." There had to be *something* here. There just had to be.

"Well, now here's something interesting, Reb Reuven."

"Yes?"

"It's not verse sixteen, but it's interesting. Starting in

pasuk eleven, Hashem gives Kayin the consequences of his actions." R. Friedler kept his right hand on the text, and raised his left, listing the punishments out on his fingers. "First, 'You are cursed from the ground.' In the next *pasuk*, He explains that means when Kayin works the ground it will no longer 'give its strength' to him. Second, 'You will be a vagrant and a wanderer'. And-- that's it! Just those two things!"

"I don't get it; you think God is being too lenient?"

"No, no," replied R. Friedler, "It's just-- look at *pasuk* thirteen which follows. Here Kayin says that his sin is too large to bear. And then Kayin repeats back to Hashem the consequences, but Kayin's list is *longer*." R. Friedler reset his fingers for a new count. "First, 'You have banished me from the face of the earth'. Okay, presumably that is a paraphrase of being cursed from the ground, Hashem's first punishment. But then, 'from before Your Face I will be hidden'! Where did *that* come from? None of the major commentators say anything here. Then, Kayin's third point, 'I will be a vagrant and a wanderer', which lines back up with Hashem's second curse. And then, 'whoever meets me will kill me.' Which is Kayin's fear, rather than Hashem's decree, and in the next *pasuk*, Hashem addresses that."

"Wait, so what was that extra one in there?"

"Kayin says to Hashem, '*Lifney panecha esasair*'. 'From before Your Face, I will be hidden.' Kayin is saying that Hashem is cutting him off! Hashem gave Kayin two consequences as punishment for killing Hevel, and here Kayin has added a third. He thinks Hashem is ending the relationship."

"But if that's Kayin's crime, then shouldn't I have seen *that* verse on my clock every morning. 4:14 instead of 4:16?"

"Hmm. A good question." Rabbi Friedler examined the Hebrew of verse 4:16 more closely. "*Vayetze Kayin mi'lifney Hashem...*"

"What does that mean exactly?"

"*Vayetze* means 'he went forth'. It's used..." Rabbi Friedler was struck by a thought. He searched the shelves for another book, which looked like a thesaurus of sorts. Using it as a cross-index, he started flipping to different sections of the Chumash. I waited as patiently as I could.

Finally, he looked up. "Well, this is certainly interesting, Reb Reuven."

"What is? What did you find?"

"Well, the pasuk says, '*vayetze mi'lifney*', which is generally translated as 'he went forth'. Now, this gets rather technical. There are other ways you could say 'he went', other Hebrew verbs that would convey a similar meaning. To understand the full import and connotation of the choice '*vayetze*', we look at other places it's used in the Torah."

"Yes, we do that in law as well."

"Okay, so in most places, we see '*vayetze*' is used when there's friction between the person and the situation he's leaving. For example, we see '*vayetze*' a few times where Moses left Pharoah, often in anger; no love lost there."

R. Friedler considered, "But between Kayin and Hashem, we have '*vayetze mi'lifney*'."

"What's the difference?"

"Well, *'vayetze'* by itself means to go forth. *'Lifney'* has the root of *'panah'* or 'face'. So together *'vayetze mi'lifney'* means 'going forth from the face of'; it has more the connotation of turning your back on someone's face!"

"So, wait; I'm trying to put this together. First, Cain assumes that God is ending the relationship, and then he turns his back and leaves God's Face?"

"Exactly! Doesn't that sound like a crime? Turning your back on God's Presence!"

"Yes, but..."

"Hmm?"

"If God is supposed to be everywhere, how could Cain leave His Presence like that? Isn't that impossible?"

"Of course it's impossible!" cried Rabbi Friedler, "Of course! But that doesn't stop us from thinking we've done it. In our mind, we create an entire world where Hashem doesn't exist. Then we enter into that fabricated world, we don't see Hashem anywhere, and we blame *Hashem* for abandoning *us*!"

"So you think that's the 'crime of Kayin', then? Not just Kayin *thinking* God is going to end the relationship, but then Kayin actually *acting* on that belief by removing himself from the relationship first? That's why it's 4:16, and not that earlier 4:14 verse where he mistakenly adds to the punishment list?"

"Exactly!"

"But why wouldn't God just say, 'Cain, I'm not abandoning you at all!'?"

"Perhaps," R. Friedler suggested tentatively, "Kayin needs to figure that out himself."

"Maybe."

"But the bigger question is: Does this interpretation sound plausible to *you*; does it fit with your dreams?"

I thought. It was all very strange, very confusing. It was one thing to have some kind of nightmare about being in court and not knowing what to do. That made sense to me. But this? If God really existed, was He expecting me to dream-defend Josh against the 'crime' of leaving some kind of personal relationship with Him? It was crazy. And it was all I had.

I shrugged. "I don't know, Rabbi; I'm out of my depth here. I don't know what to think."

"Well, it's a nice piece of learning, Reb Reuven, regardless of whether it ends up applying to your court case." Rabbi Friedler traversed the table to put his arm around my shoulder, which was a bit of a stretch for his height. "Well done, Reb Reuven; well done."

Suddenly, I felt tired and worn out. I slumped. If Josh were really being charged with the crime of abandoning God... what kind of a defense would even be possible?

55—

Driving to Dr. Silverberger's office, I tried to remember where our therapy session had left off on Friday. It seemed like a long time ago. We had talked about family, in the middle of which he had gotten called out for that emergency.

There was a lot to catch up on. I had sent the email to my uncle Friday afternoon, written in my journal the story of the past few weeks, spent the Shabbos with the Friedlers, done all the legal preparation Sunday, and had the confusing dream last night. And then there was the whole 4:16 business this morning. How much of that could I fit into a fifty-minute session?

It turned out that Dr. Silverberger had an agenda of his own. I had barely sat down and given him an overview of the intervening events, when he shifted uncomfortably in his chair and introduced his own topic of discussion.

"You know, Larry, before we get into your experiences today, I have an idea that I want to put on the table. You're probably not going to like it --you may even think it's stupid-- but I would be remiss if I didn't point out a possibility to you..."

I noticed Dr. Silverberger habitually guessed at what I might feel. *You may feel this way, you may feel that way.*

"In psychology, we have a concept called 'transference'. Sometimes old feelings are triggered by current circumstances which resemble old emotionally-laden situations. An arising experience resembles the old traumatic one, and we get a rush of emotion that is really left over from the old unresolved ordeal. Sometimes when that happens, we don't realize it. We attribute our current emotional reaction to the present external circumstances, or to other people's actions, rather than realizing that strong emotions from the past have been triggered internally, and are coming from inside ourselves."

If he was getting at something in particular, it eluded me.

"So on Friday, when I had to step out to take that emergency call..."

"Yeah?"

"Well, I would naturally expect you to feel inconvenienced, but the intensity of your reaction made me think you might have had some strong feelings arise, and, if so, perhaps they were the result of transference."

"Nothing special came up on Friday, just annoyance at having the session interrupted." An annoyance I was re-experiencing now, being forced now to talk about that, instead of my own agenda.

"Well, it's a good thing to be on the lookout for this transference," suggested Dr. Silverberger. "It's an indicator there's some material that needs attention." He looked at me as if I might have some view on his psychological paradigm. I said nothing.

"Did Friday's experience remind you of any other similar situations where you might have been left alone suddenly?"

I stared at the wheels of his chair. "No."

The word sat awkwardly in the expanding silence. I

waited.

Dr. Silverberger shifted his weight again, his chair creaking. "I see. Well, perhaps we can revisit that another time. So what would you like to focus on today, Larry?"

"Well, I emailed my uncle after our last session."

"Very good. And how did that feel?"

"It felt all right. It felt good." I paused. "So how would I know for sure know if any of this transference stuff is really going on?" I asked.

Dr. Silverberger nodded. I could almost hear Rabbi Friedler saying, "It's a good question!" The good doctor leaned forward, "I tell you what, Larry, how about we try an experiment and see what we find out?"

"What kind of experiment?"

"If you're open to it, I'll get up and leave the room for one minute, and we'll see if it stirs anything up for you."

"You mean, you just stand out in the hallway for a minute?"

"Yes. I would be right on the other side of the closed door. Sixty seconds. Would you like to try it?"

I shrugged. "Okay."

Abruptly, Dr. Silverberger rose and went out, closing the door behind him.

I looked at his empty chair. Brown faux leather with padded armrests, creases where he had been sitting moments earlier. The seat was probably still warm. It would probably cool rapidly, though. I resisted the urge to reach out and feel it.

It seemed silly to be paying him $150 for fifty minutes, just to stare at his empty office chair. That worked out to three dollars for this wasted minute. A minute to "see what we would find out." Well, I was not feeling anything special at the moment except irritation. That's what we were finding out. When a therapist walks out on his patient, his patient gets irritated.

The emptiness of the office chair echoed in the bare office. He said he would be back in sixty seconds. Surely he was just outside the door.

I rubbed the itch in my right eye. It would be fine. It would be fine. Not a big deal. I stared at the brown leather seat. My stomach contracted.

I looked up to see Dr. Silverberger regarding me from the doorway. He eased into his chair, his eyes on my face. "So how was that for you, Larry?"

"Um, I guess it was..." I covered my face momentarily with my palms and took a breath. "It was okay."

"Mmm. How are you feeling now?"

"Empty."

"Mm-hmm." Dr. Silverberger nodded slowly. "Tell me more about how that emptiness feels. Maybe nauseous, or hollow, or a numb tingling?"

"Hollow."

"Mmm. And is there a place in your body you feel that most strongly?"

I pointed to my lower chest.

"Very good, Larry; very good. If you're feeling up to it, Larry, I'd like you to focus in for a few moments on that hollow sensation, that emptiness in your chest."

I nodded. It felt like a hole going right through my body, just a few inches under my heart.

"And as you feel that hollowness, Larry, tell me if any

memories come to mind, or if any strong feelings arise."

And there it was, all in a moment, the sunlight streaming down through a crowd of people gathered on that spring day, the brightness illuminating the lower left corner of a simple pine box as it slowly descended into the ground.

I covered my face again. Tears were flowing down my cheeks. I shook my head, but they wouldn't stop.

"It's okay, Larry," Dr. Silverberger's hand was on my shoulder. "Tell me what you're remembering."

"It was my father's funeral. The day they buried him." I grabbed at the tissue box, drying my face and wiping my nose. "Just a second, I've got something in my eye." I stumbled out to the hallway bathroom. After running some cold water over my forehead, eyes and cheeks, I took a deep breath and looked at myself in the mirror. Red-eyed and flushed, but I was okay. I would be all right. I returned to the doctor.

"Wow, that was something." I said as I retook my seat.

Dr. Silverberger nodded. "It can feel overwhelming when these feelings first come to the surface. You did very well."

"So I guess I do have some of this transference stuff going on, huh?"

"It would seem so." Dr. Silverberger smiled. "How are you feeling now?"

"Oh, I'm okay. Just a little... surprised, I guess."

"Very understandable."

"So, what now?"

"Well, when you're ready, we can bring up these

feelings again in a controlled way, and explore the connection between the loss of your father and your subsequent childhood experiences. In doing so, we can help you heal from the past wounds so they don't interfere so much with the present."

"Okay," I said, "but can we talk about something else for right now?"

"Sure," said Dr. Silverberger, showing a toothy smile. "What would you like to talk about?"

"Well, this last dream was quite something." I launched into the details of my defense. Dr. Silverberger listened carefully.

When I was finished, he leaned back thoughtfully. "So part of your dream defense was that Cain didn't know death was possible?"

"Yes," I smiled. "You see, nobody had ever died before!"

"So Cain might not have even known that his brother died?"

"Exactly! In theory, Cain could have just struck him and left, never imagining that Abel actually died from the blow."

Dr. Silverberger considered. I expected him to appreciate the originality of the legal defense, but instead he took a different direction. "If Cain didn't know Abel had died, it must have been a shock when he actually found out. How do you suppose that happened?"

The question took me by surprise. Maybe Cain never saw his parents again before he was banished. Maybe he lost his brother and both his parents in one day. In my mind there flashed an image of my mother and me on the couch together, when she told me my father had died. But maybe Cain never got any comfort at all.

I realized that Dr. Silverberger was tying the court dream back to my childhood events. He was well-intentioned. But how could a psychological interpretation of these dreams be reconciled with what I had just gone through with Rabbi Friedler?

You don't have to believe in him to ask for his help.

Yeah, but what if he thinks I'm crazy?

Asking is zee first baby step. Ask him to talk to you.

"Some crazy things happened this morning..."

Dr. Silverberger nodded encouragingly.

I told him of the morning's adventures, discovering Arthur's 4:16 sign, the subsequent 4:16 of Genesis, and the way it seemed to fit together so perfectly with the words of R. Friedler, Sr. in my dreams.

"So am I crazy to think that this is being orchestrated from On High?"

Dr. Silverberger smiled and shook his head.

"I keep an open mind about whether God exists. A lot is in our perspective. If we believe in God, we can see evidence of His existence everywhere we look. If we don't believe in God, we see other explanations for the things around us: science, nature, psychology, and even, sometimes, coincidence. I think it's healthy to consider many viewpoints when you're going through such a stressful time. On the one hand," Dr. Silverberger illustrated by cupping his right palm, "these things may really be the Hand of God, and seeing God's Hand in this may deepen your spiritual life and lead to a richer way of being."

I relaxed back into my chair. At least for the moment, the good doctor wasn't calling in the men in white coats.

"On the other hand," he opened his left hand to balance his right, "your experience of these events could stem from unresolved issues. Seeing unresolved issues behind things could lead you to some healing and a fuller emotional life."

Dr. Silverberger threw an imaginary ball from one hand to the other and back. "And they don't have to be mutually exclusive. You don't have to lock yourself in to seeing things from only one perspective for all time. You can move from one to the other as often as you like."

"So you're saying that believing in God one minute, and then thinking there's no such thing as God the next minute, is... okay?"

"Absolutely."

"So if I saw God's hand in the events of this morning..?"

Dr. Silverberger smiled, "Then you'd be no crazier than your Rabbi Friedler, or any of the millions of believers across the globe."

Fair enough. "And if I saw this all in terms of unresolved issues?"

"Then you'd probably want to look more closely at the dreams and any intense feelings that come up for you when you explore those issues."

"And you think--?"

"I think it's good to keep an open mind."

"So if these dreams stem from internal psychological sources somewhere in my mind, how do I get them to stop? How do I resolve the unresolved issues?"

"Well, there's no one set formula, but the general approach that I have used over the years seems to work well for many people. We can do some things here to help nourish you --providing some of the missing experiences you may feel empty from-- and, in the process, you learn to embrace the memories and feelings associated with your father." Dr. Silverberger leaned forward. "You can't heal from the death of a loved one by pushing them away and moving on with your life as if they no longer existed. That's not healthy; it just doesn't work. You heal from the death of a loved one by cherishing their memories, celebrating the times you had together, feeling the pain of their no longer being there, and carrying their images and their values forward in your own life. You embrace the relationship." Dr. Silverberger demonstrated with an imaginary embrace. "In a nutshell: 'Turning towards, instead of turning away.'"

"So which perspective should I choose: the will of God, or unresolved issues?"

Dr. Silverberger laughed. "That's entirely up to you, and you're even allowed to change your mind whenever you want." He tilted his head slightly in reflection. "Already, thinking of this in terms of the 'Hand of God' led you to connect to Rabbi Friedler, enjoy a Shabbat dinner, and propose an original understanding of Cain. I would count those as good things -- although I'm no rabbi." Dr. Silverberger smiled. "And, in exploring things psychologically, you've reconnected with family --your uncle-- you've looked at some of the emptiness around losing your father, and who knows what else awaits?

These dreams may be a doorway to exploring some of the memories and traditions connecting you to your father. Maybe you can draw closer to him through this."

Dr. Silverberger smiled encouragingly. Then, glancing at his watch, he observed that our time was up for today. We confirmed the Wednesday appointment, and he reminded me that he was out Friday for the second day of Rosh Hashanah.

As I was heading out the door, I reflected that Dr. Silverberger had been holding up his forefinger when he said "connecting you to your father", so I thought I should clarify his meaning.

"Not 'Father in Heaven'; you mean drawing closer to my real father, right?"

56

I sat at the diner reflecting on my session with Dr. Silverberger. I couldn't decide what made the most sense. Hard to believe all these happenings were coincidence.

I took out my phone and checked my email. Jumping out as the only personal item was an email from ncohen@csus.edu. My uncle Nate!

b"h

Dear Larry,

Great to hear from you, nephew! Thanks for reaching out; I've been terrible at keeping in touch. I like to blame it on my job-- I spend so much time in front of the screen grading papers and doing research, that I stay away from computers as much as I can when I'm off the job. But really, I'm just bad at staying in touch with people. Sorry about that.

Wonderful to hear that you're an attorney in Minneapolis! I remember that you always did like a good argument. :-) I hope they're treating you well there.

Here, the U is the same old place. My wife Miriam keeps busy with her homeopathy practice and our garden. The kids are great: Jake just started his senior year at Penn, Rachel is a sophomore at Georgetown, and Hadassah is taking the year off to

```
volunteer in Guatemala.
    It's wonderful to hear from you, and
let's keep in touch. And if you're looking
for a wife, I know some nice Jewish girls
out here...  :-)

    Love,
    Uncle Nate
```

A nice warm feeling filled my stomach. Dr. Silverberger had called this one right.

I dialed Andy's number. He answered on the second ring.

"Hi Counselor, how goes it?"

"It goes well, Counselor. Just got an email from my uncle."

"Oh?"

"Yeah, I wrote him on Friday; first time in years."

"And?"

"And he wrote back!"

"And you're surprised why?"

I took a bite of hashbrowns.

"Andy, are you ready to argue the case of the century?" I told him the latest: the dismissal of the murder charge in the dream, the 4:16, the conclusion it was all about Josh's relationship with God. It set him off.

"So lemme get this straight--"

"Look, Andy," I interrupted, "I know you think all this stuff is stupid and ridiculous and you're all wigged out because I've been studying with Rabbi Friedler, but would you just humor me? Tomorrow my friend has his cancerous head cut open for brain surgery, and, as crazy as it sounds, the only thing I can do to help him is to defend him in dream court. So be my friend here and help me figure out how to do that."

There was silence on the line. I waited.

"Say, Larry--"

"Yeah?"

"I didn't realize you were taking this so much to heart. Of course I've got your back, Counselor; I'm, you know, happy to help you out."

"Thanks, Andy. Sorry I popped my top there."

"It's fine, it's fine. So look--" Andy took in an audible breath, "I'm not sure how these dreams of yours work exactly, but with *teshuvah* --returning to God and all that-- all you need to do is make an opening the size of a needle in moving towards God, and He'll do the rest."

"The size of a needle?"

"Yeah. They made a big deal of it in the yeshiva's *mussar* class. That's where they focus on improving your character. So I would think that all you need to do is get your friend to agree to the smallest little step, and you should be good to go."

"So forget about trying to disprove that he left the relationship and just focus on the smallest step of a return? Have him testify to that one little bit?"

"You got it, Counselor."

"Thanks, Andy. You're a good friend, Counselor."

I pocketed my cell and looked down at the bacon left on my plate.

"Are you finished?"

The question I had been asking myself was now

echoed by the waiter. Would that I had the faith of Rabbi Friedler; he wouldn't even hesitate.

No questions at this time, Your Honor.

That's what he'd said in Thursday night's dream. But I still had plenty of questions, and the waiter needed an answer.

I decided to follow in the fine Jewish tradition of answering a question with a question. "Um, can I have a box?"

As the waiter left, my thoughts returned to the case. Things were coming together. Call Josh to the witness stand and have him show some small sign of return.

But could he do that? *Would* he do that?

5.7___

Josh smiled when I walked in, but I could see weariness behind his eyes. Cindy rose from his bedside to make room for me.

"How are you holding up, Buddha-man?"

"Confucius say, 'Computer programmer having surgery puts faith in operating system.'"

I groaned.

"Or, as my father always says, there are no atheists in a foxhole." Cindy said, reminding me of her family's Catholic tradition. She got up and excused herself.

How was I going to bring this up?

Josh gave me a searching look. "What's on your mind, Grasshopper-man?"

"Well, you know these dreams I've been having?"

"Cain and the courtroom?"

"Yes, well..." Here went nothing. "It turns out that Cain's crime wasn't really jealousy or murder after all."

"Really?"

"Well, I guess the real Cain --if there ever was one-- was guilty of those things. But in these dreams, I just found out that his real crime was turning away from God."

"Interesting."

"Thing is... remember when I told you... these dreams started after I requested, um, to be able to use my legal skills to restore you to health? I don't think Cain was ever the defendant here... I'm actually defending *you* in this dream court."

Josh tried connecting the dots; his face scrunched

together like he'd tasted some bitter lemonade. "So you're thinking that somehow this cancer is God's punishment for turning away from Him?"

"Well, I don't know about *that*--"

"It's okay, dreamer-man, it's okay." He sighed, and his face relaxed. "I've been thinking a lot about karma the last day or two." His eyes focused in the distance. "Maybe in a previous life... maybe there were things I did... maybe this is part of setting them right..."

"Say, Josh--"

"Yeah?"

"Remember the other day we were talking about God, and you said you didn't believe in a personal God?"

"Sounds like something I would say."

"Well, would you reconsider it? Would you consider the possibility that the 'Oneness of the Universe' that you mentioned was actually a personal God with whom you could have a relationship?" It felt funny asking the question. I wasn't even sure I would consider it *myself*.

"Would I consider it? Well, I haven't experienced it myself, but I guess it would be hard or impossible to disprove..."

"So you'd say it was possible, then?"

"We live in a world where multiple truths are possible at the same time. Like light being both a particle and a wave..."

At that moment, Eric the nerd poked his head in. "Hey, dudes." He nodded at both of us in greeting.

"Hey, man," said Josh.

"Hi, Eric. Um, let me just finish my thought here." I turned back to Josh.

"Sorry to push it, Josh, but... would you be willing to *swear* that you'll at least ponder the possibility?"

Josh chuckled at my persistence. "I give you my word, Larry; I'll contemplate it with an open mind."

He turned his attention to Eric, who stepped closer to the bed. As I moved aside, I noticed his T-shirt du jour was emblazoned with an Einstein quote:

Everything should be made as simple as possible-- but not simpler.

At least that one I understood.

"What's that about light?" Eric inquired.

"Just sharing with Larry here that light is both a particle beam and a wave, depending on how you look at it."

"Yeah, it's the weirdest thing," Eric agreed. "It's all around us, yet defies our understanding." He explained that one physics test proved light was a beam of particles, another that it was a wave, and it couldn't be both. "The birth of the wave-particle theory of quantum physics." Eric concluded. He looked from me to Josh and back. "So how did that come up?"

"Larry asked about the existence of God, and--"

"Omniscient and omnipotent, *that* whole god deal?"

"I think that was the idea," Josh concurred.

"I see."

Cindy returned with a nurse in her wake, so Eric and I started making our farewells.

"Say, Josh, one other thing." I tried to sound light and off-the-cuff. "What's your full Hebrew name?"

58

Eric pushed the elevator call button and we waited. "I didn't want to say anything in front of Josh, but this whole God thing..."

"Yeah?"

"It's just a bunch of superstitions people tell themselves to keep from being afraid."

The elevator doors opened. We got in and Eric pressed '1'.

"I can prove your omnipotent God doesn't exist."

"How's that?"

"Can God make a stone so heavy He can't lift it?"

"Um, I don't know." Did I look like a rabbi?

"Here's the thing: If you say He can't make such a stone, then there's something God can't do. Poof! No omnipotent god." Eric flared his fingers like fireworks exploding. "And if you say He *can* make a stone too heavy for Him to lift, then there's still something He can't do --he can't lift that stone He just created. Again, poof! Either way, the omnipotent 'God' goes up in a puff of smoke, killed off by the simple application of logic and reason."

Somehow I felt both irritated and defeated at the same time. The elevator doors opened, releasing me from the smothering intellect of Eric the Geek.

59

I went home to prepare the case. Ideally, I would have rehearsed the testimony with Josh, but even if he were willing, there clearly wasn't a good opportunity on this day before surgery. And it was strange to think about it in any event. Would Josh *himself* show up in my dreams if I called him as a witness, or would it just be my own conception of my friend, my own mental construct? If it was the latter, then I could practice his responses on my own.

I spent the afternoon plotting a series of questions that I felt confident I knew how Josh would answer, and which would demonstrate his openness to a personal relationship with God. I typed them up, printed them out, and put them in my manila folder. If Andy was right about just needing to show the smallest step in returning to a relationship with God, I might have a case.

But to be on the safe side, I needed to run it past Rabbi Friedler, and that was best done in person. I slipped into my M3.

I arrived at the Friedlers as they were sitting down to dinner. It was just the rabbi and his wife; the girls were helping at an after-school overnight program, and apparently Sruli had been held over in Rochester with the four other boys helping R. Gruen. Mrs. Friedler insisted I partake of her homemade lasagna, so I did the ritual washing and made the blessing over the italian garlic bread.

"Reb Reuven!" welcomed R. Friedler, "I was just about to apprise Mrs. Friedler of your amazing 4:16

exploits today. Would you tell her the story?"

In between mouthfuls of lasagna, garlic bread, string beans and salad, I narrated the day's events, starting with the trip to the shelter, finding Arthur's sign, and ending with my discoveries with Rabbi Friedler at the other end of the very table on which we were eating.

"So in the end", summarized R. Friedler to his wife, amazement and wonder in his voice, "it turns out that the court in Reb Reuven's dreams considers Kayin's 'leaving from before Hashem' to be his big crime. His abrupt transition from participating in the world of holiness to living exclusively in the world of the mundane is akin to denying Hashem's existence!"

A rather abrupt transition, don't you think? It was Rabbi Friedler, Sr., commenting on M. Sutton's courtroom etiquette. Or I had thought it was about M. Sutton's manners. Maybe it had been another clue about the text. In Thursday night's dream, R. Friedler, Sr. had posed that question right after M. Sutton had concluded his reading of the text. Immediately after M. Sutton's final words.

"How's your friend Josh doing?"

"He seems pretty good. The surgery is tomorrow. You know, while I was visiting Josh at the hospital, his friend Eric brought up a paradox that you've probably heard before: can God make a stone so heavy He can't lift it?"

R. Friedler chuckled. "Yes, He can certainly make such a stone...and then He can lift it, too!" R. Friedler patted his sauce-laden mustache with his napkin. "Logic is just a creation of Hashem. Our human minds get trapped by logic, but not His Mind. As He says, *'My thoughts are not your thoughts.'* He has no difficulty causing something to be both true and not true at the same time. We're the ones who have a problem with it!"

It occurred to me that if light could be two things, impossibly, at the same time, so could an all-powerful personal God.

If you were inclined to believe in that kind of thing.

"Speaking of having problems, my friend Andy told me that when we do repentance, we only have to make an opening the size of a needle in returning to God, and He does the rest. Is that right?"

"Your friend is a fount of information; that's exactly right!" R. Friedler launched into a celebration of God's great mercy; how little He asks of us and much He gives us in return for the smallest of efforts. "In fact, the Midrash says that Kayin was the first to do teshuvah! I take it, Reb Reuven, that you are planning to use this for your friend's defense?"

"Yes, it's my only hope." I outlined my approach. "Do you think it will work?"

"Well, I'm not sure exactly how this dream court of yours works, but from what I know of how The Abishter works, your plan should be a knockout!" R. Friedler smiled. "So, Reb Reuven, what does your psychologist make of all this?"

"Well, he thinks everything is rooted in my father dying when I was young. He takes all the dreams as symbolic of inner conflict, and thinks father-son issues permeate all my relationships. He even said something about how fathers have a tendency to show up in the most unexpected places."

"Well, our Heavenly Father certainly does show up in the most unexpected places!"

"So why do we even call God 'Father'? Shouldn't it be heretical to compare God to a mere human being?"

"Ah, it's a good question." Rabbi Friedler sat back from his plate. "You see, the Elder Rebbe tells us that our human relationships can help us practice aspects of our relationship with Hashem. And, likewise, we can learn about how to act in our human relationships by understanding them to be an expression of our God relationship."

"I don't follow you, Rabbi."

"A yid's relationship with Hashem is often compared to that of husband and wife. In what way is Hashem like a husband to me? You could say that He provides me with my every need, and expects me to make a home for Him in this world, and that would be true. But also," Rabbi Friedler leaned forward with intensity, "the intimacy that we strive for with Hashem is like the intimacy of husband and wife. When we experience that intimacy in our marital relationship, we can understand the closeness that Hashem is looking for in our relationship with Him."

Rabbi Friedler smiled like a man in love. "And we also learn that our marriage in this world should reflect qualities of our relationship with Hashem. The trust we place in Him, the faith we have that everything He does is for the best, the way we set ourselves aside to do His Will instead of our own... These are things we can put to good use with our better half in our own homes."

I had never heard God spoken of in these terms. It

sounded blasphemous, but here was Rabbi Friedler, the closest man to God that I knew, comparing his love for God with his love for his wife.

"And the same holds true for other relationships as well. The bond a boy has to his father, that absolute trust, that awe, that respect... The desire to make our father proud of us. We can extrapolate from that familial connection and appreciate the devotion and honor we want to infuse into our relationship with Him." Rabbi Friedler pointed to the heavens. "Likewise, when we thank the Abishter for our blessings, when we prostrate ourselves before Him, when we recognize that we owe our entire existence to Him... we can bring those feelings back into our relationship with our father here on earth, and it can help us with the commandment to honor our father." Rabbi Friedler's gaze landed gently on my face. "Of course, when our earthly relationships are troubled, or cut short, it makes that process more challenging. But we can still learn from our other relationships, our bonds with our mothers, siblings, friends, co-workers, and so on."

I thanked Rabbi Friedler for his explanation and we finished eating our fruit. As he rose to get the prayer booklets for our after-meal prayers, I thanked Mrs. Friedler for the delicious meal. After she expressed her pleasure with having company for dinner, we murmured our prayers. Rabbi Friedler closed his book just after I did.

"Reb Reuven, you must be happy to have such a plan for your defense."

"To tell you the truth, Rabbi, I'm mostly relieved. I

feel like it's taken me forever and a day to put all this together. And thank you again, Mrs. Friedler."

Mrs. Friedler reassured me, "Everything happens in the right time, Reb Reuven; and it hasn't taken you forever -- today was only Yom Sheni!"

Rabbi Friedler translated unnecessarily, "Monday."

"I'd better be getting home; I've got a busy day in court tonight!"

"Of course. Josh's surgery is tomorrow. May it be a complete success!"

60

I reviewed my notes before getting ready for bed. As I brushed my teeth, I caught my reflection in the bathroom mirror. Was that a man who trusted God, like Rabbi Friedler? Did he think a Master of the Universe was responsible for everything that happened in his life? The face staring back at me shook its head slowly. Was he, then, a man who believed that all the events of the day could be explained by psychology and coincidence? The mirror registered skepticism, a small shrug of the shoulders topped by a non-committal grimace. No easy answers.

Dr. Silverberger had said that going back and forth between perspectives was fine. You could believe one thing at one moment, another thing the next, and you wouldn't get locked up in the loony bin.

But what about smushing the two paradigms together and holding them with both hands in one big gooey mess?

One thing was clear, anyway. Hidden somewhere behind the face in the mirror was a cavern of tears, tapped into by the good doctor through his minute-long disappearing act. Who would have thought? Life was full of surprises.

And I had a funny feeling about dream court tonight. This defense somehow felt too easy, too straightforward. All I had to do was demonstrate that Josh was open to considering a personal God and everything would be okay? Case dismissed?

M. Sutton surely had a trick or two left up his sleeve.

He was a sly one.

I took the case notes into my bedroom and tucked the manila folder under the pillow. I recited the Shema and asked that my legal preparations should yield good results for Josh. I mean, he shouldn't suffer just because I was a tangled mess of indecision, doubt and unresolved transference issues.

I turned out the light.

I stand before The Judge, staring down at the thick manila folder containing my notes. My opposing thumbs surround the phrase, "God has placed you here for a purpose."

The purpose is obvious and urgent. A life is in the balance.

The gavel sounds. "This court is now in session. You may be seated."

We sit.

"Mr. Cohen?"

I rise behind my table. This time I am ready, Teddy.

Fuzzy Wuzzy wuz a bear.

Fuzzy Wuzzy had no hair.

Becuz Fuzzy Wuzzy wuz taking chemo for his cancer.

For fighting his cancer.

For a purpose.

I consult my notes.

"Your Honor, we call Yehoshua Binyamin ben Aharon Gershon."

And there is Josh, standing in the witness box. On his wiry frame hangs the hospital gown. No IV; no oxygen mask. Good old Josh. Alert and energetic, he takes in the courtroom in wonder.

Welcome to the court of dreams,
where nothing is, as nothing seems.
A cacophony of old-time memes,
brought together by tears which stream,
drowning the young boy's self-esteem,
until all that's left is a silent scream.

The clerk intones, "Please state your name for the record."

"Joshua Levin."

The clerk glances at The Judge, then back at Josh.

"Your Hebrew name?"

"Yehoshua Binyamin ben Aharon Gershon."

"Please raise your right hand. Do you affirm that the testimony you are about to give is the truth, the whole truth, and nothing but the truth?"

"I do."

He sits. I step forward and welcome him with a smile.

"Do you consider yourself a spiritual seeker?"

"I do."

M. Sutton's brow furrows as he eyes Josh from the prosecution's table. I focus on Josh.

"Is it true that over the course of your life you have earnestly examined matters of philosophy and spirituality, and concluded that all things in the universe are connected, are one?"

"Yes, I have."

"Yehoshua, how would you describe your relationship to this Oneness of the Universe?"

"Objection, Your Honour! Zees testimony is irrelevant."

"Your Honor! I intend to demonstrate that even though Yehoshua Binyamin ben Aharon Gershon experienced times in his life when he *was distant from God, or perhaps when he neglected his relationship with God, he has for many years now pursued that relationship most diligently, in his own way. While his vocabulary and concepts may be untraditional, the purpose is the same!"*

The Judge is silent for a single heartbeat.

"Sustained. Will counsel please approach the bench."

I feel suddenly exposed, as though again I have misjudged the court.

The ground is shifting under my feet.

I sit down at my place. The dinner table is quiet, there are no playground stories here. A leadened voice issues forth from my mother's mouth, "How was your day, Larry?"

An answer would be the same as no answer. She is not listening. The jubilant celebration quiets, the cheering crowd melts away. Micah lowers my victory arm in defeated silence. It was fine, Mom. Please pass the peas.

The grasshopper approaches The Judge.

It cannot be. It cannot be.

The front door opens and I see my mother's Shabbos dress. At each elbow she is supported by women from the community. Mrs. Goldstein rises and my mother's dress takes her place by my side.

"I have something to tell you Larry, some very difficult news..."

But this woman with the ashen face is not the

mother, not my mother. She wears her dress, but there is no life in her eyes. It's wrong, it's wrong.

Something is very wrong. Where is my mother? Where is my mother? Let go of me. I'm not going to hear it. You can't make me hear it. I clap my hands over my ears. No, no, no.

"Mr. Cohen," The Judge begins, a softness in His voice, "your desire to plead on your friend's behalf is certainly admirable--"

I burst into the pause, "Your Honor, it is my understanding that Josh's relationship with You is the issue to be decided here. I am trying to establish the context of his relationship--"

M. Sutton interrupts with irritation, "Your Honour, to save zees Court's time, we will concede that Yehoshua Binyamin ben Aharon Gershon's relationship with You is in good standing."

The Judge looks piercingly at M. Sutton. "I will not caution you this second time, M. Sutton, your words will have repercussions outside this courtroom." He raps the gavel twice to seal The Judgement. He turns to me. "Mr. Cohen, your work here defending Kayin and Yehoshua has been well-meaning --even quite effective--," He glances at M. Sutton and then back to me, "but you must now focus your defense on the defendant."

I look at the witness box. Josh is gone.

"He has no defense, Your Honour. He is wasting zees Court's time with distractions and delays. He's been doing zees his whole life; zees is just more of the same."

The Judge regards my confusion. "It was you who requested this, Mr. Cohen. From the beginning."

The courtroom swirls around me like a tornado. Fast and dizzying. Then slower. Slower. It comes to rest in a hospital scene. Spread out before me is Josh's room, when I first met Rabbi Friedler. The tefillin on my arm, the words of entreaty I prayed to be able to plead the case. In vivid detail, I relive the moment, "Master of the Universe, please grant me a hearing that I might bring my legal skills to bear in entreating You to -- restore", and the interrupting flash of lightning which leaves me gazing at my own reflection as I conclude, "...him."

I said 'him' while looking at my own image. Trapped, cornered.

I said 'him' while contemplating myself.

"It was my own suffering?" My voice rises, "My own restoration?! That's what this is about? Me? This is about me?!" Dread clenches my stomach. My legs shake. I steady myself on The Judge's railing.

The Judge answers, "You have not wanted to see it, and you have refused to hear it, but it has always been so."

It's about what it's always about.

"Cain, Josh, and now-- I'm defending myself, too? I'm supposed to-- I'm supposed to defend the world?"
I sway unsteadily. The Judge blurs, recedes.
"No!" I shake my head rapidly. "No, no, no! All this work, and now-- Impossible! It's too much. Too much!" I turn, wiping my hand across my nose, striding away--
away from the graveside,
away from the pine box,
away from the echoing strains of the mourner's kaddish--
Yisgadal, v'yiskadash...
Through my tears, I see my mother, white as chalk, pale and withdrawn at the couch by the defense table.
You don't understand, Mom! You don't understand!
Maybe the boy's just overtired, Myra.
It's the shock, the loss-- at such a tender age, poor thing.
Maybe he just needs a good rest, a good rest.
I pivot, facing The Judge one last time. "The defense rests!"
Out of here.
In slow motion,
I turn,
leaving.
Passing the table,
Rabbi Friedler stretches impossibly across, reaching for my hand,

"But you can do it, son."
I pull back.
My elbow
grazes the table,
the manila folder empties
towards the floor.
The papers swirl.
I am caught
in the whirlwind
of legal arguments.
Arms flail,
I fight forward.
Stumbling,
I run
blindly.
The back of the courtroom.
Rear door.
Exit.
My right hand clenches
the knob,
wrenching the wood panel
open.
My left foot
crossing the threshold,
the gavel thunders.

Me
Any news?

Cindy
They wheeled him to
surgery at 8:30am.
Now just waiting.

Must be tough.

It's hard. Nice to
have my mom here.

Thoughts are with you.

Thanks, Larry.

If it goes well, they
finish around noon.

Should I visit then?

They're not sure
when he'll wake up,
could be hours later.

OK.

I could text you.

That's OK; I'm sure
you have other things
to think about.
I'll check back later.

OK, thanks.

<u>Me</u>
Bridge still on?

<u>Andy</u>
You know it, Counselor

Dinner + game?

Game only.
Drinks with Katrina.

Katrina?

Usher@Ordway. Russian.
Did "eye of needle" work?

Worked 4 Josh.

?

Case turned on head.
All about ME.
Walked out.

Walked out?

Woke up throwing left leg
over side of bed,
crashing to floor.

Painful. So?

Defense rested.

Won?

Lost. Don't care.
Glad to be done.

Gotcha.

Looking forward to sleeping
through night again.

Cool. Gotta go.

Guess Dr. Silverberger was right. Dreams were about me and whatever damaged neurons are left from my childhood trauma. Unbelievable that twenty-three years later this is all catching up with me. But maybe that's what happens when your best friend goes under the scalpel for brain cancer. Stuff comes up. Weird how the psyche works: Cain, God, and all that. Would have thought dream would be an image of Dad, or funeral or something obvious.

These journal entries are a waste of time. Read back over a few of them and they're all over the place, wandering thoughts and half-baked theories on what may or may not be going on. Tripping in my mind, while Josh has been fighting for his life. Wanting to be able to "do something", when there's nothing you can do.

He's going to be okay, or he's not. Not much sense in going on and on about it in a journal, or round and round about it in my head. Dr. Silverberger may think it helps to write in here, but I don't see it. Sometimes he seems like he really knows what he's doing; sometimes he acts like a clueless, overeducated idiot.

I've been acting like a bit of an idiot myself. Dabbling in magical thinking to make sense of nonsensical dreams.

With "dream court" over, I should be able to sleep and enjoy the almost-two weeks of "vakay" I still have left. Maybe I could take a road trip somewhere.

<u>**Cindy**</u>

He's back from surgery.

<u>**Me**</u>

How did it go?

Surgeon said "clean" operation; no complications!

Great news!

What a relief!
I'm crying!

So he's in the clear?

He's still sleeping.
They'll check brain
function when he wakes,
but surgeon optimistic.

That's good.

Then radiation for six
weeks, chemo for a year.

Oh.

Yes, long road. But like he says,
"A journey of a thousand kilometers
begins with the first little step
measured in centimeters."

That's Josh all right.

I'll let you know when he wakes up.
Thanks for your support, Larry.

Welcome.

Cindy,
He woke up!

Me
Great!

Groggy from meds, but
brain functions normal!

Fantastic news!
Thanks.

Nurse suggests visitors
wait until tomorrow.

OK, will plan
to see him then.

Thanks, Larry.

Strange going to bed without preparing for the case. Funny what you get used to, I guess.

Dr. Silverberger tomorrow. Maybe he can help with this lethargic, empty feeling. Just dragging all day.

Seeing Josh might help, too.

And a good night's sleep couldn't hurt, either.

In the deserted courtroom,
an old man stoops over a puddle of papers,
scooping them slowly into a manila folder.

He straightens and sets the folder carefully on
the table.

He eases down into the wooden chair,
removing his cowboy hat and white beard.
He sets them next to the folder.

He covers his face with his hands.
Beneath the dark suit fabric, his shoulders
shake quietly.

The scene fades to black, as a mournful distant
shofar sounds.

61

Dr. Silverberger wore an expression of concern. It looked genuine enough. Maybe he practiced it in the mirror. It could be. But then again, maybe he had chosen this profession because his heart naturally engaged with total strangers who were on the verge of mental collapse.

I had narrated the events since we had last met, including the "it's about me" dream, the pervasive emptiness throughout the day that followed, and the forlorn figure in my dream last night.

He said, "It sounds like these feelings of sadness and hollowness from our last session stayed with you throughout the past two days, even seeping into your dream last night."

I nodded. "It was the saddest thing ever."

"Say more about that."

"It was like... it was like maybe Rabbi Friedler had given up on me? Like he was so disappointed with me... that he... that he just set his hat and beard down on the table and just sat there, crying." I started tearing up. "Maybe he was... done with me."

"It felt like he was giving up on you, abandoning you?"

"Kind of. I don't know. It sort of *looked* that way, but that's not quite how it felt, somehow." I couldn't pin it down. "He was definitely overflowing with sadness... You know, maybe he was sad about what had happened to me."

Dr. Silverberger gave me a few moments, and then offered, "When you first described his sitting down at the table, I thought perhaps he was so worn out from crying he had no energy left to even wear a beard or a hat."

I shrugged. "Could be." I rested my head in my hands.

"Is it possible that this figure represents a part of you that still wants to cry, that still has tears that need to be released?"

I nodded through the palms I had cupped over my face. The tears flowed freely.

Dr. Silverberger gave me a few minutes. I went through a handful of tissues. Finally, I returned my hands to my lap. I looked at the doctor. "This really sucks."

Dr. Silverberger smiled. "It's hard work, Larry."

"Is it always this painful, this filled with tears?"

"Deep work can also be uplifting, generate a feeling of wholeness," he answered. "If you're up for it, Larry, let's try something a little different that may feel more restorative." He paused. "Shall I tell you what I have in mind?"

"Sure."

"The basic idea is to experience the completion of a needed interaction that you lost out on as a child. This can sometimes be effective in training your brain along a different set of neural pathways. By going back mentally and reliving the old situation with a new ending, we free up the energy the psyche has been expending trying to figure out how to deal with an unfinished problem."

"So what does that entail?"

"Together we'll identify an old experience that you'd like to explore, and then find out what might have been missing. Then we'll replay the experience and I'll provide some of the lost interaction. Are you up for trying it?"

I nodded.

"Okay, so I want you to focus again on that empty feeling you identified last time. The hollowness in your chest... sink into that place, feel the sensations in your body..." Dr. Silverberger's voice was gently hypnotic. "Do any images come up for you?"

"It's the casket at my father's funeral... the pine box lowering into the ground..."

"Good, Larry. That was a profound loss for you... the loss of your father... Stay with that feeling of loss... And now... I want you to think of another time, another place where you experienced pain resulting from that loss. Some situation where you needed your father there, and felt the absence of his presence..."

I nodded as the image took hold.

"Tell me what you see," Dr. Silverberger prompted.

"We're at the dinner table... I have news from school... I won the playground race and I want to tell the story, want to see his smile... his laugh... his..." I trailed off.

"If he were there, one more time, what is the one thing you would want him to say or do?"

"Mmm... I would want him to turn to me, ruffle my hair the way he used to do, and say, 'Well done, little Reuven; well *done*!'"

"So let me try that out, Larry. I'm going to try rehearsing that to sound like your father, and I want you to direct me, so I get it as close as possible, okay?"

"Okay."

"Well done, little Reuven! Well done!"

"No. It's more... relaxed. Like it was the most natural thing in the world."

"Well done, little Reuven; well done!"

"Better... a little more emphasis on the 'done'."

"Well done, little Reuven; well *done*!"

"Yeah." I couldn't believe how tearful those words made me. "That's pretty good."

"Okay, now I want you to imagine that scene... dinner around the table... what's your mom putting on the table?"

"Peas... my favorite... macaroni and cheese... baked beans... milk."

"Is it warm in the room, chilly, a little drafty, stuffy?"

"Warm. A little humid. It's late spring and school is almost out."

"How does the chair feel under your legs?"

"Wooden chair, a little sticky in the heat."

"Okay, good. And now tell the playground story, just as you want your dad to hear it..."

I could feel my little chest bursting with pride; Dad would be proud. I told the story of Joey and me, racing each other around the blacktop at recess. I described the crucial moment where I dug deep inside to do my very best, and Micah holding up my arms in triumphant victory. I had been elated; I had done the impossible.

I looked to Dr. Silverberger.

"Well done, little Reuven; well *done*!"

I lost it. I cried out. I was a mess of tears. I curled up in a little ball as my chest heaved. I held my knees to my chest and bawled and bawled.

Dr. Silverberger laid his hand on my shoulder and told me I was doing great. I wadded up a ball of tissues and soaked them under each eye in turn.

The feelings came in waves, and then, finally, it all subsided.

"So how do you feel?"

"It's... like a weight lifted; I feel so light. Like I'm floating."

"And how does that hollow place feel, in your chest?"

"Better. Not so empty. A little filled in somehow."

Dr. Silverberger nodded. After a few moments, he asked, "Would you like to do that again?"

I nodded like a small child. This was the best ice cream treat ever.

We did the exercise three more times, and then it was time to wrap up. Dr. Silverberger checked in on the hollow spot, and I reported that it felt about two-thirds filled in.

He confirmed our appointment for Monday, reminding me that we were skipping Friday due to his taking off two days this year for the Jewish holiday. He reiterated that we had done some good work today. For homework, he suggested I journal about the feelings that had come up, and identify other situations where I felt a strong loss of my father.

Then he surprised me, "Shana Tovah, Larry."

"Um, Shana Tovah." I answered. "That's 'Happy New Year', right?"

He smiled. "Yes, Rosh Hashanah is tonight, so the new year is upon us."

62

I drove to the hospital. I arrived as Josh, in head bandages that made him look like a mummy, was slowly finishing the food on his hospital tray. For some reason my eyes were drawn to his 24-hour clock. 14:20. Cindy, noticing my glance, commented, "That's the exact time Josh woke up yesterday! 14:20!"

Josh seemed a bit out of it, slow to respond, sluggish in his movements. Cindy helped him with his fork, while explaining to me that this was to be expected while he was on the heavy narcotic painkillers. The nurse had said he was doing well.

Out of the corner of my eye, I caught a familiar thin figure in a black suit walk past in the hallway. "Excuse me a minute, I think I just saw somebody I know!" I poked my head into the hallway and looked to the right. "Sruli?"

He turned around. "Reb Reuven! Good to see you."

"Nice to see you, too. What brings you here?"

"I was seeing Dr. Beker."

My eyes widened. This was the oncology ward and Sruli was seeing a doctor--

"No, no." Sruli waved his hand in negation. "Dr. Beker is a PhD. Sociology or social work or something. Sweetest man you'd ever meet. I was just checking in on him for my dad. Tonight's Rosh Hashana, you know, and my dad couldn't make it over, so he sent me."

"Nice."

"You?"

"My friend Josh." I pointed to the room. "Just out of

surgery."

"How'd he do?"

"They say it went well. He's a bit sluggish from the meds, but I guess he's okay." I tried to remember what I had wanted to ask him by cell phone yesterday, while I was in the car with Rabbi Friedler. "Say, Sruli, what was it you were trying to tell me the other morning at the synagogue? You said something as you were walking out, sounded kind of like a sneeze..?"

"It's you!"

"Huh?"

"I had said, 'It's you!' You were called up to the Torah for the Kohen aliyah. Reuven ben Michael Aba, right?"

"Yeah."

"That's 416!"

"What?"

"The gematria! In Hebrew, Reuven is spelled: *Raysh-aleph-vav-beis-nun*, that's 259," Sruli's eyes got bright as he did the math. "Ben: *beis-nun* for 52, making 311. Michael: *mem-yud-chaf-alef-lamed* for 101, bringing it to 412. And lastly Aba: *alef-beis-alef* for 4, for a total of 416! See?! It's you, Reb Reuven. 416 is you!"

I steadied myself on the corridor wall. The very letters of my Hebrew name added up to 416.

I tried to compose myself. "You're, um, sure on the math?"

"I checked it a few times to be sure."

"Amazing." I felt a need to move, to leave the hallway. "Say, Sruli, you should meet my friend, Josh; he's right in here, and he's a numbers whiz, too." I started leading Sruli into the room and realized I had chosen the wrong occasion for an introduction. "Although right now," I whispered, "he's kind of out of it from the medication."

Sruli entered and I introduced him to Josh and Cindy as the son of the rabbi with whom I had been studying. "And he's amazing with numbers and Hebrew letters." I explained to Cindy the significance of 416, as a wake-up time, as a Biblical reference, and, incredibly, as the sum of the numerical values of the letters comprising my name.

"That's really something!" Cindy said appreciatively. "So then what about 1420?" She turned to Sruli. "Does that number have any special significance? That's the time Josh woke up yesterday *and* the time that Larry came in today."

Sruli looked up at the ceiling for a few long moments. "Well, nothing comes immediately to mind," he apologized. "Sometimes it takes a while to make a connection."

I said, "Maybe there's a corresponding chapter-and-verse in the Bible?"

Cindy was ready to put her Catholic education to good use. "Which book?"

"I don't know. Mine was in Genesis."

Cindy rifled through her purse, pulling out a pocket edition of the King James Bible. "Let's see, Genesis... 14:20... here it is... '*And blessed be the most high God, which hath delivered thine enemies into thy hand. And he gave him tithes of all.*'" She tried to hide her disappointment. "Doesn't seem related to Josh and his surgery, though."

I shrugged it off. "Well, it might not mean anything that the numbers on the clock displayed 14:20 when I walked in. You're sure that's when Josh woke up yesterday?"

Josh, quiet up until that point, repeated dully, "Numbers on the clock."

"*Numbers!*" Cindy paged through her Bible. Catholics were persistent. "The Book of Numbers... 14:20... '*And the LORD said, I have pardoned according to thy word.*'"

It was Sruli's turn to be surprised. "*Salachtee keedvarecha!*"

I turned. "You know the verse?"

"It's a famous *pasuk* in the Torah. Moshe Rabbeinu pleads with Hashem to once again forgive the stubborn and stiff-necked Israelites --that's us!-- and He does. In response to Moshe's prayer, Hashem says, '*Salachtee keedvarecha*'. 'I have pardoned according to your word.'"

Josh's promise from yesterday echoed in my mind. I had pressed him to swear that he would reconsider the existence of a personal God. *I give you my word I will contemplate it with an open mind.* That's what Josh had said. "I give you *my word.*"

Sruli grinned. "It's what we're all praying for on Rosh Hashanah!"

My mind shifted gears suddenly. "So, Sruli, what's the gematria for the name--" I searched my memory. "Yehoshua Binyamin ben Aharon Gershon?"

"My... name," said Josh absently. Cindy smiled down at him.

"Well, let's see. 'Yehoshua': *yud* followed by *hay-vav-shin-ayin* is 391; 'Binyamin': *bais-nun-yud-mem-yud-nun* is 162, making 553. 'Ben' is 52 again, for 605. 'Aharon': *alef-hay-raysh-nun* is 256 making 861, and finally 'Gershon': *gimmel-raysh-shin-vav-nun* is 559. And that's..." A big smile broke out on Sruli's glowing face. "1420."

Cindy looked at him in disbelief. "Really? That's amazing!"

Sruli mentally checked his math. "Yup. 1420." He smiled. Then he noticed the clock again. "Well, I'll need to leave you folks to ponder the imponderables of gematria without me; Ta is expecting me back at the house. Nice meeting you both. May you have a complete and speedy recovery, Yehoshua. A *gut yontif*, everyone; Shana Tova."

"I'll walk you out, Sruli." Over my shoulder I announced, "Back in a minute."

In the hallway, I let loose. "That's freaking unbelievable, Sruli! Josh's name is 1420. He woke up yesterday at 14:20, I walked in today at 14:20, and, in Numbers, 14:20 God proclaims, 'I pardoned according to your word'. Is *everything* a coded message? Is the whole world filled with these mathematical connections, custom-sent by God?"

"Well," Sruli hesitated, "it depends on how you want to see it. A skeptic would say that if you looked through all the books of the Bible and checked 14:20 in each one of them, you could always find some verse applicable to your situation. And they would have a point, right? You could argue that since we're expecting to find something, we interpret the verse as containing a message."

"But Josh's *name*?"

"Well, for his name, I used the standard Biblical spellings, and the gematria did total 1420. But--" Sruli shrugged, "Yehoshua is sometimes spelled with an additional *'vav'* before the last letter. So if you used that spelling, the gematria would total 1426. Nothing miraculous there, right?"

I could hardly speak from bewilderment. "Sruli, don't *you* see God's Hand in this?"

Sruli smiled at his shoes. "Sure, that's the way I see things. Every experience is brought to us by The Master." He looked up, his eyes searching my face. "But, Reb Reuven... *you* have to decide how *you* want to see things. Nobody else can do that for you."

I shook my head. "Okay, so even if I chose to be the skeptic, how could I possibly explain away my own gematria of 416?"

"Let's see... Reuven ben Michael Aba..." Sruli looked up to the ceiling for inspiration. "Ah, but you're a Kohen, right? So your full name is actually Reuven ben Michael Aba *haKohen*. Including 'haKohen' would add, um, 80 to your gematria and bring the total to 496. No relation to 416 at all."

I shook my head in disbelief. Everything was turning upside-down. Dr. Silverberger wishes me "Shana Tovah"; Sruli suggests the gematria and chapter-and-verse numbers are just coincidence. 1420 becomes 1426. 416 becomes 496. Just when you thought you knew where something stood, it moved to some other spot. Was everything in a constant state of flux? With every moment, did you have to reformulate how you were going to interpret your experience? Decide anew which frame of reference you were going to use?

Sruli interrupted the thoughts swirling in my head.

"Say, if you need a place for services tonight, you're welcome to join us. Mincha starts at 6:25."

"Thanks, Sruli."

Watching his retreating figure down the hall, I tried to imagine what it would be like to attend Rosh Hashanah services at the Neener synagogue. I would be lost in a sea of Hebrew.

It was nice to be invited. And at least their services were starting at six-twenty-something. I would have lost my grip on my dwindling sanity if they were starting at 4:16.

63

Back home, I sat in my chair. I hadn't been to Rosh Hashana services in years, but somehow it felt like I ought to go. Maybe it was the promise to Moses to be open to the tradition of my forefathers. Maybe it was the time I had been spending with Rabbi Friedler. I just had an itch, like I should be a part of it. But nothing felt right.

I flipped through the cable channels. I watched the end of an old Clint Eastwood movie, and then tried an Alfred Hitchcock that I had seen before, but there was no suspense to it. Even the sports channel had nothing good. After a few tries at comedy shows I gave up, turning off the television with vague disappointment.

I surfed the web, reading news sites, Facebook and a few blogs I followed. Nothing held my interest. I picked up my therapy journal and stared at the blank page for several minutes. Nothing.

Finally, I ate and decided to turn in early. Maybe a good night's sleep would cleanse my mind. I brushed my teeth. The man in the mirror stared back at me vacantly. Like a stranger I hadn't yet met.

I turned out the light and got into bed. The sad emptiness of last night's dream resurfaced; the old man alone in the empty courtroom. Somehow it reminded me of the lonely landscape of my life over the past few weeks.

Someday soon, surely, my life would get back to normal. Someday soon I would be back at work and back in a comforting daily routine. Someday, and it had better be soon, Larry the Lawyer would carry the day once again.

I am standing in the courtroom staring down at the table.
Two thumbs pressing on formica.
No purpose in sight.

Where have all the flowers gone
Long time passing
Where have all the flowers gone
Long time ago

The Judge sits, the gavel sounds.
"This court is now in session. You may be seated."
We sit.
"The defendant will please rise."
I stand. Why is this still going on? What's the point?
"Reuven ben Michael Aba haKohen, you have been charged with the crime of Kayin ben Odom. Given the evidence presented by the prosecution and the lack of refutation of the charges by the defense, this Court finds you guilty as charged."
Two sharp raps of the gavel seal my fate in successive heartbeats.

The Judge leans forward. "Before sentencing, Reuven ben Michael Aba haKohen, is there anything you would like to say on your own behalf?"

The sun shines down.
A simple pine box descends into the earth.
Slowly, the gathered bereaved sprinkle dirt in the rectangular opening with shovels provided for the purpose.
No one speaks.
No one knows what to say.

"No, Your Honor; there is nothing to say."

There is no compassion in this courtroom, only the heavy formality of justice impartially administered.
"In considering your sentence, The Court notes your work on behalf of Kayin ben Odom and Yehoshua Binyamin ben Aharon Gershon. Also, your recent mitzvot, including the laying of tefillin and the study of Torah, are duly acknowledged."
Great.
Thanks a lot.
Glad you noticed, Pops.
"Weighed against that, we see in your most recent behavior a continued rebellious anger that you allow to rule your actions."
I expect M. Sutton to be smiling triumphantly, but he is pallid and silent, staring blankly down at his table.
"Because of this poisonous root of anger, and the crime that has grown from it--

Behold:
Your relationships shall be cursed.
Intimacy and fellowship will not blossom for you, and you will wander from one relationship to another throughout your days."

Too much. A pariah throughout my days?
This is not right. Not right.
Rabbi Friedler, Sr., with moist eyes, squeezes my hand before I snatch it away.
The Judge raises the gavel.
No, no, no! You can't do this.
Is there no escape?
Where can I run to, where can I hide?
I crouch, my hamstrings taut.
I look to the rear door.
I look back to The Judge.
It's not fair. It's not fair!
This is a setup. It's not my fault.
It's Your doing! You're The One pulling the strings here!
You're The One running the world!
YOU KILLED MY FATHER
With all my might, I release my coiled strength, launching myself at The Judge,
flying through air,
menacing hands stretched out towards Him--

64

Wham!

My head crashed into the headboard in a painful awakening.

Slowly, I rolled over on my back. I touched my forehead gingerly. Ouch. That really hurt. Nasty. I was going to have a bad bruise.

As I got up, I noticed the clock. 4:15. I looked again. There it was, stubbornly shining in red. 4:15. Now *that* was strange.

I went to the kitchen and dug some frozen peas out of the freezer. Ah. Much better. The cold felt wonderful on my wound.

Actually, I was surprised to realize that despite the head injury, I felt pretty good all the way around. Lighter and more energetic, somehow. Even though I had lost this "court case" and been "sentenced" to the life of a pariah, I actually felt great. It was as if a burden had been lifted, my load had been lightened. I felt myself looking forward to the day.

Maybe it was because the sentencing brought distinct closure to these dreams, a tangible conclusion to the whole ordeal. Or maybe it was the result of the therapy sessions with Dr. Silverberger. I had felt a similar bounce in my step when I had left his office yesterday. No doubt Rabbi Friedler would ascribe it to the beginning of the new Jewish year -- a fresh start. To each his own.

As Sruli had said, *I* had to decide how *I* was going to see things. And I, Larry Cohen, aka Reuven ben Michael Aba *haKohen*, was deciding that I was not going to care about it. No need to figure it out at all. Let it be 4:16 every morning, or let it be 4:15, like *this* morning. Either way was fine. I wasn't going to spend my time worrying about it; I was going to spend my time enjoying the day.

And the best way to enjoy *this* morning felt like a substantial workout with weights at the JCC. I gathered my gym bag and filled my water bottle at the kitchen sink. I was just debating whether to check online to confirm that they opened at 5:30, when I realized that they would be closed for Rosh Hashana.

I put away my bag and changed into my running clothes.

I stretched out on my stoop and hit the road. There were a few joggers on the path, and dog owners on their morning walks. A large man with a small pooch looked at me accusingly. His look seemed to say, "Aren't you supposed to be getting ready for synagogue?"

A few blocks later, a professional runner in spandex, presumably training for October's marathon, looked me up and down as he passed. What was up with these people?

A thin woman leaning over her Rottweiler turned her head and said, "Are you *sure* you're not going? Everyone else will be there."

I shortened my run and looped back southwards. I shook my head at myself as I realized she must have been talking to someone else on her phone.

Back home, I showered and sat down to my laptop. I checked my email. I still hadn't responded to my uncle. I hit 'Reply' and started composing.

Dear Uncle Nate,

Great to hear back from you, and nice that things are going so well for you and your family there in California. It's funny to think of Jake as a college senior! When I last saw him, he must have been a toddler. I still remember your visit where he rode my old red tricycle up and down the sidewalk in front of our house. Over and over again he pedaled past us, so happy to have mastered the pedals. Now that I think about it, I actually have a double picture frame somewhere that captured the moment; on the right, him on the tricycle beaming, and on the left, me, at the same age, riding the same tricycle, with the same celebratory smile. If you want, I could scan it and send you a copy.

With the kids away, are you having that "empty nest" thing going? I remember Mom had the hardest time adjusting after Jessi got married and moved to Ann Arbor a year and a half ago.

Do you travel over the summer at all? It'd be great to see you again.

Love,
Larry

After I sent it, I realized that it might strike him as odd that I was using my computer on the holiday itself, but-- what can you do? It would probably be fine. He knew I wasn't Orthodox. And besides, he was family.

65

I had the whole day open. No legal preparations, no meetings with rabbis, no appointment with Dr. Silverberger. I could do whatever I wanted.

I picked up lunch at the Lunds deli and took it down to Hidden Falls.

Turning from the stone steps to walk up towards the waterfall itself, I saw a lone figure ahead of me in a dark suit, bending over the water. A smile came to my lips as I drew closer and saw a black cowboy hat over a grey beard. "Rabbi Friedler!"

He turned around, straightening at his name. "Reb Reuven! A *gut yontif!* How nice to see you."

"Shana Tova, Rabbi. Happy Rosh Hashanah. What are you doing?" I nodded at the breadcrumbs in his hand.

"Ah, this. The traditional ritual of *tashlich.* Casting our sins into the water." He smiled. "It's hard to get a grip on the sin itself, so we use a symbol to show our desire to be rid of them. Most Neeners just shake our ritual fringes towards the water, but I like to scatter breadcrumbs the way my father did, may his memory be for a blessing. We used to come down here together when I was a boy." He nodded his head slowly in fond remembrance. "I remember he would always look carefully to make sure there were no fish in the water..."

"Is that common, to follow in your father's footsteps when it comes to tradition and rituals, even if it's not what the others do?" I motioned to his breadcrumbs and his cowboy hat.

"Well, there *is* a strong emphasis on respecting your father, and continuing his practices, but there are also times to adopt the community's customs, too. It's a delicate balance."

"How did your father come to wear a cowboy hat? Was he from the South?"

Rabbi Friedler laughed. "Oh, no! My father never wore a cowboy hat. Although he *is* the reason I wear one." Rabbi Friedler smiled to himself. "Would you like to hear a story, Reb Reuven?"

"Sure."

Rabbi Friedler resumed his slow tossing of breadcrumbs into the stream.

"When I was a young boy, during my bar mitzvah preparations, I became enthralled with the Rebbe's teachings. I would secretly read his writings from the weekly Neener magazine, which I smuggled home when my school buddy was done with it. You see, Reb Reuven, my father was quite anti-Neener in those days. He thought they were cultish, close-minded, even heretical." Rabbi Friedler nodded at my surprise. "Oh, yes. In those days, Neeners were quite controversial. Well, after my bar mitzvah, my parents were considering where I should attend yeshiva. We visited different schools, sometimes together, or sometimes just me going for a Shabbos or overnight. It was quite an exciting project.

"And somehow, I got it in my mind that I wanted to attend the Neener yeshiva in New York. I knew my father would never allow it, so I made my case to my mother. She was moved by my excitement, as I had hoped she would be. She had always prayed I would go beyond mastering the forms and rituals and develop a passion for serving Hashem. So when she saw me filled with such enthusiasm, it really touched her."

Rabbi Friedler dusted his hands from the last of his breadcrumbs.

"So she and my father stayed up late into the night one Friday night, going back and forth about it. He thought it would be throwing away my future, and she argued it would be good for my soul. In the end, my father agreed to let me go visit and see what the school was like." Rabbi Friedler sighed. "It was quite a concession for him."

"So what happened?"

"Well, a week before the trip, my mother read over the list of things I was supposed to bring for my weekend stay, and it included a black hat for Shabbos. Now, my father sometimes wore a hat, but he had no tolerance for the Hassidic style of dress, and he thought wearing fancy hats was superficial and ostentatious. At first he refused to throw away good money on a hat that he was convinced I would wear only once. But then he came home, the day before my trip, with a black cowboy hat, and announced that this was my hat to wear to the Neener yeshiva."

"Wow."

"Oh, yes, it created quite a stir. My mother was abashed that he would even consider sending such a hat, and I was terrified at the teasing I would suffer if he made me take it on the visit. But he held firm. My mother put in a call to the yeshiva, and apparently they in turn called the Rebbe, and the message they returned to her was that I was to wear the hat that my father had selected for me. That was a quote directly from the Rebbe. 'He should wear the hat his father has selected for him.' And I did."

"Did the other kids make fun of you?"

"Oh, no; the head of the yeshiva saw to that. He made sure all the boys knew that the Rebbe himself had instructed me to wear this particular hat. I think some of them were actually kind of jealous." Rabbi Friedler smiled. "It's funny how things turn out."

"So what happened when you got back?"

Rabbi Friedler gestured for us to start walking back towards the stone steps. "I told my parents all about the place, no doubt gushing with all the details of the stories the rabbis told, and the warm welcome I received from the other boys there. And my father interrupted, 'And you wore that hat?'. 'Yes, sir,' I answered, 'I wore the hat my father had selected for me.' It made quite an impression on him, the respect that the Rebbe had shown him. And after that, he agreed that I could go, and he made his peace with it. Amazing, really; my father could be quite a stubborn man."

"That's quite a story."

"Well, the Rebbe is quite a rebbe," returned Rabbi Friedler. "And I've worn a cowboy hat ever since."

R. Friedler turned to face me in the shade where the stone steps led up to the street.

"That's quite a bruise you have there, Reb Reuven."

"I banged my head waking up recently."

"Mmm?"

"Last night was the sentencing in dream court; it

wasn't so pleasant."

"Oh, I'm sorry to hear that, Reb Reuven."

"Well, it's okay. At least it's over now." I looked up the steps and back to Rabbi Friedler, but he made no move to the stairs. "And the oddest thing is, I woke up at 4:15. It's off by one from the usual time. What do you make of that?"

"I could ask Sruli," offered Rabbi Friedler, still peering at my wound. "I'm afraid gematria isn't my strength."

The mention of Sruli reminded me that initially the gematria expert had approached 416 by taking 613, adding one for God, and then reversing the result. If, in gematria, the number one represented God...

"The thing is, Rabbi... waking up at 4:15... If 416 is me, then I guess 415 is... me minus one."

"Mmm?"

"Well, if God is, like, The One... Do you think that means... something about me being left without...?" I pointed upwards.

"Enh." Rabbi Friedler tilted his head with a grimace. "He does work in mysterious ways, but..." His spotted hand rose up to caress the greying beard as his eyes lost focus towards our feet. "Maybe if we look at the text..." Rabbi Friedler had no problem visualizing the text without the book in front of him. "In Bereishis, 4:16 was the *pasuk* of Kayin leaving Hashem and settling in Nod... that means 4:15 would be the preceding verse, the *pasuk* where Hashem gives Kayin the sign."

"Marking him so everybody knows he killed his brother, right?"

"No, no. Remember, Kayin was worried that anyone he met would kill him? Hashem was guarding over him. Hashem gave him a sign which announced to the world that Kayin was under Divine Protection, no matter where he might wander." Rabbi Friedler looked at me. "Perhaps, Reb Reuven, you should take 415 as a sign that Hashem is watching over you, no matter where you go."

66

I was eating dinner with Andy on Sunday evening at Jillz, and he was expressing incredulity, in his inimitable East Coast style, at the innocuous question I had put to him a moment before.

"*Of course* I'm going to services on Saturday, it's *Yom Kippur!* What kind of question is that?!"

"So Andy," I affected my best New York accent as I looked at his bacon cheeseburger, "lemme get this straight--"

"Yeah, yeah, very funny." He took a swig of his beer. "But it's tradition, Counselor. It has precedence. You don't question it, you just gotta *do* it. *Kol Nidrei!* Believe, don't believe, whatever you want. But a Jew's gotta be in shul on Yom Kippur to hear *Kol Nidrei*; that's all there is to it."

"And that's that?"

"And that's that."

I shrugged. "So what synagogue are you going to?"

"Temple Elazar. Actually, it's right near you, just off the Mississippi River Boulevard, near Randolph. Conservative, mixed seating, and the rabbi doesn't know what he's talking about, but, hey, once a year, you gotta do what you gotta do." He looked at me. "You wanna go?"

"Well..."

"They do have parts in English, if that helps."

"Yeah, sure, I guess."

"So what's the problem?"

"Well, I totally missed Rosh Hashana..."

"What, you're worried they keep score, Counselor? You think they have a clipboard at the door to know who's been naughty and who's been nice? No, they let in any yid who wants to daven there. And for some reason, every year they always send me an extra ticket." A new thought struck him. "Besides, with that lump on your forehead, you look like you just bested a thug in a bar fight; none of those aging Jews are going to mess with you!"

I looked at my last few bites of cheeseburger. "The thing is, Andy... wasn't Rosh Hashanah the Day of Judgement and all that?"

"Yeah. What's that got to do with it?"

"Well, if the judgement is already made--?"

"Oh, I see where you're going. The whole religious bit." Andy shook his head. "No, Counselor, you forget you're dealing with Jews. It even says in the prayerbook, 'On Rosh Hashanah it is written, and on *Yom Kippur* it is sealed'. See, Jews always run late. So even though they're theoretically *supposed* to spend the entire preceding month of Elul doing all of their 'fearless and searching moral inventory' and making amends to the people they've hurt, and appear all ready before The Judge on Rosh Hashanah, the Day of Judgement-- the truth is that it's not until the day actually arrives that Jews finally start *doing* anything!"

"Wait, so Rosh Hashana, the 'Day of Judgement' is just the *beginning*?"

Andy's voice took on a mocking tone. "The *theory* is that once the sensitive Jewish soul somehow hears, or senses, the severity of the decree On High, he trembles down to his very core. He's supposed to spend the days between Rosh Hashanah and Yom Kippur scurrying around fixing up his relationships. Then, on Yom Kippur, he skips gaily back into shul and begs His Almighty Holiness to change His Mind and take it easy on him in the coming year."

"That does ring a distant childhood bell. It's a second chance. Like a motion to appeal after the verdict has been handed down."

"Exactly. Speaking of which," Andy stabbed a well-manicured forefinger in my direction, "I think you should appeal your dream court case!"

I shrugged. I had brought Andy up to date on the details of the case earlier. I had left out the part about the 416 gematria of my name, but otherwise had told him everything. In truth, I was happy to be totally done with the case, and I wouldn't have a clue how to initiate an appeal, even if it were possible to do so. But it was an interesting thought experiment.

"An appeal on what grounds?"

"On the grounds that you were misled about what the whole case was about!"

"Yeah, I certainly felt misled." I finished my burger and the last few fries. "But I think that was my fault. In that first dream, I was the one who didn't hear the announcement --or didn't *want* to hear the announcement-- that the defendant was Reuven ben Michael Aba haKohen..."

"Hmm, nice name."

"Thanks." I thought I heard something more than politeness in Andy's voice. "Something unusual about it?"

"Enh, not particularly. *Your* name has 'son' in it; your *father's* name has 'father' in it." He shrugged it off.

"How's that?"

"Well..." Andy seemed reluctant to bring his yeshiva learning to bear, now that the case was over. "'Reuven' is composed of the two words *'re-oo'* and *'ben'*. The translation could be 'Behold, a son', or something like that."

"And my dad's name, 'Michael Aba'?"

"'Michael is three words *'Mi'*, *'ka'* and *'eil'* which is 'Who is like God?'. And of course *'aba'* means father."

"So together it's like asking a question, 'Who is like God, father?'"

"Yeah." Andy nodded. "Or, it's a question and answer together. 'Who is like God?', with the answer 'Father'. Whatever."

Rabbi Friedler had said a person's name alluded to the essence of their mission in this world.

"So what's your Hebrew name, Andy?"

Andy lifted his eyebrows with a shrug. "Avidan ben Tzion ben Feivel haKohen."

"Wait, that's three names. You're including your father *and* your grandfather?"

Andy smiled and shook his head. "'Bentzion' is one name. Avidan Bentzion ben Feivel."

"So what does it mean?"

He sighed. "'Avidan' is a combination of 'father' and 'judgement' or 'judge'. And 'Bentzion' is a combination of 'son' and 'Zion'."

"So *your* name has father and son in it, too."

"Yeah, I guess. I never thought of it that way."

Something felt important here, but I couldn't quite see what it might be.

"And what does 'Feivel' mean?"

"I'm not sure counselor; it's Yiddish, not Hebrew. Let's take a look at that dessert menu."

67

Dr. Silverberger seemed in good spirits; the long weekend must have rejuvenated him. I asked him how the Rosh Hashanah services had been.

"Long, but good." He smiled. "The rabbi talked about our task of healing our relationships during the next ten days, and how that would situate us for a good year. It was a little simplistic, but the overall message was a good one." He looked at me. "And how was your Rosh Hashana, Larry?"

"A bit odd, actually."

"In what way?"

I told him about my ambivalence over attending services on the Rosh Hashana, and wandering down by the riverside, where I had encountered Rabbi Friedler. As I related the story, I talked about the awkwardness I felt about the future of the relationship, now that the dreams were over.

"I used to have a reason to visit the Rabbi's house, but now..."

"But now?"

I tried to explain the problem. "I just don't... I mean, I'm not going to... commit to some kind of religious obligations that might justify taking up his time. You know?"

"I can see the difficulty. You want to spend time with him, but you're not sure what he requires of you in return?"

"Something like that."

I shifted gears and told the doctor about the

sentencing dream. He nodded with interest.

"When you flung yourself towards the judge at the end, do you remember the feeling, the emotional tenor in the dream?"

"It was an odd mixture. On the one hand, I remember anger. Outrage at the injustice of it all. Like the frustration of a child not getting his way. And also..." There was something more there. I tried to wrap words around it. "I wanted to... somehow *force* him to see my point of view, I wanted him to appreciate how *I* felt, and how... crushed I was to receive such an unfair verdict."

Dr. Silverberger was putting puzzle pieces together in his mind. I looked at his thoughtful face.

"Do you see anything interesting?" I asked.

"Well... in your previous dream, where you discovered it was all about you, the anger and frustration were manifested in running out of the courtroom. So here... these same emotions were conveyed, rather dramatically, by turning towards instead of turning away."

"So that's good?"

"I would view it as encouraging." He smiled. "Also... this leap at the judge sounded beyond your normal physical abilities, right? Is this the first time you did something physically exceptional in your dreams?"

"Yes, I think so. Is that significant?"

"Could be. The feelings might come from a deeper source..."

"Maybe it's an expression of my anger towards God for my father dying? Or anger at my father for dying and leaving me alone?"

"Could be, could be. If you're open to it, Larry, we could explore it in a similar way as the transference we examined last week. Do you think you're up for something like that?"

I sighed. "That was pretty intense."

"Yes, it was," agreed the doctor. "It might be more than you want to take on today."

I thought about it. Last week's emotional sessions were tiring. Even though I had felt lighter afterwards, it had been a draining experience. On the other hand, this week was my last week of leave before returning to the office, so it was probably good to make the most of it.

Also, the dream irritated me somehow. The "Judge" had condemned me to a life of fruitless relationships due to a 'root of anger'. Who was he to make such an edict, some figure in my dream? It rankled. I could excise that 'root of anger' if I chose; my life was my own to direct. I glanced at Dr. Silverberger. He had proven himself capable last week. Surely I could trust him to guide me through this.

"Well, let's try it out. We can always stop if it's too much, right?"

"Certainly." Dr. Silverberger shifted in his chair. "Okay, Larry, I want you to relax now. Get comfortable, and take a few breaths to let the tension drain out of your body. Good. Now, focus on that moment from the dream before you lunged towards the judge. Imagine your hands, poised to reach out, your legs crouching to spring... feel that motivation, that deep anger... and as you open yourself to feeling those sensations, tell me where you feel it most strongly in your body, where is the source?"

"There's a tightness here." I pointed to my abdomen.

"Okay, good. Now focus on that tightness... see if any picture or feeling emerges."

"I see... my mother's Shabbos dress next to me on the couch... the mask of her face... the pale skin, the vacant eyes." My hands curled into fists.

"Good, Larry; very good. You're sitting on the couch, your mother is right next to you. What is happening?"

"She just told me my father died at the hospital."

Impossibly, I didn't feel sad at all; just anger, through and through.

"And what would you like to say to your mother right now?"

I hit my right knee with my right fist. Then my left knee with my left fist. Right. Left. Right. Left. I gritted my teeth.

"What would you like to say, Larry?"

I forced my mouth open. "You can't leave, Mom. You can't leave." Right. Left.

"Say more, Larry; let it out."

"Come back here, Mom. Come back here RIGHT NOW. I NEED YOU!"

"What do you need from your mother, Larry?"

"I need... I need..." I started crying and shaking my head, faster and faster.

"Say it out loud, Larry. What do you need from her?"

"But she can't give it, she can't give it!"

"That's okay, Larry. Even if she can't give it, what do you need from her?"

"I need her to tell me... it's going to be alright. It's

going to be alright... because... she's going to be there for me."

I gulped some air. I gathered some tissues and wiped my eyes.

After a few moments my heartbeat returned to normal. I breathed more easily. "That's what it is. I need her to tell me she's going to be there... to hold me. To keep me safe."

"Okay, Larry. Very good." The doctor nodded. "Now, if you're up for it, we could do the completion exercise with this, like we did last week with the dinner table memory. How would that be?"

I nodded. "That would be nice."

"Okay, so take a few moments now... imagine yourself on the couch next to your mother and tell me exactly what you needed her to say."

I brought the scene to my mind's eye again.

"I needed her to say... "

"Yes, go ahead."

It took a few moments, and then the phrases came together.

"I needed her to say, 'I will always be here to hold you, Larry; you're safe here in my arms.'"

"Very good, Larry." Dr. Silverberger auditioned a few different intonations, and when he had tuned it accurately, we went through the visualization exercise.

"You're on the couch with your mother. Feel the fabric under your legs, the warmth of your mother right next to you... You're tense, knowing something is wrong, but you're uncertain what it is... she tells you your father died..."

I relived the moment in my mind. I nodded at the doctor.

"I'll always be here to hold you, Larry; you're safe here in my arms."

As I teared up, Dr. Silverberger came around, sitting on the left armrest of the chair, to put his arm around my shoulders.

"I'll always be here to hold you, Larry; you're safe here in my arms."

I cried and cried. I leaned in to Dr. Silverberger.

Was there no end to the tears? From a deep well they flowed, on and on. The tears of a moment past, the tears of an opportunity missed. The longing of a reassuring embrace never offered. The pining for what had never been.

A long sigh escaped my lips. Finally, I straightened up and moved aside the pile of tissues that had formed on my lap. Dr. Silverberger retook his chair. We sat a few moments in silence.

"How are you feeling, Larry?"

"Drained." I looked up. "But good."

"That was good work, Larry; very nice."

"That's just amazing. I never realized how angry I've been at her... or how much I needed her to reassure me back then."

"You've been carrying that hurt alone, for a long time."

"But why wasn't she there for me? My own mother?"

Dr. Silverberger leaned back in his chair. "Perhaps she didn't have the inner resources herself. It's possible she wasn't able to give you what you needed because she had never gotten what she needed herself." Dr. Silverberger steepled his hands and regarded me thoughtfully. "Maybe that was the best she could do."

I thought about my mother, the beautiful, smiling bride of her bedside wedding portrait and the lonely shell of a woman on the couch that day. Maybe she had needed someone to tell *her* that it would be all right and she didn't have anyone. Her parents died when she was a child, a boating accident or something. There was an older aunt or distant cousin who took her in, but they were never close.

"I never thought about it like that before. I've always just thought of my mother as kind of shallow, caught up in her own world, you know? But maybe..." I searched for the right words, "maybe she just wasn't able to deal with her world crumbling like that... just not able to move past it —or 'embrace it' as you would say— and find her way... to be there for me... for us." I looked up at Dr. Silverberger. "Maybe she's kind of... a lost soul?"

Dr. Silverberger nodded slowly. "That could be, Larry."

My anger flared from nowhere. "Lost soul or not, she should have been there."

68

"Hi, Mom."

"Larry, so nice to hear from you! How are you? How was Rosh Hashanah for you?"

"I'm doing well, Mom; doing well. How was your Rosh Hashana?"

"It was just lovely. They had the same cantorial soloists as last year, and that man has just such a sweet voice..." She went on about the musical qualities of the service, the beauty of the floral arrangements, and how hard the Ritual Committee had worked to pull off such a flawless event. Apparently even Mrs. Hammerstein had been mollified.

"Say, Mom, remember you had asked about my coming down to visit for a weekend?"

"Yes, it would be great to see you for your upcoming birthday."

"Well, it turns out my friend Andy has a legal consultation in Chicago the Monday afterwards, so we're planning to drive down together Friday afternoon. And then, if you can drop me at O'Hare, there's a cheap one-way flight back Sunday night."

"Wonderful! Just wonderful, Larry! I'm so thrilled!"

"I'll be getting in kind of late Friday night --although knowing how Andy drives, you never know. I can call you along the way so you'll know when to expect me. You don't have to wait up if it's late, though."

"Well, this is just *great* news, Larry. We'll have a nice time. A little birthday celebration here at home... And I'll introduce you to the new neighbors --they have two daughters around your age, you know, and they're both quite attractive. And if you did want to speak to Mrs. Kavitz, her son got some kind of a misdemeanor ticket for drag racing his car..."

69

As I walked in, I saw Josh had only one large bandage around his forehead, looking less like a mummy and more like a recovering patient. A week since the surgery, and he was being discharged today. He looked up. "Hi there, Grasshopper-man."

"Hi there, Bandage-man. So I hear you're planning a jailbreak?"

"Heh." He looked at me with a mischievous smile. "You might say I'm a father of young children who is ready to go— home. Ready to be on the living room couch with the family all together. The nurse is supposed to be here at noon with the wheelchair. Cindy's riding shotgun."

"Wheelchair?" I turned to Cindy.

"Oh, it's just hospital policy," she reassured me. "Josh can get around with just a little help, and he should be walking unassisted in another week."

I scrunched up my face. "Confucius say, when recuperating patient is Abel... he walk with Cain."

It took him a second, and then Josh laughed. Cindy groaned and playfully pushed my arm. "Don't encourage him, Larry! I have my hands full enough with the other two kids in my charge!"

Josh shook his head, grinning. "Speaking of two," Josh said, tilting his head at me, "Cindy tells me that this '416' thing didn't have anything to do with the number two after all. It's funny; it seemed so... saturated with the powers of two: two numbers, 4, 16... and 4:16 is 256 minutes after midnight." He turned to Cindy, "Two to the power of two is four, four to the power of two is sixteen, and sixteen to the power of two is 256." He looked back to me, "But instead it was all about relationships? All about you and this personal God you've been urging me to contemplate?"

"Yeah. Kind of funny how that all turned out."

Cindy put her arm on her husband's shoulder and smiled down on his puzzled face. "But Josh, honey, aren't all relationships fundamentally about the 'power of two'?"

70

"I've been kind of dreading today's session, doctor." It was Wednesday, and I had this and one other session with the good doctor before my leave was over and I found out if I had a job.

"Quite understandable, Larry. You've been doing some intense work here. Perhaps it would be better to try something less stressful for today? What would feel like a good use of our time?"

"Well, I'm still feeling uncomfortable about the rabbi. Somehow, ever since I found out that his father never wore a cowboy hat, I've felt let down... It feels like a loss, somehow. Plus, I don't really have a reason to visit Rabbi Friedler now that the dreams are over. I mean, what would we talk about?"

Dr. Silverberger drew me out, and I talked through my ambivalence about the relationship, the fear that Rabbi Friedler might reject me if I didn't become more religious, and various possibilities for an ongoing relationship.

I didn't come to any conclusion, but at least it was helpful to think through it with someone more objective.

Then the conversation widened to other relationships, and how I might want to resolve old conflicts or reach out to people. For homework, Dr. Silverberger suggested I write a letter in my journal to each of these people, as if I were free to completely express my heart's desire for the relationship. He suggested I stick to "I" statements as much as possible, talking about my own feelings rather than focusing on other people's past actions, or what they may have done wrong.

Finally, he broached the topic of our own relationship.

"We're coming to the end of the three weeks we originally agreed to." Dr. Silverberger smiled. "You've done some wonderful work here, Larry, and I hope you're pleased with what you've been able to accomplish."

I nodded. "I am. This has been really great. Hard, but great."

"So, we have a few options here. One, we could wrap up on Friday, bringing our work to a close. And if, in the future, you wanted to return, of course I would be happy to see you. Two, you could continue to see me regularly, perhaps on a weekly basis; your insurance would cover another twelve sessions this year, and then another twenty next year, if you're on the same plan. Or third, we could do something in between."

"In between?"

"Yes, we could schedule a follow-up for six to eight weeks from now, and see how you're doing and what would make sense at that time. It's up to you." Dr. Silverberger leaned back in his chair. "And of course you don't have to decide right this moment; you can take some time to consider what feels right for you."

I decided to answer the question with a question. "How about we make a decision on Friday?"

.71

At the diner, I opened my notebook and composed some letters. The first was to Mrs. Goldstein, apologizing for not staying in touch, and expressing my hope that I would see her in ten days when I came to visit.

This was followed by a note to Mary. Just a journal entry, I reminded myself, not something I was really going to send.

> Dear Mary,
> I'm not writing to try and get back together, but I felt I owed you an apology. Even though you brought the subject of marriage up in a rather backhand way, I shouldn't have exploded. I wish I had handled that better and that we had been able to talk about our relationship more rationally.

It was a start, but I knew Dr. Silverberger would suggest I use more "I" statements without blaming her for being who she was. We had enjoyed each other's company when we were doing things together, but deeper communication never really clicked. I could remember her freckled face when she first asked about my friendship with Andy.

"So how did you two meet?"

"Uncle Hugo's."

Her eyebrows had furrowed under her neatly parted

red hair. "*Your* uncle Hugo or *his* uncle Hugo? Or are you two related?"

"No, no, the book store. Uncle Hugo's science fiction book store. It's down on Chicago."

"So you met in Chicago?"

I had explained, none too patiently, that the book store was in Minneapolis on Chicago *Avenue*, a joint building with Uncle Edgar's mystery bookstore.

"I was picking up a few books set aside for me, and Andy, standing by the register, heard the guy confirm my name, 'It's Larry Cohen?'. Not being shy, Andy asks, 'So you're a Kohen, too?!'"

She had interrupted, "Wait, so you *are* related?"

"No, we're both *Kohens*, that's the Jewish priest lineage. My last name is Cohen, his is Katz. No relation." Unless you went back umpteen years to some ancient leaders of the Jewish people or something. But of course, Mary wouldn't have known that; she had a Lutheran upbringing. I wished I could take back some of the frustration I had vented that day.

I wrote a letter to my sister Jessi, which closely resembled my apology to Mrs. Goldstein for losing contact for so long a time.

I closed the notebook, reflecting on the work I had done with Dr. Silverberger and whether it made sense to continue seeing him after this week. On the one hand, on the other hand.

I debated if I should send any of the letters I had just written. For Mrs. Goldstein it didn't make sense; I would be seeing her soon enough in person. It was surprisingly easy to send the email off to Jessi. But, then, I knew she would read it and receive it with an open heart.

But the one to Mary was harder to figure out. If I did email her, how would she take it? Still, she deserved an apology, so I tried again. After a few more attempts, I decided it was ready to send.

Dear Mary,
I hope this email finds you happy and well.
I know it might feel odd to hear from me out of the blue, but I went to see Dr. Silverberger, as you recommended, and as a result I've been reflecting on all of my relationships. Thank you for pointing me in that direction.

I want to apologize for getting so angry and harsh when you introduced the idea of marriage. You deserved to be able to discuss our relationship and its possibilities, and I am sorry I was not able to. I didn't realize how loaded the subject of marriage was for me until quite recently. Again, please accept my sincere regret.

I hope you are doing well, and I wish you joy and happiness.

Larry

.72

At home in my easy chair, I flipped through cable channels and, finding nothing, clicked the TV off. The unaddressed issue was Rabbi Friedler. I hadn't yet written to him in my journal, and I wasn't sure what I would say. He hadn't done anything wrong. Neither had I, for that matter. But somehow, with the ending of the dreams and the revelation that his father never wore a cowboy hat, the more "mystical" interpretations of my dreams had fallen flat. The hat thing really shouldn't be that important. Even setting that aside, I was still left in an awkward position where I appreciated the relationship, but had nothing to talk to him about. What do you say to somebody in that situation?

Dr. Silverberger had suggested I could thank him for his help over the past two weeks, and, if I wanted, just leave it at that. It was the best idea I had. I texted him to see when I could see him, and he suggested I come over for lunch tomorrow around noon. Consulting my busy Thursday social calendar and finding it barren, I agreed. Lunch it would be.

73—

Mrs. Friedler served grilled cheese sandwiches with sliced tomato and lettuce inside. I smiled at my thought that these were like BLTs without the bacon. Rounding out the meal was a spinach and avocado salad with creamy dressing, and sweet potato chips. The rabbi and I had the table to ourselves; Mrs. Friedler was busy in the kitchen, and Sruli was running errands. I observed that Rabbi Friedler's beard was remarkably clear of the gooey cheese filling, although a little salad dressing adhered to his mustache. He expounded on the days between Rosh Hashanah and Yom Kippur.

"We have a tradition to repair relationships during the ten days... even when we think everything is fine, and to our knowledge we haven't hurt our fellow, we still extend an apology for anything we may have inadvertently done, or left undone. Sometimes an idle remark, a word meant one way but taken another, or even a conversation brought to a close too abruptly, these can lead to a feeling of hurt, unbeknownst to us. The kind of thing that's hard to bring up, because, as we ourselves know, it is easy to feel embarrassed that such a small thing would wound us. And so during these ten days, we tend to assume that we've hurt our friends or family in some way, and we apologize, we make amends.

"So in that spirit, Reb Reuven, let me ask you for forgiveness for any way in which I might have hurt your feelings or failed to make you feel welcome or slighted you in any way." Rabbi Friedler looked directly into my eyes. "Will you accept my apology, Reb Reuven?"

"Well, I-- I mean there's nothing I can think of that you should apologize for, Rabbi Friedler. You've been only kind and helpful..."

Rabbi Friedler's cell phone rang, but he ignored it. After a few rings it was quiet again. "But, Reb Reuven, would you please accept my apology anyway, in case there might be something that you just don't recall at the moment?" Rabbi Friedler smiled into my confusion, his moist eyes crinkling into lines at the corners.

"Um, sure. I accept your apology." I was moved by the old man's sincerity. "Actually, Rabbi Friedler, I think I'm the one who owes *you* an apology."

"How's that?"

"Well, I just..." How could I explain this? "Ever since the dreams ended, I haven't really had an urgent reason to study with you, so I haven't been in touch, and it's felt, well, kind of abrupt just to stop calling. So I wanted to thank you for all your help, and say I'm sorry for just disappearing like that."

"Ah, I see." Rabbi Friedler nodded in understanding. "Well, there's no need for an apology there, either, but I will accept yours anyway, Reb Reuven. I forgive you; I forgive you; I forgive you. That's our traditional way of accepting an apology. I do confess that I've missed our study sessions; your enthusiasm has been quite invigorating for an old man."

"Well, thank you, Rabbi."

"And, Reb Reuven, any time you would like to stop by, to study or to just visit, please feel free. We would love to have you. Dreams or no dreams."

My eyes teared up. R. Friedler was a sweet man,

father figure or not. He continued, "Speaking of which, I was thinking about your dreams, Reb Reuven, and how the Judge had warned the Sutton about consequences outside the courtroom. You remember you mentioned that?"

"Yes?"

"Well, maybe your defense of Cain was more effective than you thought."

"What do you mean?"

"When you think about it, murdering his brother should have earned Cain the death penalty. So why was he instead allowed to live out his days, his only punishment being that he had to wander, and that the earth would not yield its produce to him?" Rabbi Friedler smiled a mischievous grin. "Maybe he had a good lawyer!'

"But he was punished long before my dreams ever came along."

"To The Master of the Universe, time is not so linear. He *invented* time, and His Heavenly Court stands completely outside it." R. Friedler punctuated his declaration with a strong upward thrust of his wrinkled right forefinger. "And your friend Josh is recovering--?"

"I'm sorry to interrupt," said Mrs. Friedler, poking her head out from the kitchen, "but Mrs. Beker is on the line--"

"Oh, I see. Excuse me, Reb Reuven," said R. Friedler, rising. "Let me see about this for just a minute."

And suddenly the vibrant dining room and study hall was empty and still. I was alone at the table. Rabbi Friedler's chair was empty and angled slightly to the left;

in his rising to leave he must have turned it unintentionally. It pointed towards the kitchen doorway through which he had disappeared.

It suddenly occurred to me that I had no doubt that he would return momentarily, as he had said. Unlike last week's transference exercise with Dr. Silverberger, I now only felt the slightest discomfort at his having left so suddenly. I smiled.

Rabbi Friedler returned a few moments later, taking his chair with a more somber expression on his face.

"Is everything all right, Rabbi?"

"*Baruch dayan haEmes*, Reb Reuven, blessed is The True Judge. And today He has sent some difficult news." Rabbi Friedler tilted his head slightly and looked out the window behind me. His eyes seemed to trace the sunlight shining down, from the sky to the autumn leaves, laying freshly fallen on the ground. He nodded slowly to himself. "Hashem has made a beautiful day, Reb Reuven, a beautiful day indeed. Let's make sure we enjoy it to the fullest."

After we said the after-meal prayers, Rabbi Friedler invited me to Yom Kippur services. "Tomorrow, *Kol Nidrei* is scheduled for 6:08, and we'd love to have you, Reb Reuven. Even if you can't make the service, you're welcome to join us for the pre-fast meal. With Hashem's help, we'll start at 4:30."

I had forgotten that Yom Kippur was a day of fasting. That felt like a bit much; something bigger than a baby step in the direction of the traditions of my forefathers. Maybe I would just eat a little less or something.

"Thank you, Rabbi Friedler. I'm actually planning to

go to services with my friend Andy. At Temple Elazar, just up the way."

"Wonderful! I'm glad to hear you two can go together."

"Say, that reminds me, Rabbi, do you know what the name 'Feivel' means?"

"'Bright' or 'brilliant'," responded R. Friedler immediately.

I nodded. It certainly fit Andy's father to have such a name. He was, after all, a prominent New York psychologist. But, like Cindy in the hospital room initially looking up 14:20 in the Book of Genesis, I felt a small disappointment that the name's meaning didn't speak to me in a powerful way.

When Andy and I had discussed our names, there had been a stirring, as if something might be important. I realized I had been hoping that with R. Friedler's answer I would again feel there was some divine plan unfolding all around me. I sighed to myself. Maybe there was a divine plan, and maybe there wasn't, but today it just felt like lunch was over, and it was time to leave.

74

At home, I checked my email; Uncle Nate and Mary had both replied. I decided to read Mary's message first, in case I needed Uncle Nate's as a pick-up afterwards. It was hard to say how she might have responded; she had been so hurt when we had broken up. With a small twinge in my stomach, I double-clicked to open her email.

Dear Larry,
It felt kind of strange to get your email, since Todd and I have been going out for almost five weeks now. He treats me royally, and my parents like him, too. We started going to church together Sunday mornings and, well, things look promising.
I accept your apology, and I wish you all the best.

Mary

Well, it was something at least. I read it over a second time. *I accept your apology,* she had written. *I wish you all the best.* It could have been worse. She could have retorted, "You jerk, how dare you even write to me." Or, she could have just not replied altogether. I decided I would count it as a plus. It did feel good to have apologized, to have resolved some lingering undone interaction; it felt like sitting down after the closing arguments in a case, being completely done. And having closure on that relationship somehow opened up the future. There were wide open spaces ahead. Anything was possible.

A picture of Ruth flitted across my mind, enjoying our dinner at the Chicago restaurant next to Andy and Gayle. I smiled. That was a sweet meal. Then rational thought returned. Ruth was a person whom I had met once, who lived hundreds of miles away, and who thought who-knows-what about me. It was not quite laughable, but really... I needed to get out more. Meet people. I opened up Uncle Nate's email.

> **Dear Larry,**
> It's true that kids grow up so quickly these days. It took longer when I was a child, I'm sure of that. I would love to see a picture of you and Jake on that old red tricycle, and I'm sure he'd love seeing it, too.
> As for the empty nest, it's been a little strange, but the kids do visit over the holidays, and often in the summer. Miriam and I haven't taken a vacation in many years, but I have a sabbatical next year, and we're hoping to spend half of it in Israel, if I get a guest lecturer position I've applied for in Haifa.
> We would love to see you, and you'd be welcome to stay with us if you travel

```
westward;  we've  got  two  guest  rooms
now!
In   the   meantime,   I'm   planning   to
present  a  paper  to  a  conference  in
Chicago  in  early  November;  perhaps  we
could  meet  up  then.


Shana  Tova,  and  may  it  be  a  sweet  year,
Uncle  Nate
```

Now *there* was an email to make a person feel warm inside. *Family is an important source of strength.* It would be good to connect with Uncle Nate again. I looked through my online albums for the tricycle picture. It would be nice to send it along to him.

With a sinking feeling, I realized it had probably never been digitized. All the recent pictures were digital, and I had scanned all the old ones I had copies of, but there were a whole bunch of papers and pictures that my mother had just closed up in boxes and stacked on my father's desk in the basement. She had never sorted through them and she refused to let us disturb his old things.

On the other hand, maybe this particular picture was one she had in a frame somewhere around the house. If so, perhaps I could scan it for my uncle. It sounded like he would appreciate it.

I called my mom and left her a message about it. It was worth a shot. If she couldn't bring herself to look for it, maybe she would let me search for it when I was there for my birthday. Which was coming up soon. Nine days. The big thirty-one.

It was an odd feeling. He'd never made it that far, my father. Stopped in his tracks one week before. When he was my age, actually.

I suddenly realized that one week before my thirty-first birthday would work out to be this Saturday. Yom Kippur. The day of atonement. I sighed. All I had to do was make it through Yom Kippur. And how hard could that be?

75—

Friday morning, the last Friday of my leave, and I was finishing up with Dr. Silverberger. We had reviewed our work over the past eight sessions, and it felt like a nice wrap-up. I had decided to take a three-week break and then resume with weekly sessions. Even if I lost my job, I could extend my insurance for up to eighteen months. Dr. Silverberger had suggested an extended homework assignment of reflecting on the past eight sessions and returning with some ideas of how I wanted to use the time with him. And now it was time to go.

"Well, I see our time is up for today, Larry."

"Yeah." I stood up as the good doctor rose. "It's been an amazing three weeks."

He put out his hand. "You've done some great work, Larry, and I look forward to resuming in a few weeks."

I took his hand for a firm shake. I had an impulse to hug him, but that would probably be unprofessional on his part. He walked with me to the office door, I turned again.

"Thanks again, doctor."

I supposed if I were completely well-adjusted I would have just asked him if hugs were allowed. As it was, I gestured a vague wave motion with my right hand and walked down the hall. I would be seeing him in three weeks, anyway. An awkward moment here was not really a big deal.

In the parking lot, I sat in my car and called Andy. He answered on the first ring.

"Yes, Counselor?"

"Two questions."

"Shoot."

"First, are you fasting?"

"Well, personally, I don't really fast." Andy hesitated. "But on Yom Kippur I don't eat before going to bed. It would be kind of strange to come home and eat after *Kol Nidrei*." Andy's shrug came across the phone line. "But don't follow *my* example, Counselor!"

"Okay. Second, what do you wear to *Kol Nidrei* services?"

"Well, pretty much anything, except, traditionally, no leather shoes. *I'm* planning to wear a conservative suit and tie with sneakers, but I'm sure there'll be quite a range. Last year there were ladies that looked like they had stepped off a fashion show runway, and at the other end of the spectrum, some of the more religious men wore *kittels*, the plain white shroud-like garment that a man is married in and buried in. And there was everything in between. Really, whatever you wear will be fine."

"Sounds like a suit and tie for me."

"Whatever works for you, Counselor. Just one thing," Andy warned, "this is the one service of the year that they actually start on time. So if you want to hear *Kol Nidrei*, don't be late."

This from Andy.

.76

People were milling about the rear of the sanctuary, a large open room with a raised dais in the front. Three arm chairs lined the walls on either side of the large Hebrew-laden doors to the vestibule, which no doubt held the Torah scrolls. To the right a prayer lectern faced forward, and, to the left, the rabbi's podium overlooked the congregation, which was steadily filling the padded wooden benches occupying most the room. Overhead, large polished beams soared upward, supporting a high ceiling that angled up and forward towards a series of large windows. Outside, the sun was slowly setting.

The mood indoors was less somber than I had expected; it felt almost like a social function, and I heard the occasional laugh at a joke well told. There were some college students in the corner, one of them in jeans.

I spotted Andy in a huddle of middle-aged men in suits, their well-dressed wives conversing in an adjacent circle. When Andy saw me, he nodded and detached himself from the group.

"*Gut yontif*, Counselor. I see you found the place okay. Anybody hassle you?"

"No, it was just fine. And thanks for the ticket." I gestured to the space. "Nice place."

"Yeah, they do all right here."

"So, where are you sitting?"

"Anywhere you'd like, Counselor. I usually sit near the back so it's easier to get out at the end, but, hey, I'm flexible."

There was a noticeable influx of people at that

moment, and the rabbi assumed the podium, encouraging us to take our seats as we would be starting in three minutes. Andy and I sat down on the last bench in the middle section. I picked up a prayer book from the holder affixed to the back of the row in front of us. I pulled out the insert from the front cover.

It had information about the service, including a translation of the *Kol Nidrei* prayer itself.

All vows we make, all oaths and pledges we take between this Yom Kippur and the next Yom Kippur, we publicly renounce. Let them all be relinquished and abandoned, null and void, neither firm nor established. Let our vows, pledges and oaths be considered neither vows nor pledges nor oaths.

The paper stressed that this applied only to personal vows and cautioned us to consult with the rabbi before relying on this nullification of vows in any practical context.

I read further. After *Kol Nidrei*, the congregation would recite,

May all the people of Israel be forgiven, including all the strangers who live in their midst, for all the people are culpable. (Numbers 15:26)

The leader would then beseech:

O pardon the iniquities of this people, according to Your abundant mercy, just as You forgave this people ever since they left Egypt.

And finally, the leader and congregation would say together three times:

The Lord said, 'I have pardoned according to your words.' (Numbers 14:20)

I smiled. At least I recognized the translation of one of the prayers.

A man in a prayer shawl approached the lectern. The crowd stood in one accord, and a hush fell over the room. Two Torah scrolls were carried forward. The cantor intoned a traditional invocation and then the ancient, haunting melody filled the air. "*Kol nidrei, ve-esarei, vacharamei...*" The forlorn voice rose and fell in a minor key. A mournful cry, an unforgettable chant belonging to this eternal tribe, to this lineage transcending history by impossibly surviving through the ages. Tenaciously clinging to our traditions, to our heritage. Handing them down from father to son, father to son. Generation to generation. An unbroken chain.

"*Kol nidrei, ve-esarei, vacharamei...*" Tears came, unbidden. I looked down. I belonged to these people, this nation. This collection of tall and short, spindly and fat, well-dressed and under-dressed. This unlikely assortment of souls. This Jewish clan. My people.

"*Kol nidrei, ve-esarei, vacharamei...*" A people standing before their God and asking Him to forgive their broken promises, to overlook their failed efforts, and to take them back, to welcome them in His loving arms, as a father embraces his wayward son.

These were my people. This was my home.

77

In my bathroom, brushing my teeth, I reflected back on my conversation with Andy. He had been right. A Jew needed to hear *Kol Nidrei* on Yom Kippur, no matter what the state of his faith or his disbelief. Fasting or not fasting. Penitent, rebellious, or apathetic. I looked in the mirror at myself. A Jew needed to hear *Kol Nidrei* on Yom Kippur. And that was that.

I spat out the toothpaste and washed my face. Andy had suggested I appeal the case. It was a nice thought. I imagined arguing technical procedural issues before a three-judge panel reviewing the nightmarish case that had unfolded in my dreams over the past two weeks.

In truth, though, I felt finished with it. I had given it a good effort. Time, attention, detail. It had been enough. I had done my part.

But... there was that elusive something in that conversation about our names. Reuven ben Michael Aba. Avidan Bentzion ben Feivel. Sons and fathers, Zion and brilliance. Was there was some niggling detail left undone, some undiscovered facet that could, perhaps, be brought before an appellate court?

And, in an instant, inspiration struck. I knew what I needed to do.

In my office, I fired up the computer. My fingers flew over the keyboard and the legal phrasing came together swiftly. I printed it out on a single page. Into the manila folder, under the pillow.

I changed into my sleepwear. I had said the Shema prayer in the synagogue as part of the evening service, but it couldn't hurt to say it again before bed. *Shema Yisroel, Adonai Eloheinu, Adonai Echad.*

I decided I would make the commitment to fast the rest of Yom Kippur. After all, what was one day out of the year? It wouldn't make me a religious fanatic. And who knows? Maybe it would help my case. It certainly couldn't hurt.

I crawled into bed. *Please, O Merciful Father, answer my plea.*

I am standing in the courtroom staring down at the manila folder.
I am grateful God has brought me here for a purpose.

You can lead a horse to water,
   but you cannot make him drink.
You can give a man a good book,
   but you cannot make him think.
A grasshopper is tiny,
   but you cannot make him shrink.
A leap of faith is tempting
   and I'm standing at the brink.
Is this an ocean
   or just water in the sink?

Three identical hooded judges sit, the gavel sounds.
"This court is now in session. You may be seated."
We sit.
A voice emanates from the judges' bench, "Mr. Cohen?"
I rise. "Your honors, we have a motion--"

Gonna cause a commotion
cuz this train's locomotion
can take you to the ocean
to gather up a quotient
of the makings of a potion
that will transform every notion--

"We have a motion for a mistrial."
M. Sutton stares roundly at me, his eyes wide with incredulity and umbrage.
The judges are impassive. "On what grounds?"
"The Judge is my Father, Your Honors."

The family's in session
and you've just made your confession.

M. Sutton is on his feet, unable to contain himself. "You!" He points an accusing finger. "You have spent zee last twenty-three years denying zees relationship! You have pushed Him away, denied His existence, built your own little world, and insisted you are on your own, zat you have done everything yourself. You have rejected Him at every turn and in every possible manner! And now you want to come crying 'Daddy, Daddy' into zees court of appeals?" He draws himself up as he turns to the judges. "Your Honours, zee defendant has forsaken The King of Kings and he cannot now manipulate zees court by reaching for a relationship zat he has so emphatically and consistently repudiated."

What is a home,
    if not a place you return?
Who is your father,
    the one for whom you yearn?

Why have a teacher,
    if the pupil cannot learn?
Surely there are bridges
    impossible to burn?

"Your Honors, I— have acted as he describes." I take in a little air. "However, whether I have been a 'bad' son, or whether I had been a 'good' son, the relationship still exists, Your Honors. A father is a father, whether his son acknowledges him, respects him, trusts in him— or not."

M. Sutton stands erect, reclaiming his professional bearing.
"Your Honours, zee 'Father' relationship The Judge has with zee defendant is entirely metaphorical. It is not a reality; it is not grounds for zee mistrial."

Reality eludes my grasp,
    slipping through my fingers,
Hugs may end and kisses fade,
    and yet the love still lingers,
if your heart will open,
    a timelessness can capture
connections long thought dead and gone,
    still full of love and rapture

"Your Honors, the reason that a judge cannot hear a case when he is the father of the defendant is because that relationship makes it impossible for the judge to be impartial in the case. The same obtains in this relationship, Your Honors. The Judge is called 'Father' because He has a predisposition to compassion for his 'son'. In this court, our relationship, by whatever name, is grounds for a mistrial."

M. Sutton is unimpressed. "By zat logic, Your Honours, Zee King of Kings and Zee Judge of Judges would be barred from passing judgement on any of His children. Zee entire order of Creation would be disrupted, beginning with zee Day of Judgement He has just enacted. Surely if He had wanted a world without judgement, He would have created one!"
"Your Honors, I am not suggesting that He should not judge me. Rather, I argue that He — my Father!— cannot judge me here, in this court."

My cards are on the table,
    there is nothing up my sleeve.
My Father is my Father,
    though I sometimes disbelieve.
A tapestry of doubt and hope
    in daylight hours I weave.
But now I'm here, on trembling knees,
    Your ruling to receive.

The left judge speaks, "M. Sutton ably demonstrated that the defendant indeed committed the crime of Kayin ben Odom."

The right judge concurs, "Mr. Cohen has even confirmed his guilt here today."

Suddenly the three judges merge together to form a familiar cloaked Presence.

"But since My son, little Reuven ben Michael Aba, has now publicly proclaimed that I am his Father and has demonstrated a sincere desire to improve our relationship—" the voice contains a smile "—the conviction is vacated and the case is dismissed."

Two sharp claps of the gavel echo in the chamber.

M. Sutton throws himself at my chest in a European embrace. "I knew you could do it! I knew it!"

He releases me and pats my shoulders with his hands. "Well done, Reb Reuven; well done! Au revoir!" And he is gone.

As I turn to my right, R. Friedler rises. A smile curves his lips in fatherly delight. "Well done, little Reuven."

My eyes are drawn to his cowboy hat. It seems oddly extraneous, a costume. As I stretch out my hand to remove it, it melts away into the air, revealing rich dark hair beneath. Dark hair? My hand tugs on the long white beard, which comes away, dissolving in my hand. As I look on in disbelief, his features slowly come into focus. Can it be?

"Dad?"

"Right here, son."

I hold him tightly. Tears flow. My heart feels whole, like a small boy once again. I hold his hand as we walk towards the playground together. The swings beckon. I turn to look up at him.

"It was always you?"

"Yes, it was always me." He smiles. "I tried telling you with my first word, 'Father', but you weren't ready to hear then." He ruffles my hair. "I have been right here, little Reuven. In the most unexpected of places."

A sudden fear strikes me. "But, now that this is over-- when will I see you again?"

"Whenever you want." Dad pats my back reassuringly and lifts me up to the swing.

"You... promise?"

"I promise." Dad holds my face in both his hands and looks into my eyes. "If you look for me, you will find me, little Reuven." He keeps a hand on my shoulder as he walks around to push me from behind. "I'm always here, son. Right here. Right behind you, pushing you forward." The swing goes higher and higher, and I look out over the playground from the top of the world.

"Whenever you need me, I am here."

A smile of contentment spreads across my face. My father is here with me, and all's right with the world.

As the moment lingers, the swing flies gently

higher. The world falls away, farther and farther, a spinning orb of blue and white. Smaller and smaller the brilliant blue disc recedes... becoming the pupil in the eye of an angelic man, gazing down at me with an endlessly loving smile. My heart feels whole in the warm embrace.

A cloak of night lowers over the face, but the love and the smile linger on. The hooded Judge lifts the ram's horn, and a triumphant shofar sounds.

In the
End

78

My eyes fluttered open. Sunlight streamed in through the bedroom windows, landing gently on the bedcovers. Birds sang in the trees outside, chirping over the green lawn that I could see from the comfort of my soft pillow. I laid in bed for several minutes appreciating the peaceful morning. What a beautiful day.

I swung my legs over the side of the bed and laid my bare feet on the hardwood floor. The smooth coolness felt good to the soles. I sat thinking for a moment. Today was Yom Kippur, Day of Atonement. Or "at-one-ment", I remembered hearing some adult saying in the year of my bar mitzvah long ago. This would be the first year I would be fasting in a long time. Fasting like my father had, and his father before him. As even Andy did, in his own way.

Which reminded me of services. I wasn't sure if Andy even went to the Yom Kippur day services at Temple Elazar. It occurred to me that I could go by myself anyway. I would be at home there if I did. Or I could try the Neener synagogue. They were all Jews there, too; all part of the tribe. And it would be nice to see the Friedlers as well. I reflected on the dream. It was sweet to consider that either place I went --wherever I went, really-- my father had said he would be there. And this morning, with the cheerful sun lighting up the world, I knew that he would be.

79

I had walked the short distance to the Neener shul and had apparently just missed the reading of the Torah. I squeezed into a small space in the back. Rabbi Friedler stood up and started making an announcement, something about continuing with the *Yizkor* service, but it was hard to hear the details in the midst of so many congregants taking their children out into the hallway. And then an old dread gripped my stomach. *Yizkor.*

I looked around at the older men who remained, and remembered. On the Passover after my bar mitzvah, I had attended a *Yizkor* service with my mother at Mount Carmel. It was a brief memorial service for those who had lost a parent, but after fifteen seconds of the rabbi's inspirational introduction, I had run crying from the sanctuary.

In subsequent years, my mother had excused me from the *Yizkor* service to spare me the grief. Every year, I had filed out of the sanctuary with those who still had both their parents. And now here I was, eighteen years later. Back in the *Yizkor* service again.

I glanced at the door, just closing after the departure of the last young boys. I wasn't trapped. I could leave. I really could. Even if R. Friedler saw me exit, he would understand. It would be okay.

But as Dr. Silverberger would say, this was an opportunity, really. And Moses would no doubt agree. An opportunity to embrace the traditions of my forefathers instead of fleeing from them. *Taste, and see what is good.* And it could be a brief embrace, if I needed it to be.

I probably owed it to my father. I had never said *Yizkor* for him.

Rabbi Friedler cleared his throat. "On this most holy of days, this day of atonement, we take a moment to remember our loved ones. Those that came before us and helped bring us into this world. Who shared with us the traditions of our forefathers, who helped forge us as the next link in the eternal chain of the Jewish people throughout the ages." Rabbi Friedler surveyed the somber group of congregants. Most were older, no doubt reflecting on how their lives had been shaped by their parents in their younger days. But in the corner, I saw a younger man, pale in his dark suit, with round eyes that held the unwept tears of recent grief. My heart went out to him.

"And as we ask God to remember our parents, we give thanks to Him for giving us the opportunity to be a part of their legacy in this world. And we pray that we can make our lives a fitting tribute, a shining example of their highest ideals and aspirations, a journey they would be proud of." Rabbi Friedler opened his prayer book. "We turn to page 338."

I found my place in the siddur. The service was surprisingly short, just a page and a half in all. I read quietly to myself.

May G-d remember (yizkor) the soul of my father, my teacher _____ who has gone to His world...

May his soul be bound up in the bond of the living, with the souls of Avraham, Yitzchak and Yaakov, Sarah, Rivka, Rachel and Leah, and with the other righteous men and women in the Garden of Eden, and let us say, Amen...

As the congregation filed back in, Rabbi Friedler motioned for me to sit next to him. A new prayer leader came to the front, and the congregation started the Musaf service with an Amidah, the silent standing prayer.

Throughout the leader's repetition and the subsequent prayers, my mind lingered on my connection to my father. Last night's dream filled my mind. *I will always be here for you. Always.* Today I could feel that he was a source of strength for me. He would always be.

A wave of gratitude washed over me. My father was here for me. And, I realized, I was also here for him. I was carrying his name forward in this world. Would he be proud of my life? Would it bring that playground smile to his face? How would he gently push me forward?

And then, there we were. Rabbi Friedler shared his prayerbook with me, his ancient finger pointing to the English transliteration of the mourner's Kaddish. Together with the other mourners, we prayed the timeworn words. The pace was slow, and, though the letters swam a little through my tears, I was able to say the words out loud, honoring my father for the first time with a Kaddish spoken in his memory.

Yisgadal v'yisgadash shemay raba...

80

I broke the fast with the Friedlers, after the final *N'eelah* service at their synagogue. It had been a joyful celebration over a long meal, and even when I let myself into my empty apartment afterwards, I felt the fellowship lingering.

My cell buzzed, and I smiled at the warm feeling I got hearing Andy's voice.

"Nu, Counselor, you fasted?"

"All day long, Counselor," I answered. "You?"

"Funny you should ask. I figured if you could go without bacon, the least I could do was fast on Yom Kippur."

"Impressive."

"Don't make too much of it, Counselor, I'm already regretting the impulse."

"So you've eaten?"

"Yeah, had a little nosh at Temple Elazar."

"How was it?"

"Enh. You up for a real meal?"

Truth was, I was pretty full from the Friedlers' expansive offering, but it would be nice to hang out with Andy. This was, after all, my last Saturday before returning to the office to face Mr. Hansen.

"Sure, what do you have in mind?"

"New place in St. Louis Park. Or as we Minneapolitans call it, 'Saint Jewish Park'. Lot of yids live there, so they have a couple kosher joints. I thought it'd be right up your alley, now that you're getting all religious."

"Skipping the bacon a few times is 'all religious'?"

"Whatever. Place is Vitali's Bistro on Minnetonka Ave. Meet you there in an hour?"

"Sure."

Vitali's turned out to be a small coffee shop with a warm, Russian atmosphere. The owner himself was there, a small wiry man with a ready smile, personally ensuring that everyone was enjoying themselves. I was put off at first by the menu, an odd combination of crepes and sushi, but the food when it arrived was amazingly delicious, and Andy reported that the coffee was "actually quite good", high praise from him.

"So you ready to return to the office and face the music, Counselor?" Andy said over a mouthful of a vegetarian mushroom stroganoff crepe. "Still remember how to file a motion in the real daytime courthouse? Feel like you're ready to handle the pressure without shouting at the judge?"

"Well, it might take some getting used to," I said. "But I think I'll manage if they let me." I dipped some Greek crepe in the tangy dressing. "But if Judge Swensen shows up in court wearing a hooded black cloak, I'm going to have a breakdown."

81

I almost burst into tears when Mr. Hansen greeted me at the office. I felt so bad that I had let him down. As he ushered me into his office, he smiled and said it was good to see me, but there was a somber tenor underneath.

He talked about the importance of professionalism in the court, proper decorum and respect for the institution. Then he fell quiet.

"You should know that Judge Swensen actually considered holding you in contempt of court." He forced a small smile. "But we were able to work something through." He laid it out. I was on probation and would be reviewed every three months for the next year; if there was another 'incident' I would likely be let go.

I told him I had done a lot of thinking, and working on myself over the three-week break. I was ready for a fresh start.

Mr. Hansen said he was confident things would work out well. He patted me on the back as I left his office.

I felt like I had my life back.

Immediately, there was too much to catch up on, but it felt good to be back in the groove, contributing to the team effort. Everyone kept commenting on how good I looked, how I should take time off more often. Our secretary even asked if I'd met someone new! It was true that I was in high spirits. The week went by quickly.

And now I was ready and simply waiting. I had one small suitcase of clothes and toiletries, and a backpack with an old Gibson book and snacks. At Lunds, I had picked up some grapes and corn chips. My favorite traveling food. Sweet and salty, wet and dry, soft and crunchy. What a great combination. 12:08. Any time now.

On my phone, I re-read the long email I had received over lunch from my sister. She talked about married life, Michigan, the desire to have children, concerns about my mom. She asked how I was doing, said she hoped we would be more in touch, and ended:

> ...I wish I could be there for your birthday celebration (Mom told me you were coming down). Congratulations on making it to the big thirty-one! We're going to try and make it to Chicago for Passover this year; maybe you can come then? It would be great to see you.
> Love,
> Jessi

I imagined the dot over the "i" as the little heart-shaped figure she used to draw as a little girl.

Andy arrived and we set out in his new BMW 650i with the top down and the stereo up. This was the life. Sitting in a car that cost more than my annual salary was a thrill. To be able to ride in such a car! The handling was sublime; the acceleration impressive. And Andy had gotten the top-of-the-line sound system. Did a person get used to this?

"Not bad, huh?" Andy grinned.

"I see why you were so excited."

It was great to see Andy gleeful, like a kid in an ice cream store after getting his allowance.

I admired the beautiful foliage along the river as we crossed the bridge over the Saint Croix and entered Wisconsin. If Andy knew that Wisconsin enforced their speed limit much more vigorously than Minnesota did, he showed no sign of it.

"FYI, speed limit is 65."

"Speed limit?"

"Yes, they have them here in the Midwest."

"Counselor, I'd say that if I'm willing to pay the fine, I don't see anything wrong with going a healthy amount over the posted speed limit. Everybody --present company excluded, of course-- goes five to ten miles over as it is. You could argue that the de facto speed limit is, in fact, five or ten miles over what's posted."

"You could argue that." I smiled. "I wouldn't try it out with a Wisconsin state patrol officer, but you could argue it."

"Counselor, how come you put a moral value on secular traffic laws, but when it comes to the laws of Moses you're so inconsistent? No bacon on your cheeseburger? How come the pork is an issue, but the combining of milk and meat is okay?"

"*That* is hardly related to *this*, Counselor!" But he had a point. I was just beginning to figure out where I stood in relation to the large body of Jewish practice that was my heritage.

Andy nodded thoughtfully. He was not going to let it drop. "What about collusion, Counselor?"

"Hmm?"

"You willingly got into this car, knowing that I was planning to speed most or all the way to Chicago. In fact, you witnessed my unlawfully hasty driving on our last trip. Yet here you are, benefitting from my violation of the law. Doesn't that make you an accessory before the fact, Counselor?"

The trees continued to rush past with reckless abandon, green and gold with an occasional splash of red; the sun warmed us as the cool fall air washed over us. Life was grand.

"Shut up and drive, scofflaw."

82

My mother had made a feast of my favorite foods: brisket, peas, garlic mashed potatoes and squash with onion salt. For dessert, she presented her famous flourless chocolate torte with a layer of raspberry cream in the middle; she brought it out with thirty-one candles aflame.

"Make a wish, Larry!"

I looked down at the candles, carefully arranged on my favorite cake. I took in my mother's smiling face, softened by the dim lighting. It warmed my heart to see, reminding me of the joyful innocent expression in her wedding portrait, the happiness that had illuminated her features back then. I couldn't remember seeing her like this since my father had died. Where had this woman been when I needed her?

I took a deep breath and focused on the present. My wish. I drew in my breath, preparing to extinguish the candles. *May her heart be filled with joy.* And I made sure to blow them all out, every last one.

As I removed the candles and cut the cake, my mother brought out bowls, spoons and a scooper. She presented the bubblegum ice cream that Mrs. Goldstein had brought over earlier. I laughed out loud and loaded up with two scoops.

"I have a special birthday gift for you, Larry". She went into another room.

A poignancy overcame me. I wished my father were here to share this. In a sense, I guessed he *was* here, just as he had promised in my dream, near and dear in my thoughts and in my heart. I reflected on that last dream. My father had wanted to be with me, too; I had felt that.

It was clear to me that he had been taken before he was ready to go. It was nice to feel that we were reunited. We would always be together.

My mother returned with a large rectangular package, wrapped in gold paper and tied with a matching bow. I eased the ribbon off and considered the heft of the contents. It felt like a heavy storage box; what could possibly be inside? My hands released the taped seams on the sides, and I lifted the top. As I set it to one side, staring up at me was a framed picture of a small boy of four or five years old, grinning atop an old red tricycle, as his father squatted protectively behind him. My eyes teared up.

"Thanks, Mom."

She came to my side and showed me the bound volumes that lay beneath.

"When your father and I met in college, he said he wanted to be a writer. So I told him he should keep a journal. Well, he was probably just trying to impress me, but he started writing... I came across it looking through his desk to find that picture for you."

I put my arm around her shoulder. "Thanks, Mom; this is perfect."

* * *

It was Shabbos afternoon, and my mother wanted to show me off to the neighbors. We walked two houses down, where, in the backyard, a huge Sukkah sheltered food-laden tables and clusters of people talking everywhere. My mother found our host.

Mr. Kazinski was a large man, a bulky Russian who towered over me, nearly blocking the sun. I did not often have occasion to feel small, but this Slavic giant was at least six-foot-six, and not a pound less than 300. His beefy hand swallowed mine in greeting.

"Iss plessure to meechoo," he commanded in a thick accent.

"Nice to meet you, too, Mr. Kazinski, and thank you for sharing your Sukkah with us."

"It iss our plessure." He beamed delightedly. "Your masser has made us to feel home," complimented Mr. Kazinski. "She iss tressure, your masser."

My mother smiled and murmured something about how it was the least a neighbor could do.

"Please to meet my cheeldren," Mr. Kazinski instructed. "Dee oldest two boys are East coast. But dare iss Ari, da baby, wiss Mrs. Goldstein; he has become religious." The big man shrugged. He beckoned to a large young blonde at the drink table. "Dees iss Marina, my youngest girl..." Marina turned at the sound of her name, and came towards her father. She had his proportions, in miniature, and an earthy sensibility that welcomed conversation. There was something vaguely familiar about her face. "Marina, meet Lahree. Lahree, my daughter Marina." She smiled shyly and looked slightly embarrassed at the formal introduction. Her handshake was firm and moist. "Nice to meet you, Larry."

"Nice to meet you, Marina."

Mr. Kazinski was looking around for his middle child.

"Ivana--!" He turned and collected someone from behind him. As he rotated back to face me, he said apologetically, "But perhaps I should introduce you wiss your Hebrew name? Lahree, dees iss Nechama Roos." And there, presented protectively on her father's arm, was none other than my green-eyed, dark-haired Ruth. My mouth opened silently as her cheeks colored.

"You know my Roos?"

"We met a few weeks ago," I stammered, "at the, at a tournament."

"I had not heard of such a ting."

"Oh, Papa!" Ruth's lips parted in an enchanting smile. "It's nice to see you again, Larry."

"The pleasure is truly mine!"

My mother was delighted with the turn of events. "Why, Larry, I had no idea that you two kids had met. How wonderful!" She turned to Ruth. "I don't know if Larry told you, but he's a lawyer up there in Minnesota. He handled the *Hernandez* case!"

"You mean the one with the twins?" asked Marina with disbelief. "It was in all the papers."

"Yes, that very one. Without him, it would have ended ve-ry differently, I can assure you."

My lips said, "Oh, Mom--!" but in my heart I was grateful that she wanted to present me in the best light to the radiant Ruth and her family. I let my gaze pass over the backyard scene.

Mrs. Goldstein, sitting in the shade near the dessert table, beckoned me from a distance. She seemed so much older than I remembered, and frail under her grey hair.

I excused myself from the group and crossed the

lawn. As I took her hand, I was inspired to lean over and kiss her cheek. She smiled as I sat down. "It's great to see you, little Reuven. Ah, but you're not so little anymore. And your mother says you go by 'Larry' now? That might be hard for me to remember."

"It's okay, Mrs. Goldstein, you can call me 'Reuven'." I took in the caring expression on her wrinkled face. "It's great to see you; I've been thinking about you a lot lately."

"Indeed?" She smiled. "So tell me all about yourself, young man! What ever have you been doing?!"

I caught her up on the major events of recent years. She smiled and laughed at my storytelling.

"That sounds wonderful, Reuven," she exclaimed. "What great adventures."

I asked her how things were for her, and she reviewed the life events of her nieces and nephews and their children, who were graduating colleges, getting married, and otherwise making grand plans.

"And happy birthday, Reuven. I'm so glad you've made it to this milestone day. I know your mother is greatly relieved as well." Mrs. Goldstein patted my hand. "And I'm sure your father is smiling down on you from the heavens. He'd be proud of you, you know."

"Yes," I concurred, "I think he is."

A comfortable silence followed, and we watched neighbors picking over the dessert table.

"I think maybe you should join them," suggested Mrs. Goldstein, nodding towards the distance behind me. I turned. Ruth and Ari were conversing, and he was occasionally looking in my direction.

"Wonderful to see you, Mrs. Goldstein." I said, rising.

"Lovely to visit with you, Reuven."

I walked across the lawn to join Ruth and her brother.

Ruth introduced us, and I asked Ari about his yeshiva experience and what his plans were for the future. He explained his likely course of study in some detail, and how compelling it was to be living in Israel.

"So how did all this start?"

"Oh, it began with a Birthright trip, ten intense days in The Holy Land." He looked up at me with enthusiasm. "I just didn't want to leave! And then the rabbi at the yeshiva we visited suggested I stay and learn, and I felt like I-- like that was where I was supposed to be!" His eyes asked if I understood him.

"I know what you mean."

And I did. Standing here at the Kazinskis, with my mother and Mrs. Goldstein nearby, celebrating my thirty-first birthday on Shabbos in a Sukkah, I felt like I was exactly where I was supposed to be. Perhaps it was God's Plan unfolding, or perhaps it was what Josh would call karma. Either way, it felt good to be at just the right place at just the right time.

Ari realized he had been dominating the conversation and good-naturedly changed the subject. "So Ruth tells me that you two actually met weeks ago at a bridge tournament?"

"That's right."

Ruth shook her head in wonder. "I can't believe that your mother lives just two doors down from my parents, Larry. It's almost... miraculous!"

Ari smiled broadly. "It *is* miraculous, Ruthie. Everything is. Every beautiful moment that Hashem brings us is miraculous!"

"Zo now you see Divine Pravidenz in *everysink*?!" questioned Mr. Kazinski, suddenly appearing out of thin air. Even though their father's tone was light, Ari looked uncomfortable, and Ruth blushed slightly.

"Well, you have to admit," I said, feeling strangely at home gazing up at this large Russian patriarch, "Fathers do have a tendency of showing up... in the most unexpected places."

From the Author

A few words

Let me tell you about the making of this manuscript, and thank some of the many people who have helped form it. (My apologies in advance for those whom I have inadvertently left out of these paragraphs, and let me stress that I alone am responsible for all defects, errors or deficiencies in the manuscript.)

The idea for this story grew out of love and study. Because my late wife and I were married in the week where Jews the world over study the first section of the Bible, for our second anniversary I wanted to chant that portion from the scrolls. It was a daunting task, because the scrolls have no vowels, no punctuation, and no musical notations. To prepare, I had to go over and over the verses, which included the story of Cain and Abel. The more I repeated those words, the more questions arose, and I found myself peeling away various layers of possible interpretations and exploring different understandings. Eventually, I was looking at the story from an original point of view. I wanted to share the insights I had discovered, but, being no scholar, I had no idea how to do so.

Then the idea burst forth: a story of a young man going through the same discovery process I had. It would have to be someone new to the Bible, with little formal religious background, but why would he want to study the story of Cain and Abel? Something unusual would have to compel him... Thus, <u>Defending Cain</u> was born.

My deep and abiding thanks to the Feller families (may they live and be well); their dedication and joyful service were a tremendous inspiration. The most endearing qualities of Rabbi Friedler come mostly from R. Moshe Feller and his oldest son R. Mendel Feller. The Shabbos scenes are a testament to the generous hospitality of these rabbis and their wives.

I started writing <u>Defending Cain</u> as a screenplay, because the dream sequences could lend themselves to wonderful special effects. But I quickly realized that (a) I didn't know anything about how to write a screenplay, (b) even if I finished it, I would be one of thousands running around clutching their screenplay, hoping to find a producer willing to make it into a film, and (c) there was no way that I could take on the making of such a film myself.

So family and friends encouraged me to write a book. That made more sense. I had read many novels, and I suspected I could write at least as well as the bad ones I had encountered! And so I started down the path of writing the manuscript in my spare time, while I worked as a programmer during the day.

Dr. Jerry Beker (z"l), my warm friend with the lovely smile and gentle wisdom, gave encouraging feedback and expressed an interest in the characters. May your soul ascend ever higher. I so wish I could have shared more of it with you before you left us.

I well remember when Marc Zaffran —family friend and best-selling author in France— told me that I should not write the book from start to finish (as I had set out doing). Rather, he said, I should write "the spine" of the book first, and then go back and flesh out the body. That was the soundest advice for me with regard to this book, and without that redirection, I shudder to think what shambles might have resulted. So I set aside the meandering beginning which introduced the main characters, and wrote out the dream sequences.

My mother was both encouraging and a great editor in

the early going. It was she who first commented that the dream sequences needed to be "dreamier". She also suggested I re-think the original opening, which was b-o-r-i-n-g.

Rabbi Joseph Shagalow (may he live and be well) waded into a very rough early version and encouraged me to continue. He directed me to the one rabbinic source I have seen that has a somewhat similar view to the position I describe in the book. I was relieved to find a scholar who drew similar conclusions from some of the language of the Biblical narration. Rabbi Yosef Heisler (may he live and be well) reviewed the manuscript carefully, pointing out inconsistencies with Jewish law and custom, as well as checking the gematria and the Hebrew transliterations. Any mistakes that remain in the printed version are solely my responsibility.

Steve Wilson, PhD sat next to me on a plane ride and contributed to the therapy sessions in the book; I thank him for shaping some of Dr. Silverberger's interventions. Also helpful in the psychological department was Jeanna Eichenbaum, LCSW.

On the legal side, attorneys Laura and Kelly Olmstead were invaluable in reviewing language and procedure.

I have a warm place in my heart for Vitali at Vitali's Bistro, the cafe where I spent most of my writing time. I would walk in with my 24" iMac tucked under my arm and set up my workspace at my favorite table in the back, working hours on end while consuming those delicious milkshakes. May you have great success, my friend.

Thank you to the many other friends who reviewed the manuscript and gave suggestions and encouragement.

I had several professional writers give me feedback on the

manuscript. First and foremost, Scott Edelstein (friend, editor and writing coach — look him up at scottedelstein.com) whose sharp editing tightened the book considerably. Also, thank you to both Barbara Costa and Mary Gardner, who gave me helpful feedback.

Thanks also to my son Josh who tolerated a manuscript-addled father in the house and gave feedback on word choice for the cover text.

For the beautiful cover, my thanks to my daughter Alethia for helping tweak the front cover graphic.

Many thanks to my son Emmet for putting up with a project-absorbed father during the final writing stages, and for all your work on the photos, the graphics and stitching the cover together. It all turned out beautifully, thank G*d.

All the love of my heart and gratitude for her help to my loving soulmate, Sue Rubin, whose unfailing support, encouragement and cheerleading for the manuscript made it possible to finish and publish it.

As I write this Afterword, my heart is filled with gratitude for the many blessings of friends, family and kind-hearted strangers who have helped form this manuscript. I thank the Master of the Universe for all of them, and for bringing this book to you, my dear reader. Beyond the pleasant story, may you find some lingering food for thought —nourishment for the next step of your journey— wherever your path may lead you.

— Shimon
Sept 2020; Oakland, California

Discussion Questions

For those wishing to continue the experience of Defending Cain beyond reading the last page of the book, here are some questions to think about and/or discuss with friends.

1) Larry's circle of friends have different views on where his dreams originate and why he is having them. What is your opinion, and did it change over the course of the book?

2) What advice would you have given Larry on how to handle the dreams? What would you have done yourself if you'd been in Larry's place?

3) Was Andy right to warn Larry about Rabbi Friedler? What would you have advised a friend in similar circumstances?

4) Larry is urged to consider taking small steps to explore the traditions of his ancestors. What would it look like for you to do that? What are reasons that you would or would not do so? What internal obstacles might arise? What external impediments might you encounter?

5) Over Shabbos dinner, Rabbi Friedler reflects that while some people think that religion is a comforting escape from a cruel world, the rabbi finds a relationship with God can be most challenging. Karl

Marx famously described religion as "opium for the masses". What are your views on and experiences with religious life?

6) Have you ever had experiences where, in the moment, you felt in touch with God (or a Power greater than yourself), and then later reinterpreted the event(s) with a more rational paradigm? Similarly, have you ever looked back on seemingly mundane events and detected a Guiding Hand at work?

7) Larry's experiences with religious rituals in the book (e.g. making the blessing over the Sabbath bread, attending Kol Nidrei services) are generally positive. How do you feel about rituals? Do you find your experiences most shaped by (a) external communal/ social factors (who attends, location, etc), (b) intrinsic ritual considerations (the form of the ritual), (c) your internal state (how you are feeling, what you are thinking), and/or (d) theological considerations (do you believe the ritual worthwhile and does it accord with your worldview)?

8) Were there any events in the book that seemed too improbable to believe? What would your reaction have been to the gematria from Sruli, or the 4:16 on Arthur's sign if they had happened to you?

9) What would you predict for Larry in the next year? In ten years? What are your hopes for Larry? For Andy?

For other characters?

10) Which character in the book has a view of God most similar to your own? Have there been times when you would have identified with a different character's views?

11) All the major characters in the book are male. Did that affect you as you read the book? What other lack of diversity stood out to you? Would including more diverse characters have enriched your experience of the book?

12) Rabbi Friedler espouses the view that each moment of life is about a person's relationship with God. What do you think of that statement? What kind of statement would you make?

13) If M. Sutton were to try and prosecute a case against you, what charges do you think he would bring? How would you defend yourself?

14) In what ways does Larry's journey parallel Cain's experiences (as Larry comes to understand them)? In what ways are they different?